A Fine Italian Hand

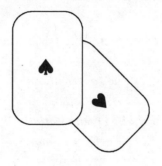

A FINE ITALIAN HAND

A SHIFTY LOU ANDERSON MYSTERY

WILLIAM MURRAY

M. EVANS AND COMPANY, INC.
New York

M. Evans and Company, Inc.
216 East 49th Street
New York, New York 10017

Library of Congress Cataloging-in-Publication Data

Murray, William, 1926–
    A fine Italian hand / William Murray.
        p.   cm.
    ISBN 0–87131–797–4
    1. Anderson, Shifty Lou (Fictitious character) — Fiction.
2. Americans — Travel — Italy — Milan — Fiction.   3. Magicians — Italy —
Milan — Fiction.   4. Milan (Italy) — Fiction.   I. Title.
PS3563.U8F56   1996
813′.54—dc20   95-49582
                                                                              CIP

TEXT DESIGN BY BERNARD SCHLEIFER
Typeset by Alabama Book Composition

Manufactured in the United States of America
9 8 7 6 5 4 3 2 1

FOR ALICE, AGAIN

We desire nothing so much as what we ought not to have.
—PUBLILIUS SYRUS

Many killings are attempted, but few are accomplished.
—PITTSBURG PHIL

FRESHENING

"You're going to Italy tomorrow? What for?"

"Some lectures and demonstrations," I said. "For the I.B.M."

"You're going to lecture for I.B.M.?"

"International Brotherhood of Magicians," I explained.

"Oh, not the computer guys."

"No. I'm not going to make any money, but it'll just about cover my expenses. And I've never been to Italy."

"You going to go racing over there?"

"I doubt it. Anyway, I need to get away for a while, Jay. I've been losing my ass here."

Jay nodded glumly. "Yeah, it's been a dismal meet so far, after Santa Anita." He snapped one of his big black notebooks shut and set it down on the empty seat between us, on top of a pile of other big black notebooks containing all the past-performance statistics for Southern California's three major racetracks for the past three years. Jay Fox was nothing if not thorough; very little was left to mere chance. I raised my binoculars to check out the field on its way to the starting gate. It was a clammy, overcast day, and across Hollywood Park's smog-enshrouded infield the horses, cheap three-year-old maidens running in a meaningless sprint, looked like moving shadows, the bright silks of their jockeys shining like small beacons of light above them. I stood up.

"Where are you going?" Jay asked. "There's nothing to bet on here. Sit down."

"A place bet on the favorite. Some long shot could easily run second and I might get even money."

"A desperate move," Jay said. "You're ready to ship out. Go to Italy, but don't bet this dog. Where's the value?"

"Jay, I need to cash a ticket," I explained. "This is the only horse in the field who can run even a little bit. And he's being ignored in the place pool."

"He's trained by a magician," Jay said, "one of those guys who can make any horse disappear by the eighth pole."

I hesitated, then sat down as the horses began filing into the starting gate. Arnie Wolfenden, carrying a large container of pink lemonade and a hot dog, eased himself into the seat behind me. "Anybody risk any money here?" he asked.

"I was going to," I admitted, "but Jay talked me out of it."

"Cal-bred maiden claimers," Arnie said. "Shifty, you're living dangerously these days."

"It's time for him to go to Italy," Jay said. "He needs freshening."

"Italy," Arnie said, with a sigh. "I was in Italy right after the war, with the occupation troops. What's it like now?"

"I'll tell you when I get back."

"Nothing worked then," Arnie said. "No electricity, bombed-out villages, very little public transport. But you know what? We sure ate well. I'll never forget the food."

"The horses have reached the starting gate," the announcer called out.

We all raised our binoculars to watch the race. The favorite broke on top, opened up two lengths, held the lead to the sixteenth pole, was passed by the second choice, and barely lasted for second over a fifty-to-one shot lumbering down the lane on the outside. "I'd have cashed," I said.

Jay turned to look at me. "Shifty, what's the matter with you?" he said. "Look at the board. He's going to pay two eighty to place. Is that the kind of bet you're making now? I'll go through life passing horses like that and save enough money every year to pay off my credit cards."

He was right, of course, and I knew it. But I had failed to cash a ticket in three days, eleven consecutive losing wagers on horses that hadn't even raised a gallop. I didn't want to carry the burden of that losing streak off with me to Italy; I'd have been nervous about getting on the plane. This particular day, with one of the weakest cards of contestants competing I'd ever seen at a major racetrack, I had yet to make a bet, and now we were coming up to the seventh. I had spent nearly three hours handicapping the night before and I had nothing to show for it, not a single horse at any price that looked like a solid wager. I stood up again. "Maybe I will go home," I said. "I haven't even packed."

"A salubrious decision," Arnie Wolfenden observed, popping the last of his hot dog into his mouth.

Jay shook my hand. "When are you coming back?"

"I have an open ticket," I said. "Maybe in three, four weeks."

"Well, enjoy yourself," he said. "When you get back, the two-year-olds will be running. We always do well with the two-year-olds. They haven't had a chance to screw them up yet."

"You're turning into a cynic, Jay. It's not like you."

"Yeah, well, the Hollywood spring meet so far has been a grind," he said. "All the good three-year-olds are back East for the Triple Crown races, and most of the good jockeys, too. I may take a little vacation myself, go off on a cruise or something."

"My idea of living death," Arnie said. "I'd rather be flogged naked in a public square than go on a cruise. Jay, surely you jest, my friend."

"I've also thought about maybe going on safari to Africa," Jay said. "Two weeks in the game parks."

"Gazing at animals you can't bet on," Arnie said, "the ultimate frustration."

"I can't bet on these either, Arnie."

"True, but there's always tomorrow, Jay. Every day a new adventure. What's in Africa? Flies, and a lot of other insects. Where are the horses?"

"They have racing in Nairobi," I said.

"What kind of animals? Horses that would make this last bunch look like Secretariats," Arnie said. "Come on, Jay, cool it. This is your habitat, my friend—the racetrack, the biggest game park in the world. Soft prey, big cats, little cats, hippos, crocs, hyenas, jackals, vultures, all right here for our enjoyment. Who needs Africa?"

"I'll see you guys."

"Take it easy, Shifty," Jay said, with a last wave of his hand.

"Hey, look at the board," I heard Arnie say, as I walked out of the box, "look at the action on the eight horse. Check him out, Jay. Maybe we overlooked something."

I walked out of Hollywood Park through the clubhouse that last afternoon in early May, leaving my racetrack cronies to their calculations. I wasn't sorry to go, I was happy to be leaving for Italy, but still I felt a twinge of melancholy. I love magic and I love the horses, and walking early out of any racetrack is like leaving a bit of myself behind. As I skirted the clubhouse bar, I spotted Angles Beltrami, the other permanent member of our grandstand box. He was pressed up against a soft-looking plump blonde in a tiny black miniskirt, black pumps, and a sleeveless pink jersey that barely covered a formidable bosom. I waved to him, but either he didn't see me or he chose to ignore me. "The eight horse in here, babe," I heard him say as I passed. "Can't lose. So what about tonight? Can't you tell your husband you got a PTA meeting or something?"

I went downstairs, but before heading to the parking lot I checked the tote board. The eight horse had been backed down to nine to two from a morning line of twenty to one. I turned around, walked to a betting window, and bought a ten-dollar win ticket on the eight, then I lingered by a television monitor long enough to watch the race.

The eight horse ran five wide around both turns of the tight turf course and lost by a neck to a forty-to-one shot. I tore up my ticket and left the premises. Jay was right. I needed freshening, I needed Italy.

1

FANDANGO

She had the face of a fallen angel. When I first saw her she was sitting by herself in a corner of the room, holding a glass of champagne with both hands as if it were a chalice. She seemed also to be poised for flight, like a young bird on a branch, unsure of herself, a little afraid. It was that quality of vulnerability that attracted me to her. And then, too, she was sexy in an earthy way, with fleshy lips and something wounded in her eyes. I knew immediately she was American, one of three or four at the party, but she wasn't like any of the other women there; nothing sleek or lacquered about her, a country girl in city clothing. I'd been in Milan for only four days and this was my third party, and so far they'd been much the same, flesh markets, people selling themselves and one another, people buying. She didn't look like someone in the path of easy commerce.

I asked Carlo Ravelli about her, and of course, he knew something. "Ah, that one," he said. "She has only been here a few months."

"American, right?"

"Extremely," Ravelli said. "Embarrassingly so."

"Embarrassingly? In what way?"

Ravelli smiled and casually flicked cigarette ashes onto a very expensive Oriental rug. "Speak to her," he said. "You will see what I mean." He glanced at her and gave a little shrug of the shoulders.

Something about her bothered him or annoyed him, I wasn't sure which, but then I didn't know Ravelli that well. "Adriano is mad for her," he said, "but you know Adriano. He only wishes to fuck her."

"I don't know Adriano."

"Adriano Barone, your host."

"And why hasn't he?"

"She doesn't like him. She's afraid of him."

"She a model?"

"She is trying."

"What's her name?"

Ravelli smiled. "That is part of the problem," he said. "Bobby Jo. Amusing, no? That could only be American. There is the sound of banjos in the air. You wish to meet her? No problem. Speak to her. They are all here to be spoken to. Excuse me, *caro.*" And he left me to go talk to someone across the room. Ravelli wasn't much of a magician, but he was a whiz at social gatherings; he seemed to know everyone. I didn't respect him at all as an artist, but he was the right man to be representing the International Brotherhood of Magicians in Italy; he had a talent for opening doors.

I decided to get another glass of wine before introducing myself to her. I was still fighting jet lag and I wasn't sure why I had agreed to come to this party. It was exactly like the other ones I'd been to since my arrival, and I found them boring, especially since I couldn't speak much Italian. Everyone seemed to be playing a part, posing for an invisible photographer. I went to the bar at the far end of the huge room and poured some *pinot grigio* into my glass.

Outside, the rain fell softly against the panes of the tall French doors leading to a terrace that overlooked a garden. The palazzo, like all the other ones I'd seen in this old part of the city, presented a shabby exterior to the street, but inside the rooms screamed of old money. This main living room, with its high paneled ceiling showing medieval religious scenes, was typical, I gathered, full of antiques and objets d'art and apparently handed down from one generation of Barones to another and now to Adriano, the heir to all this ancient history. Elsewhere in the palazzo, Ravelli had told me, lived Adriano's relatives—aunts, uncles, cousins, in flats of their own, but at a distance so far removed from Adriano that not even blood could bridge the gap. "Adriano despises them all," Ravelli had told me. "His life has become a fandango of bodies."

I hadn't even met him. Ravelli had pointed him out to me when we'd arrived, but had not bothered to introduce me. He was a tall, broad-shouldered man in his early thirties with long black hair that tumbled nearly to his shoulders, a quick, nervous smile, and dark, flashing eyes that probed the room as if searching for prey. He was dressed informally, in gray slacks and a navy blue pullover, and looked like an athlete going to seed, with a little too much weight in his once lean face and body. I'd forgotten all about him five minutes after I'd arrived and begun to mingle a bit, with Ravelli introducing me here and there as *"il famoso mago americano"* and *"il più grande prestidigiatatore del mondo,"* which I was not. But let him talk; nobody seemed to care anyway.

As I left the bar, I caught another glimpse of her and decided to go over and talk to her. Of all the young, very beautiful women in this room, moving like gazelles through these carnivores, only this girl looked somehow in danger. She was now leaning against the wall, still holding the glass in both hands in front of her, and looking down at a fat, bald, hairy little man who was talking at her rather than to her, thrusting himself toward her as he spoke, his head bobbing in time to his words, as if they were drumbeats. She looked dismayed; she couldn't believe what she was hearing. When he'd finished and moved away, she stared after him in amazement.

"You all right?" I asked, as I came up to her. "You look a little strange."

"I don't believe it," she said. "Do you know what he just asked me?"

"I can guess."

"He wanted to know if I'd go to bed with him tonight," she said. "He told me he could help me. And then, when I said no, he offered me money."

"Who is he?"

"I only met him once, at another party," she said. "His name's

Gianpaolo Caruso. He's a jeweler. He's got a shop on the Via Manzoni, near the Grand Hotel. Can you believe this guy?"

"I guess some girls will go for it in this town," I said. "His looks and charm won't carry him very far."

"That's the truth." She held out her hand. "Hi. I'm Bobby Jo Dawson. Who are you?"

"Lou Anderson," I said. "My friends call me Shifty. That's because I deal cards pretty well."

"You a gambler or something?"

"No, I'm a magician. Close-up. You know, cards, coins, cups, this and that."

"Wow," she said, "really? What are you doing here?"

"It's an I.B.M. deal."

She looked puzzled. "I.B.M.? Computers and stuff?"

I smiled and shook my head. "International Brotherhood of Magicians," I explained. "I came over to give a series of lectures on prestidigitation."

"Presti-what?"

"Sleight of hand. You know, like this." I reached into my pocket, produced a couple of hundred-lire coins, and flashed them at her. "See? Two coins, right?" I clapped my hands together, then held out my closed fists toward her. "Which hand?"

She smiled shyly, then reached out and touched my right one. I opened my hand to reveal it was empty. "See?"

"Wow. That's good."

"Wait. Want to see where they are?"

"Oh, sure."

I opened my left hand. It was empty. Then I reached up behind her ears. "Here they are," I said. I held the two coins out to her. "See? They were caught in your hair."

"Hey, you *are* good. What else do you do?"

"Oh, I've got a lot of moves, more than you have time for tonight."

"No, I mean, you make a living doing this stuff?"

"I squeak by. I also like to bet on horses."

Her eyes opened wide with surprise. "You're kidding. My dad's a breeder and trainer, Jake Dawson."

"Dawson? I know him. From Kentucky, right?"

"Yeah, near Lexington. You're a friend of his?"

"We had breakfast together. I met him through Charlie Pickard. You heard of him?"

"No, sorry."

"He's retired now, but he used to train a horse for me in L.A., where I live," I said. "Your dad came into town for the Breeder's Cup two years ago, and Charlie introduced him to me on the backstretch. We watched the workouts and then had breakfast in the track kitchen."

"Yeah. Gee, well, it's a small world, isn't it?"

"I heard it was and I keep getting proof of it all the time. So how'd you wind up in Italy? You're a model?"

"I'm trying. I just started. I've been here nearly three months now."

"And how are you doing?"

"Not too good." She smiled, a bit uneasily. "I haven't been very lucky. Piero, my agent, says it takes time."

"Piero is a swine," Carlo Ravelli said, coming up behind me with another man. "Do not trust him."

"That's what my friend Parker says, but then I don't have much choice. I mean, the agency advanced me the money for my room and board and all that."

"*Cara*, I want you to meet my friend Teddy Amendola," Ravelli said. "And, Teddy, this is Shifty Anderson. He is a magician, a very great one."

Teddy nodded to Bobby Jo and shook hands with me. "A magician?" he said, smiling. "You predict the future?"

"Don't be a *cretino*, Teddy," Ravelli said. "È un vero mago, un prestidigiatatore formidabile. You must come tomorrow to the lecture."

"Yes, perhaps," Teddy Amendola said, obviously not interested. He was small and slight, with a pale, sharp face and a shock of unruly thin blond hair. He was obviously gay, but seemed to be sizing up Bobby Jo the way a butcher might look at a well-hung carcass.

"Teddy is a photographer," Ravelli said to Bobby Jo. "He wished to meet you."

"I take pictures and I sell them to the magazines," Teddy explained. "I am quite well known."

"He is famous," Ravelli said.

"Oh," Bobby Jo said. "What do you charge?"

"What do *I* charge? Do you know anything at all?"

"Not a lot," she admitted, tossing back her mane of thick blond hair and gazing at him out of innocent blue eyes. Or perhaps not innocent, only naive. "I'm sorry. I don't mean to sound stupid or anything. I guess you must be important, after all. I mean, sure, it would be nice to get some new pictures."

"It could be more than nice," he said, handing her a business card. "You must call me. I would like to shoot a few rolls, mostly black and white. You are interesting, but, of course, on film one never knows. What do you have to wear?"

"Just my clothes that I came with," she said. "Nothing great. I just don't have any money right now."

Ravelli laughed. "Ah, and Piero is loaning you enough to live on."

"He's helped me, but I need to get some work soon."

"Yes, or Piero will sell you on the market like a piece of meat," Ravelli said, looking beyond her to someone else. He waved and swooped away again.

"Piero's been okay, honest," Bobby Jo said. "It's just hard getting started." She shrugged again and smiled. "I knew it would be."

Teddy Amendola looked at her closely. She had big shoulders, long legs and arms, strong, like those of a swimmer. "I would like to shoot some nudes," he said.

She flinched and looked away from him, like an animal startled by an unexpected sound in the underbrush. "Gee, I don't know. . . . Piero sent me last week to a studio and they wanted . . . well, a lot of stuff I didn't want to do." She turned those innocent eyes on him again. "I don't do porn. I—"

"This is not pornography, you stupid girl," Teddy Amendola

said. "If I photograph you in the nude, if you have the body for it, I will pay you two hundred dollars an hour. Don't you know who I am? What did you think, I photograph *fumetti*?"

"Pho-what? I'm sorry, I don't get it."

"Never mind," he said. "You call me tomorrow, you come to my studio and I will take some pictures. Perhaps they will be good, perhaps not. The nudes are for me, but they will not be pornographic or even *spinti*. You know what that is?"

"No."

"Not for photo strips, not for *Playboy*, not for any magazine," he explained. "For me. I am preparing a show of my work. Perhaps for that. I am famous for my nudes."

"Well, okay, thanks." She glanced at his card. "Teddy. Is that your real name?"

"Teodoro," he said, "but everyone calls me Teddy, and that is also my professional name." He smiled and shook her hand, then mine. "Good-bye. Be careful."

"Don't worry about him," I said, after he'd gone. "I don't think sex is on his mind. This must be a tough world you move in."

"You don't know the half of it," the tall brunette said, coming up beside Bobby Jo and slipping an arm through hers. "Hi, I'm Parker Williams, who are you?"

I introduced myself.

"That's a funny name," Parker Williams said. "What do you do?"

"He's a magician," Bobby Jo said. "He's good."

"No shit. What won't they think of next. Change some of these assholes into rocks, will you, or make them disappear."

She was tall, elegantly thin, with the sort of bones that photograph well and a nice smile, but she also looked worn, with too many wrinkles around the eyes and an air of having been to too many places, heard and seen a little too much. "It's too bad," she said, when I told her I only worked with cards and small objects. "Maybe I'll just make myself vanish, but that's what I tell myself every year."

"Parker lives here half the year," Bobby Jo explained. "She's a regular. You've probably seen her pictures. She's in all the magazines."

"I probably have," I said, "though I don't look at fashion magazines much."

"Why would you?" Parker Williams said. "You probably wouldn't recognize me anyway. They usually slap big hats on me that hide half my face and make me stand like a giraffe in heat."

"She's got fabulous legs," Bobby Jo said. "Last year she was on the cover of *Elle*. She photographs terrific."

"Now I'm doing the shows, mainly," Parker Williams said. "I'm getting a little too old for the gays who run these magazines. We're all supposed to look like sixteen-year-old boys. This is it for me. Really. Next year I'll stay home, find me a rich man with a ranch somewhere."

"There's always this guy Caruso," I said.

She grimaced. "Ain't he a horror? There are a lot of pigs like him around. He's not the worst, believe me."

"I don't know what I'd have done without Parker, honest," Bobby Jo said. "I came here, I didn't know anyone. The agency put me up in this hotel and Parker was staying there, too. I guess she felt sorry for me."

"I never met anyone who knew less about anything than Bobby Jo," Parker Williams said. "I figured she'd get chewed up here pretty fast if I didn't wise her up." She grimaced again and cast a sidelong glance at the angel. "I still think you ought to go home. This is no place for you, baby."

"I'm going to stick it out one more month," Bobby Jo said. "I have just enough money and I've got my ticket home, just in case. But I want to give this a chance."

"Where's home?" I asked.

She hesitated before answering, her eyes gazing nervously around the room, as if seeking an answer from someone else. "Nowhere right now," she said. "I was in New York, but things didn't work out there. I kind of had to get away."

"Is your family all in Kentucky?"

"No, my folks divorced. My mom remarried and is living in California, near L.A. My dad runs the farm and is mostly into breeding now, but he's been having a hard time the last couple of years. My folks and I don't see each other much, not since I left home five years ago. My dad wanted me to go to college, but I wanted to get away. So I just left. He was pretty mad."

"Are you an only child?"

"No, I got a younger sister, Ellie. She's still at home."

"With your mom?"

"No, with Dad. He raised us both, after my mom took off." She had begun to pick at her hands as she talked about her family back in the States, and I noticed that her nails were bitten short. "Hey, gee, this is pretty boring, isn't it?" she said, with a hard little laugh. "Let's talk about you, Shifty. Tell me about your magic."

"Listen, babe," Parker Williams said, "Swifty here is just passing through. You're supposed to mingle at these parties, that's what they're for. Come on, let me introduce you to Tortorini, one of our less arrogant art directors. He's with *Grazia*. You don't mind, do you, Swifty?"

"Not if it's work. By the way, it's Shifty."

"What kind of a name is that?"

"It's about cards. I'll show you a couple of moves sometime, then you'll understand," I said. "Go mingle."

"But it's rude," Bobby Jo began, as Parker started to tug her away into the heart of the party.

"No, it's not. Can I call you? I don't know anyone here except Ravelli, and he's wearing me down with these parties."

"Sure. I'm at the Piccolo Milan, behind the cathedral."

"Okay, I'll call you. You can come, too, Parker."

"Where?"

"Dinner, maybe. Tomorrow night?"

"Why not? You paying?"

"If I can afford it. It's pretty expensive here."

"We'll go dutch," Parker said. "I know a little cheap trattoria not far from the hotel."

"Great. I'll show you a few moves."

"Keep 'em clean," Parker said. "It's been a dirty week."

"How long you going to be here?" Bobby Jo asked.

"I don't know," I said. "I finish up tomorrow, but then I may go to Rome. I'm taking a month to look around. I haven't been in Europe for ten years, and then I was in Italy for only five days. I want to do a little sight-seeing."

"Gee, that's nice. I like Rome, but the jobs are in Milan."

"Speaking of jobs," Parker said, "Tortorini is over there by himself. You have to meet him."

She pulled the angel away with her across the room to where the art director sat. I watched them go, the pro and the amateur. "I can see why Adriano is hot for her," Ravelli said, reappearing again at my side, a glass of champagne in his hand, the usual cigarette in his mouth. "She has the most beautiful *culo*. Ass, you understand?"

"Yes, Carlo, I understand."

He laughed. "Soon you will be speaking Italian like a native."

"The language of sex is international," I said.

But he had already drifted away from me, back into his whirl and glitter. The rain was still falling when I left the party twenty minutes later, without bothering to say good night to anyone, and walked the half mile or so back to my hotel.

2

CHIAROSCURO

I wasn't sure how I felt about Milan. It was an ugly city and, I thought, a depressing one, even in the middle of town around its great wedding cake of a cathedral. Part of my trouble with the place was that it had been raining ever since I arrived and I was sick of umbrellas and raincoats and the sound of water splashing down the street outside my hotel at night. My room looked out on a public park, but I could barely see it through the fog and the dampness that seemed permanently to enshroud it. Trolley cars rumbled along silent avenues crowded by grim people on their way to and from their jobs, and a sludge of traffic moved at a snail's pace through the streets outside the ancient walls of the *centro stòrico*, mostly closed to all but residents and public transport. Everywhere, however, reckless citizens on noisy motorcycles and scooters wove through cars and buses and trolleys and pedestrians, like cockroaches scurrying across a kitchen floor. It was a busy city, but without laughter in it, populated by people evidently dedicated to commerce and inured to gloom.

But then there was the food. I had yet to have a bad meal anywhere. My first night in town, just off the plane from L.A. and groggy from an unsatisfying nap in my hotel room, I'd been whisked off by Ravelli and two other magicians to a Tuscan restaurant lost in a maze of narrow streets somewhere past the ruins of a castle surrounded by a park. I had no idea where I was, but I didn't care. I ate my way to satiety, through a risotto with mushrooms, asparagus basted in sweet butter and parmigiano, a salad of endive and rugola, a succulent pear, strawberries, ice cream, and a cappuccino. And every meal since then had been a delight, with or without Ravelli and his friends. Twice I had wandered by myself into small, innocuous-looking eateries to be ravished by perfectly cooked pasta, tender veal, fresh vegetables, ripe fruit not picked before its time, succulent sweets I had never even heard of. "Is it like this all over Italy?" I asked Ravelli, on our second night and third meal together. "Milan must be the culinary capital of the world."

"The only thing in Italy America has not yet corrupted is our food," Ravelli said, "But that will happen, too, eventually, when this horde of barbarian youths comes of age and the old generation of restaurant owners dies off. But perhaps I will not live to see that, thank the fates."

In addition to eating well, I also had the pleasure of being able to hang around La Scala, in my mind the operatic capital of the world. I didn't know much about opera, having only come to it lately, from having been involved a few years earlier with an Italian tenor who owned racehorses, but I'd fallen in love with the music of Verdi, and through the music with the man himself. I'd read a couple of biographies and I'd begun to collect CDs of his work. La Scala was where the maestro had enjoyed some of his greatest triumphs, as well as a fiasco or two, and I'd regarded the unprepossessing building, with its squat facade of dark stone pillars and dirt-yellow walls, as a shrine. The management was about to produce there a definitive, restored version of *Rigoletto*, supposedly exactly as the maestro had composed it, free of the embellishments and corruptions encrusted upon it over the years by singers eager to show off their high notes and athletic prowess, but I'd given up any hope of being able to attend a performance; seats had been sold out for months, the porter at my hotel had informed me, and I'd have had to pay a scalper four or five hundred dollars even for a perch in one of the top balconies. That was a sum I could have afforded maybe only after hitting a giant exacta or bringing in a Pick Six, say, but I'd never gone racing in Italy and had no idea how to bet. The money I was being paid for my lectures barely covered my basic expenses, including, of course, my airfare.

I resigned myself to not going, but I was able at least to visit the museum on the premises, with its thousands of mementos of great operatic nights, and was able to get into the auditorium itself one morning. I stood by the orchestra pit and looked back up at the circular rows of cream and gold boxes soaring upward above the stage where most of the world's great singers had risked everything in song. A failure here, I'd been told, was a disaster from which few careers recovered. A merciless public of cognoscenti, quick to whistle its displeasure, fiercely committed to its favorites. As a close-up artist, I was used to small rooms, quiet audiences of innocents and devotees. I'd have died having to face that sort of challenge.

My lectures had gone well, even though we never attracted more than thirty or forty people to them. "It is the weather," Ravelli had informed me. "May can be bearable in Milan, but most of the time it rains. A pathetic climate, Luigi. But what you are doing is marvelous, *formidabile*." And it was true, I had been in good form; I was able to show off some deals and moves with cards few of the local magicians had seen. What drove them crazy was my Three Card Monte, a gambling game very popular in Italy and widely played on street corners in the major cities, I'd been told. When I pulled the move using only two cards instead of the usual three, the room broke into applause and several shouts of "bravo." I then performed the move again as the old familiar shell game, using a small rubber ball under three matchboxes, then only two. More applause and shouts, and I began to understand a bit of what it must be like at La Scala to win over an Italian public. No frozen, dull-witted Anglos here, but passionate partisans, fans committed to their enthusiasms. I forgot about how few we had in the room. I reminded myself of a quote I had come across somewhere by a French writer who called himself Stendhal to the effect that ultimately in life, if you're any good at what you do, you perform for "the happy few."

As a magician, Carlo Ravelli was less than a mediocrity. He had mastered about eight very basic moves, including a primitive Cups and Balls, which he insisted on performing as part of his introduction of me and his spiel on magic in general. But his ineptitude and cynical patter, which he used to cover his clumsiness, made me look even better than I was, so I didn't mind. And he was a zealous host, almost to the point of suffocation. He seemed to live for his party-going and to know everyone and everyone's secrets. I wasn't sure how I felt about him, but I had to admit he could be amusing and he did knock himself out for me. Anyway, in Rome I figured I'd be free of him and so I tolerated him and his view of the world as a giant cesspool. "You know, Carlo, you'd be a better magician," I told him on the morning of my next-to-last lecture and demonstration, "if you could believe in magic." He didn't understand what I was talking about, but then I hardly expected him to. He was thirty-five, but looked ten years older, as if his contempt for others had etched itself into his features, in the deep lines around his eyes and the corners of his mouth. I almost felt sorry for him.

The lecture, given in a room on the second floor of the Hilton, drew the biggest audience, about sixty people, probably because it had to do with cheating. Ravelli had told me that several of the casinos on the Italian Riviera, as well as one in Sempione on Lake Lugano, would be sending supervisors, who, I gathered, were the equivalent of pit bosses in the States. About a dozen of them showed up, dark, serious-looking men with the eyes of hawks, and they sat in the first two rows of chairs, silent as statues as I showed them what could happen to them. I scratched little marks along the edges of cards, indented them with a ring, marked them at the corners. I demonstrated a variety of ways crooked dealers could work in cahoots with players, palming cards out of the boxes, switching them so rapidly no one but an expert could have spotted the move. What really entranced them, though, was when I got them all up from their seats to stand around a craps layout while I demonstrated the slide, a dandy way of throwing the cubes so they'd spin along the felt without once tumbling over. I made thirteen straight passes until even the supervisors grunted their approval, then handed the dice to them so they could see I hadn't shaved or rounded or misspotted them. "*Formidabile*," Ravelli said, when I'd finished and was packing up the little tools of my trade as the room emptied. "Luigi, you are wasting your time as a magician, *caro*. You come and play cards with me at my club. We make a fortune."

I held out my hands to him. "See these, Carlo?" I said. "They're my working capital. I can't risk having them broken."

"Just one time, Luigi. One night, that is all."

"No, thanks, Carlo. I could have gone down that road a long time ago."

He laughed and put his arm through mine. "*Andiamo*," he said. "Tonight we are all going to the Blue Moon. Adriano is paying. We have dinner first and then you come."

"I have a date, Carlo."

"Ah." He grinned. "The one you met the other night, Bobby Jo."

"There's three of us."

"How interesting. Luigi, you are also a magician in bed, eh? *Che bravo!* Good. You have dinner, then you bring the girls to the Blue Moon. After ten. *Va bene?*"

"I don't know, maybe."

"Come on, don't be a squalid. It's Adriano's birthday and he is celebrating his victory."

"What victory?"

"His horse win today at San Siro."

"He owns a horse?"

"The best *puledro* in Italy."

"What's that?"

"A colt, three years old. He is going to win the Derby with him."

"What derby? Not ours. That was ten days ago."

"No, *stupido*, the Italian Derby, the last Sunday in May, *caro*."

"I might be there."

"Wonderful, we are all going."

"What's the name of this great horse?"

"Tiberio, after Adriano's favorite emperor. He has won five times. His father give this horse to Adriano for his birthday last year. He wants him to occupy his time with the stable."

"And does he?"

Ravelli laughed. "No, he is a big playboy, a big gambler. Adriano is only interested in having a good time."

"Like you, Carlo."

"Yes, like me. Exactly like me, only he have the money to do anything he wants. Me, I have to work."

"You, Carlo? You work? I'm impressed."

He shrugged and laughed again, a little nervously. "For my father. He is an engineer. Very boring. We won't talk about it. So we see you later, right?"

"Maybe."

"Oh, yes, you come, and bring the *bimbe*. We have a real good time and Adriano will invite you to the races. You like the races, eh?"

"I'm a committed horseplayer, Carlo."

"Committed? What does that mean? You also gamble?"

"Doesn't everyone?"

That was the afternoon Bobby Jo went to Teddy Amendola's studio to be photographed. He had already decided to shoot only nudes of her, because, as he explained to her, he thought she could never have a career as a fashion model. She was too big in the shoulders, too carnal, but he was sure she had a wonderful body, he told her, full of planes and hollows and interesting contrasts of bone and muscle. "I am putting together this show for the Aurora Gallery, and you will provide another dimension, I am certain," he told her. "Flesh and innocence, it will be fascinating to photograph."

She was nervous, so he made a drink for her, a double vodka on the rocks, and told her to take it easy, to relax. Holding the vodka in her hand, she made a brief tour of the room where he had mounted a series of blowups he had shot for *Elle* the previous fall, elegant women stylishly posed in the cobblestoned streets of a mountain village somewhere in the Abruzzi, southeast of Rome. She could tell he was an artist with a camera, not just a fashion photographer. She told him so and he said, "I take pictures, that's all. Whatever is there, I try to bring it out. Sometimes it is easy, sometimes not."

It was an hour before he began to shoot. She was not a good model, because he could never get her to relax. She hadn't eaten since breakfast and the vodka hit her hard. She seemed not to exist inside her own body, to be looking at herself in action, like a character in a play. She had a beautiful body, she knew that, with those strong shoulders and high breasts, big hips, a classical female form, but she had never learned how to feel comfortable inside it. "You move as if it does not belong to you," Teddy Amendola said, as he pushed and prodded her and posed her for each shot. She felt like a mannequin in a store window, lifeless, trapped in a false reality.

Teddy Amendola worked hard with her. He used lights and shadows, became abstract in his approach to her, as if using her body for an essay in chiaroscuro. He never shot her face at all, though he used her long hair at one point as a prop, a veil tumbling back over one shoulder to accentuate the solidity of bone and muscle, the firm upward thrust of a hip outlined against a black background. I saw the pictures he shot of her much later, and you could see what he was trying for.

When the session was over, he paid her a million lire, well over six hundred dollars, in cash for three hours of her time. It was more money than she had expected and she had been grateful. "Oh, thanks, Teddy," she said. "Are you sure this is right? We didn't work that long, did we? I mean, I don't need charity."

"Be quiet," he said, "I'll pay you what I wish to pay you. Don't be stupid."

"Well, okay, that's very nice." She looked away from him briefly, feeling close to tears.

"Listen, my dear, I am going to tell you something," he said.

"Sure. Sure, Teddy."

"Go home," he said. "This life here is not for you. You are very beautiful, but there are so many beautiful girls everywhere. Not everyone can be successful, understand? It is hard here and cruel. Go home to America."

She looked stunned, he recalled later, as if he had suggested something outrageous, something inconceivable. "I don't want to go home," she said. "I have to do this, don't you see? It's my only chance."

"Your chance for what? Fame? Fortune? Dreams, my dear."

"No, just to *do* something, to *be* something for once on my own. I—oh, shit!" Again she looked away from him, and this time he was sure she would cry, but she didn't. When she faced him once more, her jaw was set and her eyes were dark with passion. "I'm not going to give up, never," she said. "I've come a ways, believe you me."

Teddy Amendola immediately disengaged himself. "Well, of course, my dear, you must do what you think best," he said, smiling. "It's your life, yes?"

It was nearly eight when she left his studio. She had paused in the entrance hall, her eye suddenly caught by the dark, handsome face of a boy looming out of the shadows to her left, from inside the recessed wall beside the front door. The eyes seemed haunted, his head framed in a light that struck her as unearthly, as if the head of the figure itself created an aura for its own existence. "Wow, who's that?" she said. "He's beautiful."

"His name was Silvio," Teddy Amendola said. "Like you, he came here in pursuit of a dream."

"What happened to him?"

"He's dead," Teddy Amendola said, withdrawing himself into the safety of his studio. "Remember what I told you. Good night."

He shut his studio door on her and she let herself out.

3

TENDERNESS

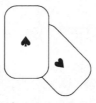

"So what kind of magic can you do?" Parker Williams asked about halfway through our dinner together that night.

"What kind would you like to see?"

"The kind I'm sure you can't do, like changing my agent into the pig he ought to be, or turning Adriano into a eunuch," Parker said. "But I'll settle for something amusing. Only no cards. I can't stand card tricks."

"Why not?"

"I had an uncle who did card tricks and I hated him. He was the most boring man I ever met, and believe me, I've met thousands of boring men. No, do something fun, something I haven't seen before."

"Honestly, Parker," Bobby Jo said, "you're rude. Shifty is a great magician."

"How do you know?" she asked. "What have you seen him do apart from a simple little coin trick?"

"Hold still!" I said to Parker. "Hold still and you won't get hurt!"

Parker stiffened in her chair. "What is it?"

"Easy does it," I said. "Don't move." I slowly, carefully reached out toward the top of her head, then lunged forward.

Parker screamed. "It's okay, I got it," I said, opening my hand to reveal a big black rubber spider I had supposedly just plucked from her scalp. "It's a tame one." I dropped it on the table in front of her.

Bobby Jo laughed and Parker conceded me a smile. "Not bad, Shifty," she said, "but hardly world class."

"Hey, I'm not being paid to do this. I'm sort of on vacation."

"Do another, Shifty," Bobby Jo said. "I could watch you all night."

So I did Ring on a Stick, Hopping Thimbles, Cups and Balls, Backfire Reverse, two or three others, and by the end of my stint we had the waiters grouped around our table. Two of them applauded. "See?" Bobby Jo said. "He's great."

Parker smiled. "You're okay, Shifty," she said. "We could use you in this town. Comedy relief."

"If it's so horrible here, why don't you all go home?" I asked.

"To become what, a cocktail waitress?" Parker answered. "No, this is easy, if you make it, and the money's good. It's just there are so many sleazeballs around."

"Everybody keeps telling me to go home," Bobby Jo said. "Even Teddy Amendola today. I guess I must look like I can't make it or something. One more month, that's what I'm giving myself." She told us about the photo session with Amendola. "He was real sweet, but kind of sad. There was a big blowup of this very handsome guy on his wall, Silvio?"

"Yeah, that was his boyfriend, the love of his life," Parker said. "He met him four or five years ago. He was a model."

"He died, Teddy said."

"Yeah. Silvio used to sleep around a lot."

"Where does that leave Teddy?" I asked.

"Who knows?" Parker said. "Who cares? They're all big boys, aren't they? They want to dip their wicks in each other's behinds, they have to be ready to take the consequences."

"You're a tough cookie, Parker," I said.

"No, just a survivor," she said. "I've had to wade through a lot of shit in this business and I got burned a couple of times. Then I stopped going out with these guys. All they want is to get laid, anyway. I string them along, you have to, but I keep my legs crossed." She laughed. "They call me the Ice Princess. But that's how I've survived here. I do my job, I'm nice to everyone, I go to their parties, but I don't do drugs and I don't fuck around. It's work, that's all."

It was nearly eleven o'clock by the time we finished eating. It had been another unforgettable meal, featuring a risotto cooked with succulent porcini mushrooms. The trattoria Parker had picked out was a mile or so away from their hotel, along one of the main avenues leading out of town, and it looked uninviting, just a couple of sparsely furnished rooms illuminated by harsh neon lighting. But it was run by the owner's wife, a plump, pink-cheeked woman who presided over her kitchen as if it were her own home; every dish was prepared as if she were cooking for her children, and at a modest price of about twenty dollars per customer. Parker and some of the other models in town were regulars there, and the family treated them like long-lost relatives. "Great people," Parker had explained, "the best. Italians in general are wonderful, Shifty, except for the politicians, the rich, and people in the movies and fashion worlds. You'll find out."

"Isn't that true everywhere?" I asked. "I don't know any great human beings in politics or the upper levels of show biz. It's the same all over, isn't it?"

"It sure is in New York," Bobby Jo said. "Wow, it's really bad there."

"I don't know," Parker said, pouring the last of the house white wine into our glasses. "Here it's so naked, so crass. Milan isn't as big as New York or Paris, so maybe that's why it seems more brutal. The modeling agencies here attract people from all over, a lot of them, like Bobby Jo, from the States. They show up here with little money, promises of work, an introduction or two to a couple of art directors and photographers. They don't know anything and they don't speak the language. They're dependent on the kindness of strangers, most of whom want to exploit them one way or another. Like me. I came here ten years ago, maybe eleven, but I caught on fast. And I was lucky. I got a break right away, doing a *Playboy* fashion spread, the Italian edition. A lot of people aren't lucky."

"What happens?"

"Well, they come over thinking it's all going to be easy. The agencies con them. Sometimes they pay their airfares, put them up in cheap hotels, loan them money while they're out making the rounds," Parker continued. "They charge commissions as high as forty-eight percent till they get their money back. It's kind of like white slavery. These kids are plunged into a world they're totally unprepared for—a big party scene, fast cars, easy money, drugs. The guys who run this scene are rich, or their families are rich. They make their own rules. You have to learn how to survive here. You have to be lucky as well as talented. You have to be able to say no."

"Some of them are all right," Bobby Jo said. "They all want you to go to bed with them, but you say no and it's okay. They don't hassle you all that much."

Parker snickered. "Don't count on it, honey," she said. "Some of these guys'll do anything, believe me."

"What about Carlo Ravelli?" I asked.

"He's sweet," Bobby Jo said. "He just likes to party all the time. And he works."

"Not at magic," I said.

"He's what the Italians call a *figlio di papà*, a daddy's boy," Parker said. "He works for his dad because he doesn't have any money of his own, but he doesn't do anything. His dad's a builder, public works, mainly. The word is he's all mixed up in this big scandal that's going on now."

"What big scandal? You mean, the one I keep reading about in the papers back home?"

"Yeah," Parker said. "Old man Ravelli was one of those who kicked back money to get government contracts. They've been doing that since the beginning of time here, but now it's all coming out and people are going to jail."

"Carlo says nothing's going to happen," Bobby Jo said. "They'd have to put half of Italy in jail. And he says his dad wasn't one of the main guys, anyway. His firm is like not a very big one and a lot of his business is abroad, like in Africa or Asia or somewhere. Carlo thinks nothing's going to happen."

"Maybe not to him," Parker said, "but a lot of businessmen and politicians are going to the slammer here. The trials have just begun.

They've got a new government now, you know. All the old guys are in big trouble. They call it Kickback City here."

"What about this guy Adriano?" I asked, turning to Bobby Jo. "The one who has the hots for you? Is he involved in all this stuff?"

"I don't know. He's real rich, I know that."

"He's bad news," Parker said. "I've been telling Bobby Jo to stay away from him."

"He comes on to me all the time," Bobby Jo said, "like he's obsessed with me or something. I think he's a little scary."

"You bet he is," Parker said. "He beats up on people."

"So why are we going to the Blue Moon tonight?" I asked.

"Why are you?" Parker echoed me. "I'm not. I'm going home. I've got a ten-o'clock appointment."

"Maybe we should all go home," I said.

"Yeah, me, too," Bobby Jo agreed. "I'm tired. I got a little drunk at Teddy's and my head hurts."

It had finally stopped raining and we walked back to the hotel in the soft spring night. A full moon had broken through the clouds and touched the old, grimy-looking buildings of the *centro* with silver. For the first time since my arrival I felt rested, free of lingering jet lag. I wasn't sleepy at all. Bobby Jo took my hand and we strolled happily along, with Parker Williams on the other side of me, her face a pale blur in the light reflected off the shiny, slick surfaces of the street. "I think I could get to like Milan," I said, as we turned in to the cobblestoned alley leading to the hotel.

"That's because you're with me," Parker said. "And you think you're going to get laid."

"Parker, honest," Bobby Jo said. "You're really bad."

"I don't rush things, Parker," I said. "I just let the current carry me along."

"Sure you do," Parker said, laughing.

Carlo Ravelli was waiting for us in the lobby of the hotel. He'd been sitting by himself, nursing a whiskey and water while watching the news on the small TV set in a corner of the room, next to the self-service bar. The Piccolo lived up to its name; it was small, only thirty-eight rooms, with a lobby that could accommodate no more than eight people. Carlo was alone in it. The minute he saw us he bounced to his feet, smiling broadly. "There you are," he said. "I've been waiting for you!"

"What for?" I asked.

"The Blue Moon, we are all expecting you," he explained. "It is nearly eleven-thirty. Adriano wants you very much to come. He sent me here to remind you."

"Good night, kids," Parker said, heading for the elevator. "Have a good time. Watch yourself, honey. Shifty, you're okay."

Ravelli made no effort to stop her, but concentrated on us. "Come on now, Adriano will be very disappointed. He wants so much to meet you, Luigi. I have told him all about you and how you love the horses. He is fascinated."

"Carlo, it's Bobby Jo he wants, right?" I said.

"*Beh*, her, too, of course. But you must come. It's a very nice party, really. Adriano is paying for everything."

"That's very nice of him, but I think I'll pass, Carlo."

"Bobby Jo? Adriano is waiting."

"Gee, I don't think so, Carlo," she said, "but please thank him for me. I'm really tired."

"But Adriano insists—" Ravelli began.

"Hey, Carlo, why did he send you? Couldn't he come himself?" I asked.

"Well, it *is* a party," Ravelli said. "He *is* the host, no? So I told him I'd try to find you." He looked back and forth from me to Bobby Jo. "Ah, *capisco*. I do not insist. Eh, *l'amore, l'amore* . . ."

"Carlo, isn't it possible we just don't want to come to the party?" I said. "It's nothing personal. Just tell your friend Adriano that you couldn't find us. We didn't come back to the hotel, okay?"

"Okay," he said, grinning broadly. He kissed Bobby Jo on both cheeks. "*Bella.*" He turned to me. "Luigi, I don't tell Adriano nothing. He gets mad, you know? *Bravo*, Luigi. I see you tomorrow. You go to Rome?"

"Maybe. I'm not sure yet."

"I call you or you call me, okay?"

"Okay."

"*Ciao.*" He slipped out into the night, and seconds later I heard him roar away up the street in his cream-colored Ferrari.

"I guess what Adriano wants, he usually gets," I said. "And I guess Adriano wants you, Bobby Jo."

She picked up her key at the front desk and I walked her to the elevator. "So you may go to Rome tomorrow?" she asked.

"Probably," I said. "I do want to see some things. I don't know anybody there, but Carlo said he'd give me a couple of introductions. I'm sort of playing it by ear, Bobby Jo. I don't have a fixed itinerary or anything like that. I have to be back here for one more lecture before I leave, but I don't want to spend all my time in Milan."

We reached the elevator. "You want to come with me for a while?" she asked, taking my hand again.

"You sure you want me to?"

"Yes, I'm sure," she said, as we got into the elevator. "I guess you want to, huh?"

She lived in a tiny room on the third floor with a single bed and a window that looked out on a courtyard. There were hooks in the wall to hang her clothes from, a chest of drawers, a small table, and straight-backed wooden chair. There were no pictures on the wall and no TV set. The bathroom was the size of a broom closet, with a showerhead protruding from the wall. "It gets everything wet," she said, as I peered into the room, "but at least I can stay clean." She paid about eighty dollars a night for the place, a special rate arranged by her agency. "But I get breakfast, too," she said. "Coffee and a roll, usually."

"It looks like a jail cell," I said.

"Yeah, well, it's not so bad," she said. "If I start making some money, I can move. And it's right in the middle of town and all. Of course, the bed is kind of small." She kissed me and began to undress.

We started to make love that night, but it wasn't very satisfactory. She had a beautiful body that made me want to take her, but she was a passive recipient and not a participator, as if she were repaying me simply for being nice to her. And then, before I could enter her, the phone rang. She pushed me away, picked up the receiver, and sat up on the side of the bed. "*Sì?*"

I could hear a male voice barking into her ear. She nodded and said, "Yes, yes, I understand. . . . No, I didn't see him there. . . . No, not yesterday. It is tonight. . . . Yes, I will, I will. Good-bye." She hung up and leaned over, hugging herself with both arms.

"Who was it? You all right?" I asked.

She shook her head. "We should have gone to the party tonight," she said. "They expected me to."

"Who did? Adriano?"

"No, no." She began to cry.

"Hey, Bobby Jo, we don't have to do this," I said, putting my hand on her shoulder. "We can even go to the party, if you have to. Come on, we'll get dressed. I'll take you there."

"No, I don't have to now," she said. "It's too late."

"Too late for what?"

Instead of answering, she turned and put her arms around me. "Oh, Shifty, you're so nice and all," she said. "I don't know what's happening to me. I'm—I'm so kind of lost or something."

I sat up and patted her, as if she were a child. "Look, you're just depressed. Maybe Parker's right, Bobby Jo. Maybe you ought to go home."

"I can't," she said. "I don't want to. You don't understand. I've got to make this work."

"Okay, but give yourself a break," I said. "It's not the end of the world if you don't make it here. You're young, you're really beautiful. You have a long road ahead of you. You're pushing yourself too hard, you've got too much wrapped up in this. Am I wrong?"

She shook her head, her eyes still full of tears. "I can't help it, Shifty," she said. "I've never done anything right. This has got to work out for me. You don't know."

"No, I don't," I said. "But you can talk to me about it, if you want to."

"No, it's okay, honest." She sat up and shook her head. "I'm so mad at myself."

"Forget that," I said. "Anger just poisons the old system. Lose it."

For the next half hour or so, I played child psychologist and counselor, and eventually she stopped crying. I put my clothes on, told her I'd call her when I got back from Rome, and let myself out. I wasn't sure I would call her or ever see her again; she had problems I knew nothing about, and I wasn't so enamored of her that I wanted to make them my own. I'd give her a ring, I told myself, maybe before I flew home from Milan in three weeks or so. I felt sorry for her, but I had decided to be selfish about my own life for a while. I was still bleeding a little from an involvement I'd had recently with a lady cop back in California. Out in the street, it had begun to rain again, a misty drizzle through which I walked glumly back to my hotel.

4

INHIBITIONS

My departure for Rome was delayed for a day by the porter at my hotel, who had somehow managed to acquire a ticket for me in the *loggione*, the topmost gallery of La Scala, for that night's performance of *Rigoletto*. It cost me $150 including the tip to the porter, but I decided it was a once-in-a-lifetime opportunity that I couldn't pass up. From where I sat that night, way up in the next-to-last row and off to the side, the stage seemed to be at the bottom of a well, but my racetrack binoculars enabled me to bring the singers into focus. The sound was glorious, with the voices soaring up through the tubular shape of the great house to ravish the senses. The baritone in the title part, a veteran whose name even I had heard of, broke slowly out of the gate in Act One but closed strongly to prove best by a couple of *fioriture* over the rest of a strong field of warblers. As for the music itself, well, it was old man Verdi again, touching the heart and mind with melodies rooted in a deep understanding of human passions and pain. I left the theater humming.

Carlo Ravelli had also tried to delay my departure by inviting me to another party. When I told him I had a ticket for the opera that night, he said, "*Formidabile,* you will come after the performance. Nothing begins until midnight anyway." I said I'd see how I felt after the final curtain, but he insisted that I couldn't cheat myself of this ultimate Milanese experience. "Dino and Allegra's parties are always fabulous," he said. "They have very much money and they make all their parties an event. You must come, *caro*. You will never forget this, I promise you."

I was too charged up from the opera to want to go immediately to bed that night, so I took a taxi to the Palazzo Pelagra, named after our hosts. It was a small, elegant four-story Renaissance building behind the Corso Magenta, a main avenue, and overlooking a public park, the handsomest I'd seen in Milan, with sculpted hedges, ancient trees, and great banks of flowers. The Pelagras lived in a duplex on the top two floors, a sanctuary they had designed for themselves, according to Ravelli, and accessible only by a private elevator from the story below. It opened directly into their vestibule, and from there you stepped down into a large sunken living room, very dark and comfortably furnished with low divans and couches, fat pillows, burning incense, a room apparently designed to seduce.

It was nearly midnight when I arrived and the party was well under way. The living room was full of bodies dressed in elaborate costumes, but I couldn't make out anyone's features. Luckily, Carlo Ravelli soared up from the gloom to greet me. He was dressed as a pirate, in boots and black pants, with a cutlass thrust into his sash and his shirt slashed open to the waist. "Ah, Luigi, you have arrived," he said, grinning and pumping my hand up and down. "Come, you must right away get into your costume."

"What costume?"

"Everyone must wear a costume tonight," he explained. "Oh, Allegra, I wish you to meet a famous *mago*, Luigi Anderson."

Allegra Pelagra had a body like a snake. She seemed to have coiled into her dress, which was all black leather and swastikas and chains and high boots, something out of a fetishist magazine. Her thighs and arms were bare and her shirt was slit open to her belt, from which dangled a set of black leather cuffs. Her long black hair had been pulled straight back into a bun and her blue eyes glowed out of the pale skin of her long, angular face like those of a feral cat. "Darling," she said, as she opened her arms to embrace me, "you must immediately put on your costume. This way. You'll find them all ready for you in the upper bedroom, over there. Then do join us down below." She kissed me on the cheek. "I'm so pleased Carlo invited you. I have such a treat in store for us all this evening."

"I assume the costume is required," I said.

"But of course," Allegra answered. "Didn't Carlo explain? This is a costume party. Such fun. We all change identities and become other people in different clothes. Hurry up now! We're all waiting for you."

Bobby Jo Dawson came down the stairs from the upper bedroom. Apparently she had decided to portray some sort of water nymph. Her outfit was woven out of netting, with strands of green seaweed and bits of shells and starfish and seahorses sewn here and there to make her appear to have emerged from the depths of the ocean floor. "My dear, you look simply spectacular," Allegra said, taking her hand and tugging her away from us toward the living room. "I knew I had chosen the perfect one for you. Come now, I have friends who are excited to meet you." And she pulled Bobby Jo behind her down into the party.

I went upstairs and found myself offered a choice between a slave costume, which consisted of little more than a loincloth, and a wedding dress, complete with bridal veil and bouquet. My first instinct was to bolt, but I decided to hang around long enough to find out what would happen. After all, I'd never been to an orgy before and I figured my racetrack pals back in L.A. might never forgive me if I just walked out on one. I opened a closet door and found a long, black feather boa, draped it around my neck, and returned to the living room.

It was very dark, with the only light coming from shielded bulbs set above into the walls themselves. An enormous ancient golden Buddha Dino and Allegra had brought back from Thailand or some-where sat on his throne against the rear wall, while at the other end of the room a long, low table held all sorts of edible tidbits and drinks. There was a faint pink smoke of incense that blurred my view of the scene. I decided not to taste anything but the wine that a manservant was pouring directly out of a bottle. Carlo had warned me that Dino and Allegra liked to ensure the success of their scenarios by putting substances into the refreshments, and I didn't want to be drugged.

The manservant was dressed like a satyr and looked ridiculous. He was in his fifties and fat, but he played his role to the hilt, ogling and leering at the guests.

I found a seat on a couch across from the Buddha and next to a woman in her forties who was dressed in tights, a furry sweater, and a cat mask that covered her face from the nose up. "*Ciao, chi sei?*" she said.

"I'm sorry, I don't speak Italian," I said.

"Ah, I see. What are you supposed to be? A transvestite?"

"No. I'm just a guy with a feather boa around his neck."

"Well, you look stupid."

"I figure I'm not the only one, lady. What's the point of all this? Who are all these people?"

The woman laughed. She had a dark, hoarse voice ruined by decades of smoking. "Ah, they are all most distinguished," she said. "That man over there, dressed like an ape, is Franco Bellinzona, everyone's favorite investment banker. The fat man in the toga is Tommaso Cataldi, the Socialist deputy and ex-foreign minister. The woman next to him is his girlfriend, Marisa Tempelli, the television talk-show hostess. She is a hyena and, of course, Allegra's closest friend." The Tempelli woman was dressed in a short brown tunic and sandals laced up to her knees. "She likes to look like a boy. She is a famous bisexual."

"You seem to know everybody," I said. "Who are you?"

"I am married to the banker, but we do not sleep together anymore."

"That's too bad."

"No, it is liberating. Franco is a pig."

"So whom do you sleep with?"

"No one," she said. "I am happy with myself and to look at the follies of others."

"That must be rewarding. What is the occasion for this party?"

"I have no idea," she answered, "but usually there is a human sacrifice. The women will let us know."

"The women?"

"Yes, Allegra and her friends. They are the ones who perform.

Sometimes Dino will join in, but not always. We are here for the entertainment value. It is a game and it has rules, though I have no idea what they are." She inhaled deeply from her cigarette and blew smoke into my face. "Did you come here hoping to be included?"

"I don't know why I'm here," I said. "I don't think I'm going to be around very long."

The woman lost interest in me and conversation languished. I decided to stay put, not knowing what might happen if I got up and mingled. I felt like someone who has blundered unwittingly into a fetishist bar or a club reunion of old queens. I sipped my wine and waited, not sure what I would do. I wondered whether I should try to rescue Bobby Jo and get her out of there, but I couldn't see her anywhere. She seemed to have disappeared.

It must have been about an hour later that I sensed a stirring of bodies at the far end of the room, below a short flight of steps leading up to the master bedroom. Something was happening. Ravelli loomed over me. "Come, Luigi, the fantasy is beginning," he said, urging me up out of my seat.

I dropped my feather boa on the floor and followed him into the bedroom where most of the party had now gathered. Bobby Jo was lying on the bed between Allegra and Marisa, who were kissing and caressing her. She was resisting, but only feebly, as if unable to defend herself, and her eyes seemed made of glass. She had obviously been drugged.

There were ten or eleven people in the room, mostly men, watching. Cataldi was there, bug-eyed, his mouth parted in anticipation, and so was Bellinzona, standing rigidly in a corner in his ape suit. I grabbed Ravelli's arm. "Carlo, let's get her out of here," I said. "She's been drugged."

"Luigi, where is your costume?"

"I'm wearing it. Carlo, this is nasty stuff. She doesn't know what's going on."

"It is part of the festivity, Luigi."

"This isn't festive, Carlo. It's called rape."

Dino Pelagra smiled at us from across the room and put a finger to his lips. I walked over to the bed and took Bobby Jo's arm. "Come on, Bobby Jo, let's get out of here," I said, trying to pull her upright.

Allegra pushed me angrily away. "Stop!" she said. "You stop! You must leave now!"

I leaned over Bobby Jo again. "Bobby Jo, come on, let's go," I said. "Let's go home now."

Somebody grabbed me from behind and pulled me away. I turned around and found myself confronted by Dino Pelagra. His face was contorted with rage. "You go now!" he said. "You do not belong here!"

"No, and neither does she," I said. "You've drugged her."

Ravelli came up beside me. "Luigi, there is no harm here," he said. "No one is hurt."

"Carlo, this is a bad scene. It would be only ridiculous, but what they're doing to Bobby Jo is criminal. Now help me——"

I was seized from behind and my right arm was twisted up behind my shoulder blades. Dino Pelagra said something in Italian and I was quickly hustled out of the room. I caught a glimpse of the woman I had been talking to on the sofa. She was lying on the floor, deeply involved with two men. Elsewhere in the room other guests were pairing off. No one even looked up as I was propelled toward the elevator. My escort was the manservant, whose fat evidently concealed a lot of muscle and who had obviously had some sort of professional training in handling unruly citizens. He kept a firm grip on me until the elevator door opened and he thrust me into it.

As the door started to close on me, Ravelli came up behind him. He appeared distraught. "Luigi, I am sorry," he called out. "Nothing bad will happen. Don't——" But I was on my way down and couldn't hear what else he said. My arm ached from the force of the man's hold on me.

It was raining hard outside and I got soaked getting back to my hotel. I caught a bad cold and had to delay my departure for Rome for a couple of days. Ravelli called the next afternoon. "Luigi, I am sorry. Are you all right?"

"Yes," I said, "How's Bobby Jo?"

"She is fine. It was most amusing, Luigi. It was only for fun, you know."

"Some fun. If I were Bobby Jo, I'd go to the police."

"Don't be absurd, *caro*. Who would believe her? She has not even the proper work papers, you know. Dino and Allegra are very well known."

"I can imagine."

"Like so many Americans, you are a prude," Ravelli said. "I am disappointed in you. You see, Dino and Allegra are also magicians. They can make all inhibitions disappear."

"Was Adriano there?"

"No, and he's furious about it."

"Why?"

"He was reserving the girl for himself. When he learned of the party, he couldn't believe he had not been invited. He called Dino, who told him he had not been invited because he would not have fitted in with the delicate structure of the tableau. Adriano is furious. He thinks Allegra is a Lesbian, nothing more. He is utterly without fantasy. By the way, you sound terrible. Are you ill?"

"I have a cold. Does it ever stop raining in this town?"

"In June, usually. Are you going to Rome?"

"Maybe tomorrow, if I feel better."

"Good. Maybe I will see you there. Remember, the Derby is in two weeks. I will call you. Where are you staying?"

"I found a small hotel called the Portoghesi. Parker told me about it. I have to come back to Milan next week."

"I know, but that is one day, maybe two, no? Then we go to the Derby."

"I may go down to Naples and Pompeii for a few days, but I'm playing it by ear."

"Good. Enjoy yourself, Luigi. We will talk soon."

5

PICTURES

I was still hacking and coughing when I left for Rome two days later, but at least I no longer had a temperature. No sooner had I left Milan and the Po Valley than the sun began to shine. The train pulled into Rome's Stazione Termini late that afternoon under a bright blue sky, with swallows wheeling overhead. For some strange reason, even though I had never been in the city before, I felt completely at home in it. The taxi whisked me down avenues and narrow streets that seemed familiar to me, as if I had dreamed them, then dropped me off at my hotel in a tiny piazza where three streets converged beneath a medieval tower I was sure I had seen before. I realized later I had read about it, as the setting for Hawthorne's novel *The Marble Faun*, but the feeling remained strong in me that I had somehow been there at some earlier time, that I belonged to these ancient stones. I had never had such a feeling before, in any of the cities and countries I had visited, so I made the most of it.

For a week I walked everywhere, guidebook in hand, with no fixed itinerary but just allowing my fancy to dictate the route. I forgot all about Milan and Carlo Ravelli and Bobby Jo until, late on the afternoon of my seventh night in town, I walked into the lobby of the Portoghesi and saw a copy of the *Paris Tribune* on the front desk. A snapshot of Bobby Jo Dawson looked up at me from under a headline that said the body of an American model had been found on the shore of Lake Lugano, not far from the Swiss border. The story described how the body had been found and that no one had yet been arrested. I went upstairs and called Parker Williams in Milan.

"They don't know who did it yet," Parker said. "It's been all over the front pages here. The cops came to talk to me this morning. I had to call her father in Kentucky. He's coming over in a couple of days to claim her body and take her home."

"My God, Parker, who could have done this?" I told her about my last evening in Milan at the Pelagra orgy.

"I told her not to go," Parker said. "It was that friend of yours Ravelli who talked her into it. She was a nice kid, but not bright. I never met anybody with less self-esteem and common sense than that kid. I tried to help her."

"I know you did, Parker. Is there anything I can do?"

"No, not that I can think of. I hope the police go after that guy Adriano. I'm sure he knows something about this."

"Why do you think that?"

"He had a real thing about her. He'd been chasing her for weeks. The night she was killed she was at a party at his villa. I think Adriano's capable of anything."

"Did you tell the police that?"

"Yeah, but I'm not sure they'll do anything. Adriano's dad is a big wheel. He's untouchable."

"Even if he kills somebody?"

"He has an alibi, I'm sure, and he'll have plenty of witnesses to put him far from the scene. Are you coming back here?"

"Yes, but I'm not sure when. I love Rome. I may stay on for the Italian Derby, then come back for my last few days in Italy. I want to go to La Scala again."

"Okay, maybe I'll see you."

"Yeah, I'll call you. Call me here again if you find out anything more."

"Yeah, I will."

"Who found her?"

"Some old man. There was a photographer, too, Francesca Pirro.

I know her. She's a freelance, a nice gal. I told her about you, she may want to talk to you."

"Why?"

"She's on the story. It's her pictures in all the papers."

"I don't know anything."

"She's okay, you can trust her."

"But I don't know anything, Parker."

"You were at the Pelagra party. It's possible, you know, that the police will want to talk to everybody who was at that party."

"Nobody's contacted me."

"That's because they don't know where you are. I'll call you, Shifty, if anything else happens."

After she hung up, I went down to the lobby to pick up the *Tribune*.

The body was found by an old man walking his dog along the shore of Lake Lugano, on the Italian side not far from the old Swiss customs house. The old man saw the body as the dog began to bark. He was more upset by the dog's behavior than by the sight of the woman, who was lying facedown, her torso wedged between a couple of rocks, with her legs in the water. She was wearing only a pair of panties and a dark blue sweatshirt.

The old man lived with his invalid wife in a small villa about two hundred meters away, up the hillside toward Sempione. He was a retired engineer named Paolo Bartolini. He had not even gone down to look at the body, but had rushed home to call the carabinieri. Then he had gone back to the site and arrived there just as the car and Jeep full of uniformed men showed up. He had made his statement, then had retreated back up toward the road. He had left the dog at home and he was standing there, with his hands in his coat pockets, looking down at the activity below when Francesca Pirro showed up. He was the first person she talked to. "What happened?" she asked. "Who is she?"

"I don't know," the old man said. "I don't know anything."

Francesca took down his name and he told her his story. He only shrugged when she asked him why he hadn't checked to see for himself whether the woman might be alive. "I was afraid," he said. "I didn't know what to do. These young people today . . ." He looked at the photographer as if she, too, represented some sort of threat.

"Listen, I'm only a reporter," she told him. "It's all right, Signor Bartolini. Really." Then she thanked him, smiled, and started down to the shoreline, where the carabinieri were busy around the body. Up above her, on the road, she could see the flashing blue lights of an ambulance, and down below, among the cops, she spotted the white uniforms of two paramedics supervising the loading of the body onto a stretcher.

Francesca took a few pictures from up above, one of which Mezzanotte used that evening on the front page, and then she started down the slope. It was a misty morning and a light rain had begun to fall. She almost slipped on her way down, which would have been embarrassing, but then she was used to men, especially Italian men, wanting to see her fall on her face. They were always fooled by her. First they'd try to patronize her and coddle her, because she was small and, they thought, so adorable-looking, and then when they found out she wasn't so adorable and that she was a photojournalist and a tough little bitch, they'd feel betrayed and treat her like shit. She was used to it.

She got to within ten or fifteen meters of the group around the woman on the stretcher and she could see they were working on her. Nobody had spotted her yet, so she shot some more pictures. The flash got their attention and one of the carabinieri turned around and came back toward her, motioning her away. "*Via,*" he said, "no pictures! Please leave immediately!"

Francesca ignored him long enough to shoot a couple more. She had caught a glimpse of the woman's face in profile under the oxygen mask they had clamped over her nose. She could tell that the victim was young and that she had blond hair. One of the paramedics had set up an IV, so Francesca knew she was still alive. The close-up of the woman lying on her back with the mask over her face made the *Corriere* and then later Francesca sold it to the magazines. It was the only picture anyone had of her after she was found. Francesca made a couple of million lire from those shots, a good day's work for a freelancer. *Paparazza suprema,* she called herself.

The young cop was annoyed when she paid no attention to him. He started shouting at her and telling her he was going to confiscate her cameras. "Hey, listen, listen," she said, flashing her Milanese police pass, "it's all right. I'm a journalist."

"In Milan maybe, here no," the young cop said. "*Se ne vada!* Leave, right now!"

She spotted the *maresciallo* and waved at him. He was an old acquaintance from two years before, when she'd been sent by *Epoca* to shoot a picture story on the casino at Sempione, which is a tiny Italian lakefront town entirely inside Swiss territory. It has a gambling casino that was used to launder money for a number of criminal enterprises in Milan from all over Italy. The mayor and the whole city council were arrested. There was a big scandal and the mayor went to jail. Francesca's editor at *Epoca* had wanted a big spread on the whole scene. The *maresciallo*, the head of the carabinieri station there, took a fancy to her and had made her job so much easier. He was an old guy, maybe sixty-four, sixty-five, with a wife and kids and grandchildren, but he had an eye for the young stuff, and Francesca definitely qualified. All she had to do was act cute and sweet with him. It puffed him up like one of those balloon figures you see in parades and he'd let her shoot anywhere and everywhere, even told her a lot of background stuff about the people involved in the scandal. It was one of the easiest stories she had ever worked on and she got a lot of money for it. Now, unfortunately, she couldn't remember the *maresciallo*'s name. But he recognized her and walked up the slope to talk to her. "*Ciao*, Francesca, how are you?" he said, waving the young man away from her and taking both her hands in his. He was a big man, not tall, but heavy in his limbs, and her hands disappeared in his like swallows into their nests. "What are you doing here? How did you get here?"

She smiled, going into her cute act. "What a pleasure to see you," she said. "I was in Lugano for the weekend and I was driving back home when I picked up this call on my radio. You know I always tune in to the police channels. Well, I'm a journalist, no? So what's going on here?" She leaned in toward him, as if she were helpless and totally dependent on him. "Who's the girl? Is she alive?"

"*Cara*, one thing at a time," the *maresciallo* said, smiling. "We don't know who she is. Some old man who lives near here found her and phoned us. I put out an emergency call and here we are."

"But what do you know about her?"

"Nothing," he said. "Except that somebody beat the hell out of her."

"So she *is* dead."

"Not quite, but soon. I think maybe her skull is fractured. She's not breathing very well."

"I'd like to get some pictures, a couple of close-ups."

The *maresciallo* shook his head. "Hey, Francesca, I can't let you down there," he said. "There isn't any room, as you can see, and they're trying to keep her alive long enough to get her to a hospital."

"No identification of any kind?"

"No." And that was when he told her about the logo and the picture on her shirt.

"So maybe an American, huh?"

"Who knows?" the *maresciallo* said. "These days the kids buy these shirts from all over. It doesn't mean there's any connection, you know."

"Maybe a tourist," she ventured. "Somebody ripped her off, raped her, and dumped her here."

"It could be anything," the *maresciallo* said. "These are times of violence, Francesca. Good times for you, eh? You make money off this stuff."

"Ah, *Maresciallo*, you know I don't commit violence, I only record it," she said.

"For money."

"Sure. You're a cop, no? You get paid, don't you?"

The *maresciallo* laughed. He had big yellow teeth that gleamed under his gray mustache. He squeezed her shoulder. "Look, Francesca," he said, "you stay right here, all right? You take all the pictures you want. You be patient. When we take her out of here, they'll carry her right past you. You can get whatever you can then. All right, *cocca*?"

"Okay," she said, "but keep that buffoon off me. Where do you get such recruits?"

The *maresciallo* laughed again. "Sicily, Calabria, the Abruzzi, where else?" he said. "Poverty breeds criminals and cops, Francesca." He threw her a little mock salute and went back to his men around the stretcher, where they were still working on the girl.

From her perch above the action, she took as many pictures as she could. She had good lenses and plenty of film, but still it wasn't satisfactory. About ten minutes later, however, when the paramedics and two of the carabinieri began to carry the stretcher up the hill toward the ambulance parked on the road, she was able to get a couple of real good shots. They had the oxygen mask over her face and a blanket on her, so Francesca never got the close-up she wanted. She had to do her best, that's all. She took that one shot all the papers and magazines used, the one in which the woman's arm hung down and you could see the bruises and the rope marks on her wrist and also her face in profile, all puffed up from the beating she had taken. No fun to think about, this violence against women, but Francesca's job was to take pictures. *Mezzanotte* always wanted exclusives, but Francesca knew she'd do better this time just spreading the shots around, no exclusives to anyone. It wasn't often you were the only person on the scene of a crime like this one. She had to make the most of it. She shot three rolls of film.

Francesca followed the stretcher party up to the road and took pictures of the girl being loaded into the ambulance and then of them all driving away. "Where are they taking her?" she asked the *maresciallo*, as he came puffing up the hill after her.

"There's a clinic in Sempione," he said, "but if they can make it, it will be a hospital, either in Lugano or the nearest ones in Milan. You know the Salvator Mundi? Maybe there." He shrugged and sighed. "It makes no difference," he added, looking sad. "She can't last very long, not in the condition she's in."

"Do you think she was raped?"

"Who knows?" the *maresciallo* said. "In these cases, one always assumes the worst. There will be an autopsy and a report, of course."

Francesca made no effort to follow the ambulance. Instead she drove like hell to the nearest pay phone, up the road a couple of kilometers, and called in her story to *Mezzanotte*. Giulio Camerini was on the news desk and she spilled it all to him. "And I've got a lot of pictures," she told him. "Can we make the early edition?"

"Certainly," he said, sounding not too concerned. It was just another body found lying somewhere, after all, so what was so terrific about that? "You know who she is?"

"Probably not Italian," she said, "but young and pretty. Blond."

"Ah, blond, well, that's something," Giulio said. "A model?"

"Possibly. Has anyone been reported missing?"

"I'll check." He burped in her ear; Giulio was such a pig. "No tits? Only a bare arm?" he asked. "That's not exciting."

"Giulio, you're a shithead," she said. "She's been beaten up, probably raped. There are rope marks on her wrists."

"Ah, that's interesting," he said. "You have pictures of that?"

"Yes, if they come out. I had to shoot from a distance, mostly," she explained.

"Well, we'll see. Where are you?"

"I'll be in town within an hour. You want me to come straight to the paper?"

"Of course. We'll develop the film here."

"Okay, but no exclusives. You get first crack, that's all."

"What is she, a diva of the movies? Come on, Francesca!"

"We'll find out, Giulio. No exclusives. You'll beat everybody to it, if you break it early enough."

"Francesca, there may be no story."

"A nearly naked blond beauty found beaten, ravished, tortured, and dying on the lakefront and you tell me there's no story," she said. "Giulio, you must think I'm a cretin. Be an editor and stop trying to screw me out of money. What a shithead you are!" He laughed and she hung up on him.

By the time she got to the paper, maybe an hour later, they were waiting for her. No sooner had she handed in the film to the lab than Giulio called her from the newsroom. "Get your behind up here, Francesca," he said. "I want to talk to you."

"You found out who she is."

"It's not certain, but there's a girl missing."

"Who is it?"

"Some American girl, a model. A friend of hers called the police early this morning. She said this girl called her last night and she was very upset. She wanted her friend to call the police if she wasn't home by two A.M."

"Who's the friend?"

"Some Anglo-Saxon name," Giulio said. "Come up here."

"What's the girl's name? Do we know?"

"Dosan, something like that."

"Sounds Japanese, but, of course, it isn't," she said. "Where is she? Where did they take her?"

"No one seems to know," Giulio said. "I checked your *maresciallo* and he didn't know and neither did the cops. I've assigned Scarponi to the story and he wants to talk to you. He's going to call in. Come on up."

"Is she dead?"

"We don't know. We're checking. Hey, move your ass!"

By the time she got up to his office five minutes later, he'd had a call from Scarponi. The girl's name was Bobby Jo Dawson, a twenty-five-year-old American model. She had been in Milan for only a few months and she was dead. That's all Scarponi knew about her at the time. You could not get to the body because they were performing an autopsy. No one would tell him where, but that was to be expected. Still, the news exasperated Giulio, who was sitting behind his desk in shirtsleeves and sweating profusely into his collar when Francesca walked in the door. Giulio was short and fat and he sweated so much, she wondered he didn't melt away in front of her. "Get on this story with Scarponi," he said. "Find this dead *bimba* and get some good pictures this time. You understand me, Francesca? Fuck somebody, if you have to."

"Giulio, you're a pig," she said.

"I don't care what you think," he said. "I want the body, naked, if possible. Something to match Scarponi's story."

"He has no story."

"Not yet. But you know Scarponi. He'll have his story."

"Yes," she said, "even if he has to invent one. Where's this friend, the one who called the police?"

"Scarponi's looking for her."

"He'll invent good quotes from her, I'm sure."

"Ah, Francesca," Giulio said. "Francesca, Francesca, we're selling newspapers here. What do you think we are doing? Stories about the goodness of man?" He reached into his desk, pulled out a towel, and mopped himself. "Go, *bella*. And those pictures of yours better be good."

6

HELP

Jake Dawson arrived in Milan the morning after my return. I had
checked into the Piccolo, which was a lot cheaper than where I'd
been staying, and given my last lecture that night. I had told Parker
I was coming back for a day or two at most and was planning to leave
again that evening. She called my room at about noon and told me
Dawson wanted to see me. I didn't know what more I could tell him
about his daughter than Parker had, but I agreed to come. I met
them in the bar of the Grand Hotel on the Via Manzoni, where
Dawson had taken a room. It was a rendezvous for people from the
fashion business, but I fell in love with the place at once because it
had a large oil painting of Giuseppe Verdi mounted on an easel in the
lobby. The composer had died in the hotel, and all of Milan had
paraded past his window during his last few days of life. I'd have
stayed there myself, but found out it was much too expensive.

Parker and Dawson were already there when I arrived and I
recognized him at once. He was a big man, heavyset, with spiky
iron-gray hair and big hands, and his face was ruddy from a life spent
mostly outdoors. He was dressed in gray slacks and a blue sport jacket
that seemed too tight for him, as if he'd outgrown them. He rose to
his feet to greet me and his handshake was firm. He seemed ill at
ease, out of place in such civilized surroundings. As we talked, his
eyes kept straying to the comings and goings of the sleek-looking

people who frequented the hotel. "Thanks for coming," he said. "I sure appreciate it and I'm sorry to spoil your holiday, but Parker here said you could tell me a few things about my daughter."

"Not much that you don't know already," I said. "I'm very sorry about what happened, Jake. Parker always said this was a tough town for a girl on her own."

"I guess I know that. I told her not to come here, but she wouldn't listen. She never did listen to me."

"I told Jake about the party you were at," Parker said.

"Can you tell me anything else about it, like who was there and all?" he asked.

I told him everything I'd witnessed and gave him the names of the people Ravelli had identified for me. "Bobby Jo was drugged, I'm sure of it," I said. "She never would have consented to what they did to her."

"I guess I know that. What about this guy Adriano Parker told me about?"

"He wasn't there," I said. "From what I heard he was pretty mad about not having been invited. He had a thing about Bobby Jo, maybe because she wouldn't go out with him."

"She was afraid of him," Parker said.

"Have you talked to the police?" I asked.

"A couple of detectives met me at the plane and took me to an office here in town, but they didn't tell me a hell of a lot and only one of them spoke any English. I'm going to the consulate tomorrow morning to see some guy there, fellow named Branch Nevins."

"You might get some help there, I guess."

"Yeah, maybe. I also want to talk to this guy Adriano."

"He might be hard to get to," Parker said. "He's not even mentioned in the stories about Bobby Jo, which means, I guess, that he's not part of the investigation."

"I'll sure as hell find out about that," Dawson said. "I want to talk to him."

"I have to go out of town tomorrow," Parker said. "To Monte Carlo for a few days for a fashion convention and show. I'm sorry I won't be around to help out."

"You've been great," Dawson said, then looked at me. "What about you, Anderson? Can I impose a little on your time?"

"How can I help?"

"I got to get out of here day after tomorrow," Dawson explained. "We're in the middle of the breeding and foaling season back home. I got eighty-five mares to take care of plus four stallions and all these weanlings. And I'm shorthanded. Things haven't been good in the industry for a while and I've got to stay on top of things. I can't hang around here. I need to delegate somebody to make sure Bobby Jo's body comes home, so we can give her a proper funeral and all. I'll pay you for your time, Anderson."

"Jake, I don't know. I was going to go home myself next week, right after the Italian Derby in Rome. I need to get back to work."

"I'll pay you five thousand dollars plus expenses for a month of your time," Dawson said. "I guess I can get some kind of notarized document that empowers you to act for me, maybe at the consulate tomorrow. What do you say?"

I hesitated. I wasn't sure I wanted to become involved in this painful business, but then I didn't see how I could refuse Dawson. The five thousand dollars would help pay for my trip and it was also more than I could earn as a performer, too, unless I had a TV or movie gig waiting for me back home, which seemed unlikely or I'd have heard something from my intrepid agent, Happy Hal Mancuso. "Jake, I'm not sure," I said. "You know, I don't know much more than you about how things work over here and I don't speak Italian."

"I don't either," Dawson said. "I thought I did. My family was Italian, from somewhere down South, and I grew up hearing what I thought was Italian around the house. Found out later it was some kind of local dialect. I can't understand what anybody says around here."

"Dawson? That's not an Italian name," Parker observed.

"It was Danise," Dawson explained. "They Americanized it after a while. They wanted to be pure American." Dawson smiled wanly. "How about it, Anderson?"

"Let me think about it overnight, okay?"

"Sure. I'd like you to come to the consulate with me, if you wouldn't mind. I'm due over there at nine-thirty."

"I'll meet you in the lobby here at nine o'clock and we can go together," I said.

"That'll be fine," Dawson said, standing up. "Now, if you two will forgive me, I'm going to grab some sleep. I only got a couple of hours on the plane and I'm beat."

After he'd gone, Parker and I lingered through another drink. She looked cool and elegant, with her long legs crossed and a martini in her hand, her eyes shaded under the brim of a bright spring hat. "This is it for me," she said. "This is my last year here. It's become too sleazy and corrupt, Shifty, even for me. That poor kid never had a chance."

"Old Jake doesn't seem too broken up about it," I said.

"He's keeping it all inside, and they didn't get along too well," Parker explained. "She said he loved her a lot, but that he was a tyrant and a bully while she was growing up. She couldn't seem to please him, no matter what she did. And sometimes he'd hit her."

"You think I should take his offer?"

"That's up to you, but why not? If you have no compelling reason to go home right now. You could be a big help to him. You know, you should talk to Francesca."

"Who's that?"

"The photographer who took the pictures. She's a freelance, what they call a paparazza, but she's okay. She used to cover some of the shows, which is how I met her. She knows everybody and where a lot of skeletons are buried. She even dated Ravelli for a while, though I think she despises him now. She could be helpful. Just a thought."

"Sounds like a good one. Maybe we can get to her before Dawson leaves town."

"She's not hard to find. Call *Mezzanotte*. I may even have her home number."

"Want to get some dinner somewhere?"

"Okay. We can walk back to the hotel. There are a couple of good trattorias along the way."

I paid for the drinks and we walked out into a cool spring night.

Amazingly, the sky was clear overhead. The old red cobblestones of the Via Manzoni gleamed in the soft light as a trolley car rumbled by on its way toward Piazza della Scala. We strolled along in its wake, Parker's high heels clicking sharply on the sidewalk, heading for the heart of the ancient city. "I like a lot of things about this town," Parker said.

"Like what?"

"It's alive, it's the real capital of this country," she explained. "Everything works here, everyone's involved. I like that. It reminds me of New York in that way. People on the hustle, you know, but it's a tough town, too tough for me now, Shifty."

We emerged into the piazza where the old opera house crouched in the shadows like a huge yellow cat. Ahead of us loomed the vaulted arches of the Galleria, and beyond, the curlicued spires of the Duomo. The streetlights bathed the scene in a soft glow, as homeward-bound stragglers scurried off toward taxis, buses, and trolley cars. "Yes," I agreed, "I could get to like this part of town a lot. If somebody offered me a subscription to the opera, I could just maybe spend a few months. I guess I could use the five grand. Do you really think we'll ever find out how Bobby Jo died?"

"I doubt it," Parker said, "but you could help. Dawson doesn't seem like too bad a guy. Just badly fucked up, like a lot of fathers."

"I wouldn't know. I've never been one."

"Poor Bobby Jo," Parker said. "Basically, she died of innocence."

Branch Nevins sat behind a large wooden desk in a second-floor office with a view over the street and a small public park. Jake Dawson and I sat in leather armchairs facing him and the wall on which hung the Great Seal of the United States. Nevins looked like an ad for a Brooks Brothers spring sale. He was in his mid-thirties, freckled, with a full head of nicely trimmed sand-colored hair and pale blue eyes sheltered behind horn-rimmed glasses. He was wearing a dark green gabardine suit and a green and gray striped necktie. His manner was affable but guarded, as if he had reason to be suspicious of our motive for disrupting his morning routine. "I'm awfully sorry about your daughter," he said, after we had introduced ourselves. "A shocking business. Have you talked to the police?"

"Yeah," Dawson said. "It wasn't very satisfactory."

"What happened?"

"They wouldn't tell me anything. They said the case was under investigation. They did show me photographs."

"Photographs? Of your daughter?"

"Yeah. The ones taken at the scene and then some shots of her at the hospital."

"What can we do for you, Mr. Dawson?"

"You're the American consul here in Milan," Dawson said. "I figured you could help us."

"In what way? Oh, and I'm not the consul, just the acting consul. Mr. Weatherby is on vacation. He'll be back at the end of the month."

"Okay, I understand. What I mean is, you could help me get some real answers from the cops here. I asked about my daughter's body and they wouldn't even tell me where it was."

"They must have a reason, Mr. Dawson."

"Maybe you could find out for me what that reason is. I also want to know how she died and who killed her. That matters to me."

"Well, of course it would," Nevins said. "I imagine there is a very thorough investigation going on. I gather your daughter may have been involved in some sort of party scene involving drugs. I'm sorry to be so blunt about it."

"I've read the papers," Dawson said, "but I think that's mostly bullshit. Bobby Jo wrote me a couple of letters since she's been here, and I got the feeling she was really trying to turn her life around, that she was making a go of it here. Or at least had hopes of making a go of it."

"Well, the Italian press is notoriously sensationalist," Nevins said. "I'm sure they've blown things up out of proportion."

"You bet they have."

"But I'm afraid there isn't much I can do to be of help right now. It's a criminal investigation, you see, and our hands are pretty well tied."

"You expect me to do nothing about my daughter's death?"

Nevins smiled sadly and tapped the fingers of one hand on the surface of his desk, as if marking time till our departure. We were spoiling his day. "Of course not, Mr. Dawson," he said. "I can make a couple of calls for you, perhaps find out what exactly the status is and when you could expect to arrange to take your daughter's body home. I presume that's what you'd like to do?"

"Yeah, you got it. That would help. I'm not about to let this slide by, Nevins."

"Mr. Dawson, my advice would be to remain patient and let the investigation run its course. I'm sure there will have to be an autopsy. We can't interfere with Italian policy and legal procedures. I imagine it will be a week or two at least before we hear anything definitive."

"I can't wait that long, Nevins. I run a horse farm back home and this is the busiest time of the year for me. I have to get back there tomorrow or the day after, at the latest. I asked Mr. Anderson here to handle matters for me and to represent me. I guess he'll need some kind of notarized document or a power of attorney."

"Yes, a *procura*, which is equivalent to a power of attorney. I can arrange that," Nevins said. "It's a simple procedure, basically." He looked at me with curiosity. "You live here in Milan?"

"No, just passing through," I said. "But I agreed to help out. I'm on vacation, but I can stay on for a while, maybe a month."

"We should certainly have some answers by then. You're a lawyer?"

"No, I'm a magician."

Nevins blinked with surprise. "Really? How curious." But he didn't pursue the matter and I saw no need to enlighten him. "Well," he said, rising to his feet, "let me take you both downstairs and get this *procura* business under way. It may take a day or two. Can you come back tomorrow?"

"Sure," Dawson said.

"By then I may have some information for you."

"Good. I'd appreciate it."

"I'm sorry I can't be more helpful, Mr. Dawson," Nevins said, as he ushered us out of his office. "We have to play by the rules here. I'm sure you understand."

"I guess you'll do what you can," Dawson said. "We are taxpayers, ain't we?"

Nevins smiled feebly. "Yes, of course. This way."

He led us to the ground floor and left us in the charge of a Miss Lois Robinson, a gray-haired middle-aged woman who sat in a windowless office to the right of the main entrance from where she could look out into the street and see the marine guards outside the door. She asked for our passports, punched the numbers into her computer, glanced at the information that appeared on her screen, and began to type it into a document she had produced from one of the drawers in her desk. "No need for you to stay," she said. "This will take a while and we'll have to get it approved tomorrow morning at court. Come back about four tomorrow."

"Do you think we accomplished much?" Jake Dawson asked me, as we stepped out onto the sidewalk. "I wonder what that asshole Nevins does most of the time."

"Lives off the fat of the land on our tax money," I said.

"Like everybody else in the damn government," Dawson said. "Let's get the hell out of here. Want a drink?"

"Not till later," I said. "It's against my religion."

"What religion is that?"

"I live by my hands and my wits, Jake," I said, "so I worship the old body."

"Shit, you can come and watch me drink. They got any good bourbon in this town?"

"Probably."

"And I'll buy you lunch."

"An offer no one could refuse."

7

SISTERS

Angela Tedeschi was a tall, slim woman in her mid-thirties who wore very little makeup and her long black hair coiled back into a bun. She sat behind a huge, dark antique table piled high with dossiers and under a portrait of a fierce-looking old man dressed in a general's uniform. Her office was furnished with several padded armchairs, and a large medieval tapestry hung across the wall facing her. Two windows looked out on a broad avenue teeming with traffic and pedestrians, but somehow even the noise from the street could not dispel the feeling that I had intruded into another century, nor could the computer and printer and fax machine that sat on a corner of the table. Angela Tedeschi gave the impression of having stepped out of the past; her face, with its long aquiline nose and broad sweep of thin eyebrows, could have been painted by Pinturicchio. Only her manner was briskly modern, unsmiling and coldly rational. Dawson had taken an instant dislike to her.

"What the hell's happened to my daughter?" were his first words to her.

"I beg your pardon?" Angela Tedeschi answered in flawless English, with hardly the trace of an accent.

"You heard me," Dawson said. "My daughter's been murdered, nobody even bothers to inform me, I find out about it only because a friend of hers calls me, then I come over here and get the runaround from everybody I talk to. I want to know what the hell's going on. And I want my daughter's body. I'm going to take her home."

"Mr. Dawson, it would help if you would calm yourself," Angela Tedeschi said. "I know how you must be distressed by what has happened. You must understand that there is an investigation going on. Unfortunately, part of that investigation, a very necessary part, is an autopsy. That could not be avoided. Surely you must understand that it is essential to know how she died. Do I make myself clear?"

"Yeah, that part I get," Dawson said. "What I don't get is why I haven't been allowed to see her and why I've been getting the runaround from everybody."

"Certainly not from this office," Angela Tedeschi said. "The minute I learned that you were in Italy I made an appointment to see you. I am the investigating magistrate in this case."

"What does that mean? You're a cop?"

"No, I'm a member of the judiciary, something like your district attorney's office," she explained. "In Italy the police investigate crimes, but always under the jurisdiction of an office such as mine. The investigation is ongoing, Mr. Dawson. We believe even now that your daughter was not the victim of a simple accident."

"That shouldn't have taken you too long to figure out. What did she die of?"

"The pathology is not conclusive. We need more tests, but it appears that she died of drowning," Angela Tedeschi said. "When she was left on the lakeshore, she was almost certainly unconscious, with her face in the water. She had been badly beaten up. She had four broken ribs, several small cuts on her breasts, and bruises all over her body. Her face was swollen, her eyes blackened. Perhaps she would have died of her injuries, we don't know. But the injuries were not self-inflicted and they were not from an accident, such as a fall. Some person or persons inflicted them on her."

"It has to be this guy Andrea something-or-other, whatever the hell his name is," Dawson said. "He was after her."

"What makes you think that?"

"She wouldn't go out with him," Dawson said. "She was afraid of him. And when he found out about that party she was taken to and raped at, he was real angry he hadn't been invited."

"I see. And where did you acquire this information?"

"From her friend, Parker Williams."

"I know about Miss Williams. We have been in touch with her. We know also that she was aware of the situation with Adriano Barone."

"How can I get to this guy?"

"That will not be possible," Angela Tedeschi said. "He's in Rome at the moment, but even if he weren't, I could not allow you, Mr. Dawson, to intervene in such a reckless manner."

"You aren't going to do shit, are you?" Dawson said, his voice rising in anger. "You aren't going to go after this guy because he's connected."

"He's what?"

"Connected. His father is a big shot, right? Isn't that how it works here in Italy?"

"Not always, Mr. Dawson, and certainly not in this office. We have every intention of interrogating Signor Barone, as well as all of the people who had anything to do with your daughter. We have spoken to some of them already. As I explained to you, this will be a most complete, exhaustive investigation. Your daughter's death was a shocking act. We have every intention of bringing her murderer or murderers to justice."

"I'd hang him with my own two hands."

"Unfortunately, we do not have capital punishment in Italy," Angela Tedeschi said. "Whoever did this will undoubtedly receive a life sentence."

"And be pardoned in five or six years."

"We are not so lenient in such matters, Mr. Dawson. The perpetrators of this terrible act will be properly punished, believe me."

"When can I have my daughter's body?"

"Not for some time, I'm afraid. I understand you've made arrangements to be represented here."

Dawson glanced at me. "Anderson here."

"Yes, I am aware of Mr. Anderson." Angela Tedeschi fixed her large dark eyes on me. "I presume you will stay in touch with this office, Mr. Anderson."

"Yes, of course. I'll be here another month," I said. "I'm going to Rome for a few days, then I'll be back in Milan. I'm at the Piccolo Milan."

"I know," Angela Tedeschi said. "Have you been interrogated yet by the police?"

"No. I guess they've had a hard time finding me. I've been in Rome."

"How well did you know Miss Dawson?"

"Not well. I met her at a party here in Milan that an acquaintance of mine, Carlo Ravelli, took me to. Miss Williams was also there. Later I went out to dinner with them. And I was at the party at the Pelagras, also because Ravelli insisted I come."

"And do you always do what Mr. Ravelli insists?"

"He's been sort of my host here," I explained. "I came over here as the guest of the I.B.M., the international magicians' group, to give some lectures and demonstrations. Ravelli took me in hand."

"Signor Ravelli seems to have many talents."

"Magic is not among them."

"Oh? He is not a magician?"

"Not by my standards," I said, "but then they're admittedly high."

Angela Tedeschi looked at Dawson. "Who else have you spoken with since your arrival, Mr. Dawson?" she asked.

"No one," he said. "Parker and Anderson and Nevins and now you. Oh, yeah, a whole bunch of guys with the police again yesterday afternoon, but that got me nowhere."

"I see. And when are you leaving?"

"I'm flying out of here tomorrow morning," he said.

"Have any reporters spoken to you?"

"No. I guess they don't know I'm in town."

"Good. I would avoid any interviews, if I were you."

"I got nothing to say now anyway." Dawson shifted uneasily in his chair. "I'll have plenty to say if I have to come back here and nothing's been done."

"That's why I'm relieved that you are going home," Angela Tedeschi said. "I understand your distress, but nothing is to be gained by your involving yourself in the investigation." She looked sharply at me. "And that goes for you, too, Mr. Anderson. I would urge you not to do anything without consulting this office and I respectfully request that you avoid the press. You would not want to prejudice the investigation, I'm sure."

We rose to leave and Angela Tedeschi shook hands with us. She had a strong, manly grip. "Thank you," she said. "Rest assured, Mr. Dawson, that we are doing everything in our power to bring your daughter's killers to justice. Please believe me."

Dawson seemed suddenly drained, the bluster and hostility gone out of him. He mumbled something at the woman and shuffled from the room. At the door I glanced back at her. Angela Tedeschi was still on her feet, but already on the phone, barking orders into it in Italian. She hung up and noticed me standing there. "Yes?" she snapped, obviously surprised to find me still on the scene.

"I was wondering who the man in the painting is," I said. "Anyone I should know? It's very impressive."

"My grandfather, Enrico Armore Tedeschi," she said. "He was a general. Not a nice man and a very bad general."

"It's a terrific painting."

"He stood for everything I am opposed to," she said. "That is why I hang him in my office, to remind me of my duties."

"Oh. Thanks for sharing that."

"I beg your pardon?"

"Facetious American chatter," I explained, letting myself out of the room and closing the door behind me.

Halfway through the evening I realized that Dawson was pretty drunk. He had been boozing steadily since our first cocktail in the Grand Hotel bar at six o'clock. It was now nearly ten and he hadn't stopped, though he had switched from double shots of whiskey to red wine. We were sitting in the Biffi Scala, a restaurant next to the opera

house, at a side table against the far wall. Luckily, he had eaten an
enormous dinner to soften the effects of the alcohol on his system,
which made it possible for him to remain comprehensible, even
though he was slurring his words and his heavy head drooped over
the table. He had spent most of the evening filling me in on the
vagaries and misfortunes of the horse-breeding business, some of
which I already knew about. I gathered he'd been having a rough
time staying solvent. "It's the goddamn tax laws," he said at one
point. "Then the Arabs and the Japanese stopped buying and the
bottom fell out of the business overnight. It's been a rough time,
believe you me. I should have paid more attention to my kids, but I
was trying to stay afloat."

"Is Bobby Jo's mother dead?"

"Hell no, but she might as well be," he said. "She ran off and left
me for a cop in L.A., when the girls were twelve and eight. Didn't
want to have much to do with them after that. Hell of a thing. All she
wanted to do was fuck this dude from L.A. and then she went and
married the sonofabitch."

"So you were left to raise the girls."

"That's about it. It sure as hell wasn't easy. Especially Bobby Jo.
That kid was always in trouble. Couldn't do nothing with her. She
started running around with a bad crowd in school when she was
thirteen and it just went on from there. When she was fifteen she
went out with some guy on a motorcycle and got herself gang-raped.
The boys got off, said she was on drugs and was doing everybody, just
about. The case ran us out of town, as most of them boys were the
sons of the best families around. We had to move. I sold the farm in
Frankfurt and bought the place I got now, though I had to go into
debt with the bank for a hundred thousand. It's that damn loan
that's made the past five years such tough ones."

"What happened to Bobby Jo?"

"I sent her off to a Catholic boarding school in Little Rock. The
nuns there got her straightened out pretty quick and she got a good
education, too, only when she got out she went back to her old ways.
She hadn't been home two weeks when I threw her out. I didn't hear

from her or see her for a couple of years after that. Somehow she wound up in New York."

"What was she doing there?"

"She took some acting classes and was working as a cocktail waitress in some hotel on the west side of town," he said. "She seemed to be okay for a while, but then she met some guy in the fashion industry who told her she could make big bucks as a model. He also got her on drugs, cocaine mostly. She moved in with him. Then one night she caught him in the sack with some guy. He beat the shit out of her and threw her out in the street."

"And so she decided to come to Milan and try her luck here."

"No, she came home first. She stayed home for a couple of months, got herself off the stuff she'd been taking, even helped out around the farm. I thought she was going to be okay. I thought she'd gotten most of the nonsense out of herself. She was working real hard with the yearlings."

"She's good with horses?"

"The best. Animals just like her. She has a real touch with 'em. She was a good rider, too. You know how it is, Anderson, some people just have a touch with animals. It comes natural to 'em, like breathing. Bobby Jo had that. She could have been just fine if she'd hung around long enough to really put her life together."

"What happened?"

"It was partly my fault, I guess. There was something between me and Bobby Jo that wasn't never right. She'd say something or I'd say something and we'd be hollering and shouting at each other. Well, she forgot to do one of her chores one day and I kind of cussed her out about it. I told her she was a screwup, that she couldn't do nothing right, and she sassed me back some, so I hit her." He paused, reached for his wineglass, and took a long drink from it. Then he set it down on the table and stared gloomily into space, as if reliving the scene. I didn't say anything, mainly because I could see how painful the memory of that incident had become. It was etched into his features, into the way he slumped over the table, his hands clasped in front of him. "I'd do anything now to take that all back," he said at last. "I hit her so hard she fell against the wall or she'd have gone down. I remember her looking at me like she'd kill me, if she could. 'You aren't ever going to do that to me again,' she said. And she went upstairs to pack and left the house that same night."

"Where did she go?"

"To a motel. The next morning she caught a Greyhound bus back to New York from Louisville. I never saw her again. I sent Ellie to go talk to her for me, but it didn't do no good."

"Maybe you should have gone yourself."

"You're right, of course, I should have. I was letting Ellie carry the ball for me. I made a lot of mistakes in my life, Anderson. Bobby Jo was the one I couldn't make right or do nothing about. We loved each other, at least I loved her, but there was something between us that kept us angry at each other all the time. It was a damn shame."

"How do you get along with Ellie?"

His face softened and the pain seemed to drain out of it. "Oh, she's a sweetheart," he said. "She's my girl." He fished into his wallet and produced a color snapshot of her. "Here she is. This was taken about a year ago, on her birthday in town."

I took the picture from him. It portrayed a smiling blonde standing against a ship's railing, with a large river flowing in the background. She was smiling and I saw the resemblance to Bobby Jo in her coloring and the shape of her mouth, but she seemed like a lighter, happier version of her older sister; her eyes sparkled and her face glowed with pleasure. "She's even more beautiful than Bobby Jo," I said.

"She's always been everything better than Bobby Jo was," Dawson said. "Maybe that's part of the trouble, Anderson. Ellie always got the best grades in school. She got voted homecoming queen. She had the best-looking, smartest boys after her. Then, when she went to college at Louisville, she won all the top prizes and a scholarship. There wasn't nothing she couldn't do better than anybody else."

"And that must have hurt Bobby Jo."

"I guess it did. She just couldn't measure up to Ellie in anything she did. Except around the farm. Ellie didn't care, still doesn't, about the horses. That was the one thing Bobby Jo could do best, ride and look after the animals. I guess it wasn't enough."

"I'm sorry about your troubles, Jake," I said. "I wish I'd known something about all this when I met Bobby Jo. Maybe I could have helped, maybe I could have stopped what happened."

"How?"

"Well, I could have gotten her out of the Pelagras' that night. Her being there probably got her killed."

"How do you figure?"

"It made Adriano Barone angry," I explained. "Maybe it got her killed, if he's the one who did it. I guess we'll find out soon enough."

"You really think this woman knows what the hell's going on?"

"Yes, I do. She struck me as pretty competent. I believe her."

"Well, I don't," Dawson mumbled angrily. "I sure don't. I think she's full of shit. I think they're covering up the whole damn thing."

"Why would they do that?"

"Because this guy's connected, don't you see, Anderson? It's the same as back home. Some big wheel gets in trouble, everyone just kind of closes ranks and all. This babe who's supposed to be in charge of the investigation, she's just somebody's hired hand. She ain't going to do nothing. Hell, they won't even let me take her home." His big head sank forward on his chest, as if he might cry or go to sleep, I wasn't sure which. I waited, hoping he'd rouse himself and I could get him back to his hotel. His plane left at nine A.M. and I was afraid he might pass out on me and I wouldn't be able to get him out of there.

"Jake, I think we'd better get back to the hotel," I said when he showed no sign of coming around.

His head jerked upward. "What? Oh, yeah, sure." He reached into his pocket and pulled out a wad of crumpled lire notes. "Let's pay this goddamn bill," he said. "Here, use some of this funny money."

"I paid the bill, Jake. I used my credit card."

"Well, then, take this goddamn Monopoly money," he said. "I sure can't use it."

I gathered up the bills, about two hundred dollars in lire notes, and stuffed them in my side jacket pocket. "Expenses," I said.

"Yeah, right." He put his hands against the tabletop and heaved himself to his feet. "Let's get the hell out of here."

It was after eleven and the restaurant was nearly empty when we left. Outside, it was a cool, misty night. I put Jake into a taxi, gave the driver twenty thousand lire, and told him to drop Dawson off at the Grand, less than a half mile away. "*È sbronzo?*" the driver asked. "Drunk, no?"

"*Sbronzo, sir,*" I said. "*Attenzione.*"

The driver, a husky gnome with a beard, grinned, touched his cap with a forefinger, and sped away into the night. I stood there and watched him go, feeling saddened by the evening. Jake Dawson wasn't a bad guy, I thought, just an ignorant one. And that ignorance had contributed to his daughter's death. He knew it and it was tearing him apart. He'd have to live with it for the rest of his life.

ENCOUNTERS

"**B**obby Jo was not strong and she was not lucky," Piero Lavenante said. "I warned her, but she allowed herself to be caught up with fast people. She went to too many parties. She acquired a cocaine taste. She went to bed always with the wrong people. It was inevitable that something bad would happen to her."

I had come straight to his office from the airport and surprised the agent before he could disappear behind phone calls, secretaries, and meetings. He had put Dawson and me off for two days until the morning of Jake's departure. I had told Dawson I would drop in on Lavenante that morning and find out what I could from him, then call him at home that night if I had learned anything significant. Dawson had nodded and stumbled aboard his homeward-bound plane. He looked more dead than alive and was sweating profusely. "I don't know what they put in the booze in this country, but I ain't never been this sick," he said on the drive out of the city. "I think somebody tried to poison me."

"You had a lot to drink," I told him, "and you're under a lot of stress."

"Yeah, well, I think somebody poured something into my glass," Dawson said, "and it wasn't liquor."

Twice in the airport lobby at Malpensa, an hour north of the city, he'd had to lumber away from me to the men's room, and as he boarded he looked as if he'd barely make it to his seat before having to go again. I was anxious to get him out of town. I felt sorry for him, but I wanted him gone so I could resume my Italian vacation. I had told him I'd do what I could to find out what happened to Bobby Jo, but I expected the superefficient Signorina Angela Tedeschi to accomplish that. All I had to do was keep Dawson informed. And, of course, make a few calls and pay a few visits, such as the one to Lavenante's office this morning. I wasn't sure what the agent could tell me, but I owed Dawson something for his money and my added time in Italy. I think basically I was feeling guilty. I had taken the man's five thousand dollars, but what could I possibly do for him? Simply wait for the outcome of the investigation and then make arrangements to ship Bobby Jo's body home. Well, it had been his idea, I told myself. Why not take his money and do the best I could? Which accounted for my presence in Piero Lavenante's office that morning.

"May I ask, Signor Anderson, what is your interest in this matter?" the agent said. "You are a friend of the family?"

"Yes, that's right," I said. "Bobby Jo's father has been here. He's asked me to stay on and act for him. He had to return home this morning. We've been trying to get an appointment with you for two days."

"Yes, most unfortunate," Lavenante said. "This has been an extremely busy time for me. The fall collections, you know." He glanced at his watch, a diamond-encrusted Rolex worth more than my entire estate. "In fact, you must forgive me, but in ten minutes I am due at the Continentale for the Chigi show."

"Where is that?"

"At the hotel. It is not far from here."

"Good," I said. "I'll walk you over. Mind if I go in with you? I've never seen a fashion show."

The agent blinked uneasily, but quickly adjusted to my suggestion. "Well, of course, if you wish. We can walk over together. Excuse me for one moment." He bounded to his feet and rushed out of his office. "Elena!" he shouted. "Elena!" He gave her orders in Italian, then stuck his head back inside his office. "Two minutes," he said. "I forgot I have to call Rome. Forgive me." And he shut the door behind him.

I relaxed in my chair and gazed idly at my surroundings. Lavenante's private office was small and messy, with magazines and stacks of photo layouts piled here and there. Two large filing cabinets took up much of the space and the furnishings were nondescript, a plain metal office desk and two padded chairs. The walls were practically papered with glossy eight-by-ten photographs of young men and women peering smilingly or dramatically into the lens. Sixty or seventy prints at least and not one face that looked older than twenty-five, not a line or a wrinkle to be seen anywhere. The room had the air of a vault in which youth had been permanently enshrined and celebrated. No one in here would ever grow old or become ill, not so long as their pictures graced the walls. A single window looked out on the street, a narrow alley connected to the Via Monte Napoleone, Milan's Rodeo Drive, where luxury shops and boutiques nestled opulently next to one another in an array of affluence and conspicuous consumption. I couldn't imagine Bobby Jo in this world. I scanned the walls for her face, but it was missing.

During the walk to the Continentale, Lavenante answered my questions regarding Bobby Jo's Milanese activities by filling me in on a few of the particulars of the Italian fashion industry. He seemed to know everyone and to have an inexhaustible fund of mean-spirited stories about them. Our progress along the streets became a sort of cynic's travelogue, in which every person mentioned became identified with a secret contamination. I began to think of Lavenante as a huge crab scavenging an ocean bottom. He seemed to be scurrying sideways along the sidewalks, darting this way and that to avoid oncoming pedestrians, all the time keeping up his outpouring of scandalous observations. He began actually to look like a crab to me, with his small feet and darting hands, round pale face, strands of oily black hair in disarray over beady black eyes. By the time we reached the hotel entrance I had developed a solid dislike for the man. "Is it true you sent Bobby Jo on a call to a pornographer?" I asked, as we entered the lobby.

"But of course," he said. "What other work was she qualified for?"

"Did you tell her that when you took her money and brought her over here?"

He stared at me as if I had uttered a minor blasphemy. "I am not their guardian," he said. "They pay me, I try to find them work. This Bobby Jo was one of the dozens of girls every month. What happens to them finally is not my concern."

He shoved past me toward the main ballroom where the Chigi showing had apparently already begun. I followed him into a spacious room down which a long central runway had been erected. Young, beautiful women and men in flashy green and brown ensembles strolled down it and back, twirling this way and that to display themselves to an audience of silent, mostly middle-aged men and women, some of them taking notes, others murmuring into tiny tape recorders. Soft music, mostly that of Cole Porter, accompanied the action, a soothing carpet of sound designed to confirm, to reassure, to establish ultimate class. Cameras clicked and whirred.

I stood for a while at the back, against a wall, then made my way around to the side of the room away from Lavenante. I had spotted Teddy Amendola, the photographer, sitting in the second row near an aisle, and I positioned myself nearby so I could intercept him when he left his seat, which occurred about half an hour later during an intermission. He went straight to a small bar in a corner of the room, and I followed him. No sooner had he acquired himself a drink than I came up behind him. "Signor Amendola," I said, "excuse me."

He turned, the glass clutched in both hands, and looked blankly at me. "Yes?"

"We met at a party a couple of weeks ago," I said. "Carlo Ravelli introduced us."

"Ah, yes. You are . . . ?"

"Lou Anderson. I'm a magician."

"Yes, Carlo told me about you."

"You wanted to photograph that model, the American girl, Bobby Jo Dawson."

"Yes, very sad," he said. "I knew she would come to a bad end. I told her to go home."

"So I understand. She told us."

"Us?"

"Me and her friend, Parker Williams."

"Ah, yes. So?"

"You took some pictures of her, she said."

"Yes, very beautiful ones, although she was a difficult model, of no talent at all. Very awkward, hard to pose. Luckily, she had a most beautiful body, like a landscape in moonlight. There was an unreal quality about it."

"I'm wondering what you're planning to do with those pictures."

"Do? Why, exhibit them, of course. Not all, but two, perhaps three. I am preparing a show of my nudes for the Aurora in November. Didn't she tell you?"

"Yes, she did."

"Why do you ask?"

"I think her father might want to buy those pictures back."

"Tell him not to be concerned. I do not plan to identify her. This is an artist's show, not pornography."

"Well, he doesn't know about them. I won't tell him."

"Thank you."

"Do you know anything about Bobby Jo that might be helpful?" I asked.

"Helpful? In what way?"

"I'm acting on behalf of her father," I explained. "We're trying to find out how she died."

"How will that help him?"

"By knowing, at least, that his daughter's murderer will be brought to justice."

"Ah, justice, a fine abstract concept. Small satisfaction, no?"

"I agree, but that's what he wants. Do you know Adriano Barone?"

"Of course. Everyone knows Adriano."

"Everyone?"

"In certain circles, Signor Anderson. He is rather notorious."

"Does he beat up women?"

"Most certainly, I am sure," Amendola said. "He has a bad cocaine habit and can become very violent. His wife sued him for divorce—they have two children—because of this violence. She appeared in court with a broken arm in a cast. It was very effective. The judge was most sympathetic. She was given the two children and a great deal of money."

"He's rich."

"The family is very rich."

"Where does the money come from?"

"Ah, a very American question, isn't it? Some of it inherited from old estates in Campania, south of Naples. Then, after the war, there was much building going on everywhere. The Barone were deeply involved in the corruption of public officials to secure necessary building permits. The Barone poured concrete everywhere, enough to encase Vesuvio. Then they moved to Milan, where another branch of the family had a palazzo."

"I've been there. It's where we met."

"His father had married a Milanese *contessa, la* Nervi, and the family expanded into banking and publishing and export–import, all sorts of ventures. Luca Barone is one of the richest men in Europe. He owns a political party, always very useful in times of stress."

"Which one?"

"The Partito Conservativo, a very tiny entity but powerful because of the money behind it. It controls eleven seats in the Chamber of Deputies. That is like your Congress."

"I gather he hasn't been touched by the recent scandals."

"Oh, perhaps brushed slightly, I would say. Touched? No. The Barone are too big to be touched, you see. You don't know very much about Italy, do you?"

I shook my head. "No. I guess what I'm hearing, though, is that we're never going to know for sure who killed Bobby Jo."

"I wouldn't count on it, Signor Anderson."

"Do you know a magistrate named Angela Tedeschi?"

"Not personally, but the family is well known. Her father, Guido, was in politics. He was a Socialist, very famous, second only to Nenni after the war. The Socialists were very powerful then. They held the balance of power between the Right and the Left, you see. So Angela is a magistrate. Interesting."

"She has a big oil painting of her grandfather in her office. I gather he was a general and that she didn't like him very much."

"Ah, Armore Tedeschi, a very bad general, but a very good Fascist, very popular with Mussolini. He commanded troops during our glorious conquest of Ethiopia."

"Angela despises him."

"Then she takes after his son, her father. He also hated old Armore Tedeschi, which is why he became a Socialist. You say she is a magistrate? Is she investigating the death of this girl?"

"Yes."

"Ah, most interesting."

"Why is that?"

"Because her father was once very close to Luca Barone. For a while they were in business together, then they had a very big quarrel and Luca had Guido liquidated from his company. They have been great enemies. Guido launched many investigations of Barone, denounced him often on the floor of the Chamber, but nothing ever came of it. Then Guido died at home one afternoon, under rather mysterious circumstances, and that was that. Luca Barone, Signor Anderson, is one of the untouchables, along with the pope and Gianni Agnelli. But it is interesting that she is in charge of this case. If she thinks like her father and also hates the Barone, it will be fascinating to watch."

"You're very well informed about all this," I said.

"But everyone in Italy knows these stories," Teddy Amendola said. "Italy is a very small country entirely immersed in gossip."

The music began again and people hurried back to their seats. I said good-bye to Amendola and looked around for Lavenante, but failed to spot him. A spectacular-looking black model wearing knee-high laced sandals, a dark green miniskirt, and a silk blouse slit open to her navel appeared on the runway as the photographers went back to work. I edged my way around the crowded room toward the exit.

As I stepped through the door into the lobby, a sharp female voice called out to me. "Signor Anderson, one moment, please!"

I turned around to find myself confronted by a pixie of about thirty with a pair of cameras slung over one shoulder. She was dressed in faded jeans, a man's shirt, and a black leather jacket. Her hair was cut short like a boy's and she wore little makeup, just lipstick and a touch of mascara. Her eyes were large and very dark. From a distance she would have passed as a teenager. "Hello," she said, "I am Francesca."

"Who?"

"Francesca Pirro. I took the pictures of the girl."

"Oh, yes. I've been wanting to talk to you."

"I am sometimes hard to find."

"How did you know me?"

"I see you come in with Piero," she said. "I put two with two together."

"And two."

"What?"

"Two *and* two."

"Ah. My English is shitty, no?"

"No. Sorry, but I sometimes do that."

"Do what?"

"Correct people."

"Ah. You are forbidden."

"What?"

"Forbidden. *Scusato*, no?"

"No. Forgiven."

"Ah. *Merda*. Look, you have time to see me?"

"Sure, I want to talk to you."

"Good. Later today, all right? I have this shitty show to photograph now."

"Looks nice enough to me."

She grimaced and shook her head. "Garbage," she said. "*Mondizia*. I call you later. Where are you, at the Piccolo?"

"Yes. Dinner?"

She shrugged and smiled. "Why not? I pick you up, eight o'clock. *Va bene*?"

"*Va bene.* I'll be in the lobby."

She smiled again. It was a brilliant smile, revealing a row of dazzling white teeth and a pair of dimples. "I go now. Shit waits. I photograph shit. For money, you see? Sad, no?" She whirled and rushed back inside, then suddenly stuck her head out the door again. "Your name is Shitty?" she asked, looking slightly alarmed.

"No, Shifty, with an *f*, not a *t*."

"Ah. Good. The world is full of shitty." And she disappeared once more.

I had already begun to look forward to dinner.

9

FRANCESCA

She was forty minutes late, but I didn't mind because she looked so adorable. She had changed into an elegant dark purple pants suit with a frilled shirt and a big red bow tie that seemed to frame her small features. A pair of gold hoops dangled from her earlobes and she was wearing just enough makeup to accentuate her features and lustrous dark eyes. She carried a black leather handbag and a single camera in a leather case slung over one shoulder. "I am so sorry," she said, as she hurried in through the door and I rose to greet her, "but the traffic was, how you say, *odioso?*"

"Odious?"

"Sì, *un disastro.* There was an accident."

"That's all right. We're in no hurry, are we?"

"No, but I am ravished."

"You're what?"

"With hunger, food."

"Oh. What's the camera for?"

"I never go without my camera," she said. "Who knows when there will be a picture, no?"

"Where are we going?"

"You like fish?"

"Yes. I'll eat anything."

"Even me?"

"Francesca, that's not a question to ask a man on a first date."

"No? Why not?" Her eyes were wide with surprise. "I say something bad?"

"Intimate."

"Ah, I am always putting my foots in my mouse."

"It's okay," I said. "You make yourself understood. Shall we go?"

"Sì, andiamo."

She drove a small, battered Fiat that she maneuvered through the city's crowded streets like a child in a Dodge-'em ring. I groped about for a seat belt, failed to find one, and braced myself with both knees and hands against the dashboard. "What you do?" she asked.

"In case you hit something," I said. "I don't want to go through the windshield."

"Everyone drives like this here."

"So I've noticed," I said. "That's why I'm taking precautions. Don't you have a seat belt?"

"Why? Is so uncomforting. No worries, I am good driver. I kill no one."

She was a sensational driver, but I couldn't make myself watch where she was going. There was one memorable block that she drove up backward because, as she informed me, it was a one-way street and it would have taken too long to detour around it. Eventually, after several near misses and another cutoff that took us over a short stretch of sidewalk, she swept us out into a tiny piazza, pulled up to a flight of steps in front of a church, and parked. "Can you do that?" I asked, as we got out.

"Do what?"

"Park here."

"Why not?"

"Isn't this a church?"

"So? Who goes to church at night? Come, the trattoria is this way."

I followed her down a short, dark alley between two rows of dingy-looking apartment houses. We were no longer in the heart of the city, but somewhere on the outskirts, heading north toward the Swiss border. I wondered why she had brought me to this dismal quarter of town, a typical lower-middle-class residential district devoid of charm, but it didn't worry me. I had yet to have a bad meal during my Italian stay and I suspected Francesca had something special in mind.

I was right. The place she had chosen was a tiny trattoria at the very end of the alley. It contained no more than eight or nine tables in a single room whose walls were decorated with old photographs of Milan and the adjacent countryside that must have been shot around the turn of the century. The kitchen was at the far end of the room behind a buffet table piled high with cheeses, salamis, sausages, olives, roasted peppers, sardines, anchovies, fried zucchini, sweet-and-sour onions, mozzarella floating in brine, sautéed mushrooms, and other delicacies I couldn't immediately identify. "I think I'm going to like this place," I said, as we helped ourselves at this table of goodies before sitting down.

"Oh, yes, is very good," Francesca said, "my favorite in Milano."

"How did you happen to find it?" I asked.

"It belong to me," she said.

"Belongs to you? You own it?"

"I grew up in the *quartiere*," she explained, then waved a fork toward the blowups on the walls. "My grandfather was a photographer. Those are his pictures."

"And your father?"

"He died when I was young, maybe three years. My mother die also. But I grow up here, with my aunt Fiorentina."

Before I could hear more of her family history, a small, chunky, middle-aged citizen in a food-stained white waiter's jacket appeared from the kitchen and threw his arms around her. "Francesca," he cried, kissing her violently on both cheeks and almost causing her to drop her plate, now loaded with food. "*Come stai? Sono mesi . . .*" And he went on pouring out a flood of language while continuing periodically to hug and kiss her. Finally she was able to stop him and introduce me. "*Un giornalista?*" he asked, gazing at me out of a red-cheeked, unshaven countenance.

"No, *un mago americano*," she said. "*È molto famoso.*"

I understood what she'd said to him, that I was a famous

American magician, and I saw his expression change to one of childlike wonder. "Ah, *sì?*" he answered. "*Che meraviglia!*"

"Is marvelous, he says," she explained with a grin. "Come, we eat."

We sat at a corner table while the owner, whose name I still didn't know, bustled back into the kitchen to order our dinner. "What else are we eating?" I asked.

"Peppino and Teresa decide," she said. "There is pasta and fish. You like, no?"

"I like, yes," I said.

"Then later you do some magic, yes?"

"Sure. But how did you know I'm a magician?"

She glanced up at me, momentarily startled, then smiled. "Ravelli," she said. "I see him at a party. He tell me about you."

"Carlo is like the town crier," I said. "You tell him something, next thing you know, you're famous."

"He say you are marvelous. Is not true?"

"I'll let you judge that for yourself," I said. "But first let's eat."

"*Buon idea.*" She raised her wineglass to me. "*Salute.*"

We touched glasses and drank, then I turned my attention to the meal, which turned out to be the best one I'd had yet. Peppino and his wife, Teresa, owned the restaurant. She cooked and he waited on the customers There was no menu; you ate whatever they had decided to serve that day. You began with antipasto, then a pasta dish followed by fresh fish or veal, a salad, fruit, and cheeses. Every dish was excellent, but not heavy, so that by the end of the meal I felt fully satisfied and not satiated. "My God, Francesca, how you eat in this country," I said, over my third glass of some unsung but delicious pale white wine. "Music and food, two fields where Italy reigns supreme."

Francesca laughed. "Ah, you are right," she said. "But in politics, no."

During dinner I queried her on her background. She came from a long line of printers, lithographers, and photographers. The family had originally come from Naples sometime in the middle of the nineteenth century and settled in Milan, then as now the capital of the book and magazine publishing world. Francesca, an only child due to her father's premature demise, had simply carried on the family tradition, first in fashion photography, then, more recently, as a freelance photojournalist. "I am the best paparazza in the business," she said, with another laugh. "They hate me for it."

"Who hates you?"

"The men, *naturalmente*. I make the hard for them."

"You what?"

"The hard."

"You mean you give them a hard time."

"*Sì*. Did I say wrong?"

"It could be interpreted a little differently," I suggested. "You don't want me to tell you."

"Why not? How I learn if you not tell me?"

I explained what she could have meant and she blushed, then laughed again. She had an infectious one, a sound that seemed to bubble up from deep inside her, then explode out of her mouth. "I always make terrible what you call boo-boobs," she said. "You know, I never got English studies. I learn it from books and magazines. Then, too, I talk to everyone, you know. There are many Americans everywhere in my business. And so I learn. You correct me, please, when I make mistakes."

"I don't know," I said. "I sort of like the way you talk."

"You make the fun of me."

"No way," I assured her. "I find it very charming."

After we had finished eating, I took a deck of cards out of my pocket and began to shuffle and riffle it as we went on talking. Peppino and his wife, Teresa, a plump red-cheeked woman in a chef's outfit, came out of the kitchen to watch me. There were only three other sets of diners in the room, a slow night for this trattoria, I gathered, so I was able to show Francesca and the owners a few moves. I fanned the cards out to reveal various combinations of colors and numbers, then swept them up, reshuffled them, and fanned them out again to show other sequences. Once I spread out a blank deck, scooped it up, reshuffled, and then restored the fan to display the familiar suits in perfect order.

"*Che meraviglia!*" Peppino said, grinning broadly.

Teresa barked something at him and began to berate him in Italian. "What's she saying?" I asked.

Francesca laughed. "He is always playing cards with his friends and losing," she explained. "Teresa tell him why he doesn't learn what you are doing, so he can win."

"That's called cheating," I said.

Francesca shrugged. "So?"

"Look at this," I said, shuffling and then fanning the cards so Peppino and Teresa could see I had the deck stacked in an easily identifiable sequence. I set the pack down on the table and asked one of them to cut it. Francesca translated for me and Peppino reached out toward the cards. Teresa slapped his hand away. With a defiant look at me, she now cut the deck in four stacks and melded them together.

"Ah, *difficile*," I said, picking up the deck. I riffled it once to catch a glimpse of what she had done, then proceeded to reshuffle the deck until I had the cards back into their original sequence, a move that took no more than fifteen seconds, after which I fanned the cards to display them.

"*Mamma mia!*" Teresa exclaimed, shaking her head.

"*Basta, basta,*" Peppino said. "*Non gioco più, lo giuro.*"

"He say he not play again," Francesca translated.

"Never with strangers," I said. "You see what can happen."

I spent another twenty minutes demonstrating a variety of moves, using crimps, jogs, bottom dealing, second dealing, cull shuffling, and blinds, until they actually began to applaud. Finally I gathered up the deck, autographed the ace of diamonds, and handed it to Peppino. "For you," I said. "A present."

Peppino beamed, as if I had handed him an actual diamond, and Teresa took both my hands in hers and kissed me violently on the cheek. "*Bravo!*" she said. "*Un vero mago. Accidenti, che roba!*" And she retreated into the kitchen again, still mumbling to herself.

"Why you not do this to make money?" Francesca asked.

"You mean in real games, like poker?"

"Sure. You win much money, no?"

"Yes, until they break my hands."

"How they know?"

"Francesca, I'm not the only magician in the world who can do this," I explained. "And the casinos have experts on the premises to spot card cheats. I might get away with it for a while, but eventually somebody would catch on. I'm a magician, not a cardsharp."

"A what?"

"A cardsharp, a cheat."

"Ah, I understand. Yes, you are smart. But if I need money and I do what you do, I do it. You ever cheat?"

"Once I ran a cooler into a game, but that was a long time ago."

"A cooler?"

"That's a fixed deck," I explained. "You deal it so that everyone gets a good hand, but, of course, the person you want to win gets the best hand. The betting will be very heavy because every player thinks he has the best hand and stays in the game. But there's never any doubt who the winner will be. That's called a cooler or a cold deck."

She nodded thoughtfully. "Is very brilliant," she said. "I like it."

"Don't try it, Francesca," I advised her. "It's risky, even when I do it."

It was midnight when we left the restaurant. Instead of heading for her car, Francesca turned toward an old, ramshackle palazzo at the corner of the alley. "Where are we going?" I asked.

"My place. I show you," she said.

She lived on the top floor of the eight-story building. The elevator, an ancient contraption that could barely accommodate the two of us, lurched upward as it afforded a hair-raising view through the glass panels of the door to the stairwell below. "If I ever come back here, next time I'll walk," I said. "When was the last time the elevator was inspected?"

"Inspected? What for?"

I almost leapt out on the landing when we arrived. Francesca fished a giant mass of keys out of her purse and used three of them to unlock and unbolt her front door. "Is many thieves in the *quartiere*," she said, as she led me inside the flat. "Poor people, you know, but very good thieves."

Her apartment was a converted loft into which she had built a wooden platform, accessible by a circular stairway, that functioned as her bedroom. In one corner of the large space was her studio and darkroom, in another a tiny kitchen, while the rest of the room was furnished with battered-looking but comfortable armchairs, a marble-topped coffee table, and a long sofa. Like the trattoria, her walls were decorated with old photographs, these mostly of the Milanese countryside, shots of misty landscapes and ancient stone farmhouses framed by straight rows of poplars lining the banks of canals and streams. There were no windows, but a large skylight substituted for them. "This is very charming," I said. "How long have you been here?"

"Ah, always," she answered. "My parents lived downstairs. I sold the apartment and buy this place. Is very nice, no?"

"Yes, very."

"Come, I show you."

She led me over to her working area, opened a drawer, and pulled out a stack of photographs taken on the day Bobby Jo's body was found. As she shuffled through them she told in detail the story of how she'd happened to shoot them. "Is lucky for me, no?" she said. "I was in Sempione with friends gambling and I stay up very late, then go home. I hear the news on my car radio, police news, you know? So I hurry there and take pictures."

"You're a born paparazza."

"Ah, yes, the best one."

After the pictures of poor Bobby Jo, she opened another drawer and handed out a set of photographs of what I took to be Milanese party scenes, mostly of handsome but dissipated-looking citizens carousing at various nightspots. Carlo Ravelli was in most of them. "And this one is Adriano Barone," Francesca said, pointing out the best-looking of the men.

"A handsome devil," I said. "I've seen him." In Francesca's pictures, however, his eyes seemed both wild and dead at the same time, a curious, disturbing effect, as if he had stepped out of a scene from a Hogarthian nightmare. "He looks like very bad news."

"News?"

"Trouble."

"Ah, yes, much trouble."

"You know him?"

"Everyone know him. He is famous in Italy."

"Francesca, why are you showing me these pictures?"

"I want to help you."

"In what way?"

"I want to help you to catch him. He kill this girl."

"You're sure of that?"

"Yes, I know what he is like."

"Did he do something to you?"

She didn't answer me right away, but averted her gaze and began stuffing the pictures back into a drawer. "He rape me," she said at last, turning to look at me in anger. "Three years ago he pull me into a bedroom in his villa and he rape me."

"You were alone with him?"

"No, it was a weekend at his villa. There was twenty people maybe, but no one do nothing. It was very late and everyone is drunk or taking drugs. He pull me inside and he rape me."

"What did you do?"

"I run away."

"You didn't tell the police?"

She shook her head violently, her cheeks red with anger. "It do no good. No one say nothing. I swear one day I get this man. He is evil."

"I believe you. Where's his villa?"

"He has four. This one is near Sempione. He like to gamble there."

"On the lake then, near where the body was found?"

"Two kilometers. But I think maybe they were on the island."

"What island?"

"The father, Luca, he have an island in the lake, on the Swiss side, but is not far."

"How far?"

She shrugged. "Maybe one kilometer, maybe more, I don't know. Is very small, only Luca's villa is there. That is where the family was that night."

"You know that?"

"Yes. Luca was having a *festa* for the whole family. There was a marriage, a cousin. Adriano go to the island, too, then maybe he leave and go to his villa to join some friends."

"And you think Bobby Jo was there?"

"I know. Gianpaolo Caruso, the jeweler, he bring her. Adriano tell him. He is one of his *creature*."

"Francesca, what can we do about it?"

"We make Adriano angry. Make him think you fook Bobby Jo or something. Get to know him."

"How do I do that?"

"In Rome, next week, you meet him."

"Will you be there?"

"Yes. I take pictures, no? You want me to help?"

I thought about the pictures of Bobby Jo's body, I thought about Francesca being raped, I thought about this guy with all his money and his powerful daddy at his back, and I suddenly decided that I wanted her help in nailing Adriano Barone. Maybe Jake Dawson would get something for his money, after all. "Okay, Francesca, I'm not sure how we'll swing this, but I'll do what I can, with your help."

She smiled. "I like you, *mago*." She leaned up on tiptoe and kissed me. "You want to stay here now?"

"With you?"

"Why? You see somebody else?"

"You know what I love about Italy? People are always making you these offers no one can refuse."

"You are stupid. It is late and the drive is bad. No taxis come here now. You sleep there, okay?" She pointed to the sofa. "Maybe, if you are good, I kiss you good night."

10

BAUBLES

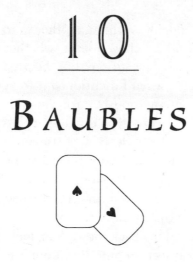

Imust have been very good, because she did more than kiss me good night. No sooner had I settled myself on her sofa under the ragged quilt she had provided than I heard her tiptoe down the stairway from her loft. She sat down beside me, kissed me, and took my hand. "Come," she said. "You don't sleep here."

I didn't argue. I followed her up the stairs to the loft. She was wearing a bathrobe, but took it off as we climbed into bed. She was naked, her body gleaming in the faint moonlight coming through the skylight. I was in my Jockey shorts and a T-shirt. "Take it off," she said. "You look stupid."

I obeyed and crawled in beside her. "Don't get ideas," she said. "We don't do fooking now. We sleep."

"You're not making it easy," I said.

"You silly, Shifty. You sleep." And she curled up around one of her pillows with her back to me and was soon sound asleep.

I decided to pretend I was a monk. I turned my back to her and tried to go to sleep, but for a long time I couldn't. Then, just as I was beginning to doze off, she turned and pressed her body against me. Her arm lay against my thigh. I waited, once again wide-awake. "Francesca, this isn't going to work," I finally said. "I think I better go back to the sofa."

"Don't be a stupid," she whispered.

I turned and suddenly, without another word being spoken, we became lovers. I found myself wondering whether I should have said something about taking precautions, but the passion of the moment swept me away. Later, when I mentioned it to her and asked if she had, she snorted contemptuously. "You Americans," she said. "Always practical. I don't worry, you don't worry." An interesting attitude, I thought, but let it pass. In any case, our lovemaking hadn't lasted more than a few minutes. It was fierce, unbounded, complete, but as brief as the coupling of a pair of squirrels. When it was over, Francesca got up, went to the bathroom, returned five minutes later, kissed me quickly on the cheek, turned over, and immediately went to sleep again. I lay on my back for a while, looking up at the stars, then dropped into a sleep so profound I don't remember anything except being awakened by her the next morning.

The studio was full of a misty, early-morning light. Francesca, again in her bathrobe, was sitting on the bed beside me with a cup of steaming *caffè latte* in her hand. "Here," she said, "drink."

I propped myself up on one elbow. "What time is it?"

"Nine o'clock. Drink."

The coffee tasted wonderful. "*Grazie*," I said. "How are you?"

"Fine," she said. "You snore. I push you to make you roll over, but you don't wake up. Luckily, you stop soon."

"Sorry. I must have been lying on my back. That was nice last night."

"Yes. Peppino's is very good food."

"I don't mean Peppino's," I said.

"Ah, our fooking. Yes, that was necessary."

"What do you mean, necessary?"

"How we sleep, eh? You lying there like a goat."

"What do you mean, a goat? Do I look like a goat?"

"No, but you all excited. We don't fook, we don't sleep. Is necessary, no? You men, you must do something with it."

"With what?"

"Your little fish there between your legs. So busy always."

"Oh, you were just making sure we got some sleep, is that it?"

"*Beh*, I do what is possible, no?"

I smiled at her. "You're a character, Fran, did you know that?"

She looked puzzled. "A character? What is that? *Un personaggio? Che vuol dire?* What you mean?"

"I mean you're unusual."

"Ah, yes, I see. You are right. Get up now, Shifty. I take you somewhere."

"Where?"

"You see."

"You got a razor?"

"*Certo.* Come on, I show you."

Twenty minutes later, we were on our way toward the Swiss border. It was early and most of the traffic was headed into town, so we made good time. "I show you where they find Bobby Jo," she explained. "You want to see, no?" She parked the car at the spot on the road where she'd left it that day and we walked down to the shoreline. "There," she said, pointing to a pebbly area where the girl's body had been spotted. "With her face down between the rocks. It was one miracle she was alive."

"When, exactly, did she die?"

"Maybe on the way to hospital."

"Has there been an official report?"

"No, not yet."

"They take their time, don't they?"

"Everything in Italy take time, *caro.* Italy is very old country. There is always much time."

"Was she badly beaten up?"

Francesca nodded. "I see many bruises, Shifty. She look bad. You see my photos, no?"

We sat down on some rocks and looked out over the lake. It was peaceful and calm, with the sun now beginning to burn the mist away. Villas, half-hidden among trees, lined the shore on either side of us. "Where's Adriano's place?" I asked.

She pointed to our right. "Over there, behind that *penìsola.* You see the one, with the little *cappella* at the end?"

"The church?"

"*Sì.* Behind that, maybe one kilometer."

"And the island?"

"Out there."

"Where?"

"You can't see it from here. This is a, how you say, *una baia*. . . ."

"A bay?"

"*Sì*. The island is around that point, then out in the water. We drive up toward Sempione, I can show you. Is very small. Only the villa is there and a place for the boats."

"And old man Luca lives there part of the time?"

"Only in the summer. He have the art collection there. The paintings and sculptures, many of them. He open them to the public two weeks a year, one week in June, one in the fall."

"Only two weeks in all?"

"Yes, it is for taxes."

"You mean, by opening the collection to the public he can claim tax deductions?"

"Of course. Everything Luca Barone do, he do for money," she said. "Always for money. He own this country."

"All by himself?"

"He and two, three others. Gianni Agnelli, the pope, and Luca Barone, they are untouching."

"Untouchable."

"Yes, that is what I mean. They own Italy. The pope owns Rome, and Luca Barone and his friends own the country. It has always been like this, ever since many centuries. One time there was much worry Italy go Communist. To Luca Barone is no difference. He own the political parties also. He give money to all of them, he buy them. Before him, under the Fascists, was the same. Always the rich own everything, everybody."

"That's pretty much the way things work everywhere, Fran. Money talks."

"It talks?"

"Money commands, that's what it means. And the poor don't vote."

"In Italy the poor people vote, Shifty, but is no difference. People like Luca Barone, they always command. But poor Luca, he have one weakness—Adriano."

"I don't care about Luca, Fran. But if Adriano killed Bobby Jo, maybe we can help him along to the slammer."

"*Cosa?*" She looked bewildered.

"The slammer is a slang term for jail."

"Ah, I like very much. Why you call me Fran?"

"It's a diminutive. Francesca seems a little cumbersome for someone so small. Do you mind?"

"No. Is funny. Like Shifty. Fran and Shifty, is amusing, no?"

"We're definitely one of the amusing couples." I leaned over and kissed her. She opened her mouth and put both arms around my neck. "I'd like to think you made love to me last night because you wanted to," I said, "and not because you needed to put me to sleep."

"Ah, you are nice to fook," she said. "Tonight we take more time. You see me tonight?"

"I'll check my calendar."

Again she looked confused. "You what? *Cosa dici?*"

"Just kidding, Fran. Of course we'll see each other tonight."

We kissed again and headed back up the slope to the car.

It was a few minutes after six o'clock that afternoon when I dropped in on Gianpaolo Caruso. The jeweler's elegant little shop was directly across the street from the Grand, where I had an appointment at seven with Francesca. She was shooting another fashion show somewhere in the neighborhood. I don't know what I expected Caruso to tell me that he hadn't already told the police, if they'd bothered to interview him, but I thought it might be useful to get the word out in the right circles that someone was asking questions regarding Bobby Jo, someone who wasn't connected to the Italian power structure.

Caruso was the first person I saw when I walked in. He was deep in conversation with an older couple with whom he'd apparently been negotiating the sale of a major bauble. He was holding it out in front of him, obviously engaged in a sales pitch, so I pretended to be looking around for something to buy on my own. A sleek-looking young saleswoman, dressed in black with a single strand of pearls around her neck, stepped out from behind the counter at the rear of the store. "May I help you?" she asked in English.

"How did you know I wasn't Italian?" I asked.

She smiled, revealing a mouthful of teeth as brilliant as her pearls. "You look very American," she said. "Is there something I can show you?"

"No, thanks," I said. "I'm waiting for Signor Caruso. I'm a friend of Carlo Ravelli."

"Ah, yes, of course," she said. "It will be a few minutes." And she retreated to the rear of the store again, leaving me to wonder what it was that had given me away as a barbarian. My clothes? The way I moved? My attitude? The incident confirmed what I'd learned during my weeks in Italy; every tradesman I'd dealt with had spoken to me first in English. It was as if I had the word "American" tattooed across my forehead. "It is because we have known so many foreigners over the centuries," Carlo Ravelli had explained to me. "Tourists, conquerors, exploiters, invaders of one sort or another. We know you in our bones."

I saw nothing in Caruso's shop for less than a million lire. Every piece was beautifully displayed, each precious stone set in designs of exquisite workmanship and imagination. I strolled to the rear of the shop and asked the woman about the merchandise. "Oh, yes," she said, "Signor Caruso designs every piece himself. Each one is a work of art, do you not think so?"

"I'm very impressed," I said, meaning it. This man, after all, was the same sweating pig who had propositioned Bobby Jo at the party where I'd first met her, treating her like a piece of meat. I couldn't put that image of him together with the skilled artisan who had designed these pieces. Another of the many paradoxes the country was providing for my entertainment.

"Yes? May I help you?"

I turned around. Caruso was standing there, smiling, his hands clasped together, his body hunched slightly forward, as if he might want at some point to kiss the hem of my garments. I wondered if he'd studied for the priesthood. "Signor Caruso, we met a couple of weeks ago at a party," I said. "I'm Lou Anderson, a friend of Ravelli's."

"Ah, yes," the jeweler said. "I remember. I was with Carlo the other night. How are you?"

We shook hands. "Another party?"

"No, no, a dinner, a boring affair, I'm afraid. Business. What can I do for you?"

"I'd like to talk to you about Bobby Jo."

His face flushed and his eyes flickered in alarm. He glanced around the store, then empty of customers. "Bobby Jo? That unfortunate girl," he said. "It was a tragedy."

"I understand you were with her that night."

"I? No, not with her. No, not at all." Again he glanced around the room, then beckoned me to follow him. "Please, not here," he said. "Come."

I followed him into his office at the rear of the store. It was a small, dark room with a single barred window looking out on an alley. Several oil paintings of Neapolitan landscapes decorated two of the walls, while books and ledgers lined the third one. Caruso sat down behind his desk and motioned me into a chair facing him. "Now, please, what is this all about? I have told the police what I know."

"Would you mind telling me? I'm a close friend of Bobby Jo's father," I said. "He couldn't stay, but he's asked me to act for him. I'd appreciate it very much. Her father is very anxious to find out what happened. You can understand, can't you?"

"Yes, of course. I see." The jeweler looked mildly stricken, as if he had just bitten into something a little too ripe for him. "Of course, it is a tragedy. No one knows what happened. She left the party early, perhaps one, one-thirty in the morning."

"She left by herself?"

"Yes."

"How could she get home? I thought she went with you."

"Well, yes, she did. That is, Adriano asked me to take her. He was not in Milan. So I called her and arranged to pick her up at her hotel. It was about eight-thirty, I believe. And then we drive to the villa."

"Oh, so you didn't go to the island?"

"The island? The commendatore's villa? Oh, no. The party was at Adriano's. It was very gay, very many people. Carlo was there, too. After I drive Bobby Jo there I did not see her again. That is, I see her from time to time during the party, but not to spend time with her. She was always with other people."

"Why would she go there? She was afraid of Adriano."

"Afraid? No, no, he was always very kind to her. He send her many flowers and then, the day before the party, he buy her a beautiful diamond pin in the shape of a quarter moon."

"He bought it from you?"

"Yes. He pay four million lire for it. He ask me to send it to her with the invitation to the party. Then he ask me to bring her. He was already at the villa. Perhaps he go to the island first, then to the villa."

"What sort of party was it?"

"What do you mean? Very nice, a big dinner affair in the open by the lake. Luckily, it is a nice night, no rain for a change. It was very beautiful, very elegant, with dancing."

"What was the occasion?"

"Adriano is always giving parties. He tell me it was a spring celebration for before the Derby. But with Adriano, who knows? There is no reason. He likes parties."

"You picked out the pin, right?"

"Yes, he ask me to do this. He tell me what he want to spend and I choose it for him."

"Why didn't he ask Ravelli to bring her?"

"I don't know. Maybe he try and he don't find Carlo. Sometimes Carlo travels with his father on business. So he call me."

"What about you?"

"Me? What do you mean?"

"How did you feel about Bobby Jo?"

"Feel about her? I don't know her."

"Come on, Signor Caruso. The night I met you, you were trying to get into Bobby Jo's pants. You were so eager to have her, you even offered her money."

He looked shaken, as if I had suggested I had caught him spitting on his mother's grave. Were all Italians born actors? I had begun to think so. "I never offer her money," he said. "Who tell you this?"

"She did. I was there."

"She is lying to you. I never offer her money. Why do I have to do that? I go out with many beautiful women. I do not treat them like prostitutes. Everybody like me. Why do you accuse me?"

"Maybe Bobby Jo exaggerated."

"Of course she exaggerate. I am very angry to hear this."

"Forget I mentioned it. Let me ask you, Signor Caruso, what do you think happened that night?"

"I don't know."

"You said that you brought Bobby Jo to the party. So how did she leave? Somebody must have driven her out of there, right?"

He shrugged. "Perhaps, but I did not see her go."

"Could she have stayed at the villa that night?"

Again he shrugged and his gaze wavered uneasily away from me, as if he were looking for an escape route. "I always assume she leave," he said. "I did not see her at the party after one or perhaps one-thirty. All this I tell to the police."

"Did you see Adriano after that time?"

"I don't follow Adriano everywhere, you know. I was enjoying myself with my friends. What Adriano is doing, I have no idea."

"Okay, well, I'm sorry to have bothered you, but nobody here tells me anything. I appreciate your seeing me."

He stood up and ushered me out into the store, where his saleswoman was now busy with a young man looking for an engagement ring. At the door Caruso shook my hand. "It was very tragic," he said. "So many young girls in Milano have this trouble. It is very difficult here. I tell you what I think. I think Bobby Jo take one of Adriano's cars and leave the party. He have several cars at the villa. Someone, some bandits, stop her. They rob her and they kill her, that is all. Milano is the crime capital of Italy. Bobby Jo is wearing her beautiful diamond pin, which no one has found. That is why. Maybe they also rape her and beat her, I don't know. That is what I think. All the criminals in Milan know who lives in these villas and they rob them all the time. They see this girl leave and they follow her. They also take the car. That is my opinion, Signor Anderson."

"Where is the car, then? The one she borrowed."

"No one has found it. Maybe in Croatia, maybe in Switzerland or Austria. That is where they take the stolen cars, over the border. Good-bye, Signor Anderson."

I stepped out into the Via Manzoni and headed toward the Grand. I was pretty sure that Gianpaolo Caruso was a skillful liar who knew far more about what had happened that night than he had bothered to tell me.

11

ABSTRACTIONS

"What are you giving me, Fran, the Grand Tour?"

"What this means?"

"It means why are we going to all these noisy, expensive, smoke-filled nightclubs?"

"I think maybe we find Adriano," she said. "You see what he does, where he goes."

"It's a tour of my idea of hell."

"Yes, is very boring, but I have to come here."

"Why?"

"My work. These places is where many celebrities comes. See, over there?" She pointed across the room to a corner table where a large man with a bulbous nose and a mane of curly gray hair sat with a thin, chesty blonde at least twenty years younger than he. Their waiter was pouring champagne for the two of them from a newly opened bottle, after which the couple touched glasses and drank.

"A celebrity," I said. "Okay, who is it?"

"Mimmo Spadolini."

"So?"

"Ah, you know nothing," Francesca said. "He is a movie director of many terrible movies, but they all make much money. The woman is not his wife."

"Who is she?"

"A very terrible actress called Lucia Malvoglio. She star in many porno films because she have big boobies."

"Who taught you that word?"

"What word?"

"Boobies."

"Ah, Scarponi. He work for *Mezzanotte*. He speak fantastic American. He teach me."

"Okay, so what about Signor Spadolini and the lady with the boobies?"

"He is fooking her. I take his picture."

"Now?"

She flashed me her most winning smile. "Sure, why not?"

"Where's your camera?"

She reached into her purse and produced a tiny camera and a light meter. She flashed the latter at the room, checked the numbers on it, adjusted the camera for the shot, and put the light meter back in her bag. "Excuse me," she said, standing up. "I go to ladies' room now."

"You're going to take a picture of him with this bimbo? What if he sees you?"

"I wish him to see me," she said. "That way maybe he pay me not to sell the photo, you understand? I sell the photo, I get maybe one hundred thousand lire. He buy it from me, I get more."

"What's the Italian word for blackmail?" I asked.

"You don't worry," she said, kissing me quickly on the cheek. "I come back soon."

I watched her thread her way through the tables skirting the dance floor toward the corner where the director sat with his floozie. As she passed their table, I saw her lean in toward the couple, then scurry away toward the rest rooms. The director rose halfway out of his seat as if to pursue her, then beckoned angrily toward the head-waiter. I waited for the drama to unfold, hoping that Francesca would keep it away from our end of the room.

The club we were in was called Il Pellicano. It was located on a side street behind the Duomo and was much like the two other spots Francesca had taken me to. It was dark, smoky, and loud. There was a bar, a sea of tiny tables crowded together around a small dance floor, a lighted booth occupied by a disk jockey who alternated between sessions of frenzied rock and old-fashioned slow pop songs to which the customers danced *"panza a panza,"* belly to belly, as Francesca put it. The clientele was older than at the other places we had visited, The Blue Moon and the Capricorn, with more men than women on hand. To accommodate the single males, Il Pellicano provided a complement of B-girls, who worked mainly in the bar area and who could be had for the night, I was told, for two or three hundred thousand lire, not including whatever bill they could persuade their dates to run up on the premises. The cheap champagne ran to fifty dollars a bottle and the minimum at the tables was fifty thousand lire per customer, about thirty-five dollars. So far I had spent over two hundred dollars of Jake Dawson's money and I had told Francesca that Il Pellicano was to be my last stop on this circuit. The smoky atmosphere was so dense that I was having trouble breathing and I also have an aversion to being swindled. "You are so difficult," Francesca observed. "Why you complain all the time?"

"I guess I'm not a fun guy," I said.

"Ah, poof, you are an *orso.*"

"What's an *orso?*"

"Big, hairy," she said, raising her arms over her head and scowling.

"A bear?"

"*Bravo, sì,* a bear."

Francesca emerged from the ladies' room and headed back toward our table. No sooner had she rejoined me than the headwaiter materialized behind her. He leaned over and said something to Francesca in Italian. She nodded, got up, and followed him over to the corner where the director and his girlfriend sat, sipping champagne. The music switched from soft pop to loud rock and a horde of dancers occupied the center of the room, heedlessly bumping and banging into one another. I got up and headed for the men's room, skirting the bar area as I did so. Carlo Ravelli reached out and grabbed me. "*Mago,*" he said, "what are you doing here?"

"Hello, Carlo," I said. "Just having a look at how the rich folks play."

He was with a small group of revelers in their thirties or early forties, four stout burghers and two large blond women, waiting for a table. They had finished dinner and it was too early to go home. Ravelli introduced me to them as "the famous magician," but none of them displayed the slightest interest in me. The men wore dark business suits, and the women, who apparently were married to two of them, sported heavy gold jewelry and diamonds. Ravelli pulled me aside. "Germans," he explained. "We are in business together, you understand? I have to be with them."

"That's a lot of expensive jewelry to be displayed in a joint like this," I observed. "Is it safe?"

Ravelli shrugged. "*Chi se ne frega,*" he said. "Who gives the shit, you understand? They have a car with a chauffeur to take them home to their hotels. They are from Bonn. They know nothing."

"Is this what you do for your father, Carlo? Entertain the visiting colleagues?"

He grimaced. "Yes. It's what I do best, no? My father goes to bed at eleven o'clock every night. All he do is work. Me, I like to amuse myself. You wish to join us?"

"No, thanks, I'm with somebody."

"Ah," he said, scanning the room. "Who?"

"A photographer named Francesca Pirro."

"*La paparazza?* Oh, you be careful, Luigi. She do anything, you know, for to take pictures."

"I know."

"You know she hate Adriano. I tell you that, no?"

"No, but I can imagine. Where is Adriano?"

"Roma, for the Derby this Saturday. You come, no?"

"Yes, I'm leaving here Thursday."

"*Bene.* Where are you?"

I gave him the name of my hotel in Rome, the Portoghesi, where I had stayed before.

"We go to the races together. Thursday night we go to Tor di Valle, and Saturday is the Derby."

"What is Tor di Valle?"

"*Il trotto*," he said. "I pick you up at your hotel at seven."

"Trotters? I hate harness racing," I said.

"No, no, Luigi, you have the good time," he said. "I guarantee it. You come with Francesca?"

"I don't think so."

"Good. I have surprise for you. Then if Adriano is there, it is bad scene. You don't bring her, okay?" He clapped me on the shoulder. "*Bravo*, Luigi, he said. "We have much fun in Rome. Adriano is giving the big party Friday night at the Osteria Greca. I bring you, okay? *Beno. Ciao.*" He leaned forward to whisper in my ear. "I have to be nice to these Germans. Shitheads, but rich."

In the men's room, one of the booths was occupied by a man obviously inhaling a substance through his nose. We were four in the room, but no one paid the slightest attention to him. "Sounds like a man with a bad cold," I observed to the citizen at the urinal next to me. Either he didn't speak English or he chose to ignore me. I decided I had had enough of the scene at Il Pellicano and resolved either to whisk Francesca out of there or escape on my own.

When I returned to our table, I found Francesca deep in conversation with a man she introduced to me as the most famous journalist in Italy. His name was Tommaso Scarponi and he was a slightly built, pale citizen of about fifty with a pair of startling blue eyes under a shock of unruly red hair. He was wearing a plaid sport jacket, gray slacks, and a black silk turtleneck shirt. "*Ciao*," he said. "Francesca tell me you are a magician."

"That's right," I said.

"Do some magic, *amico*."

I shook my head. "Not here," I said. "It's too dark and too noisy."

"What do you do in Italy?"

I glanced at Francesca. She gave a tiny, almost imperceptible shake of the head and looked away. "Seeing the sights," I said. "I'm on vacation."

Scarponi looked at Francesca. "He is lying, no?" he said.

"Why would I lie to you?" I asked.

"You are not a tourist, because you would not know Francesca."

"I give lectures on magic," I explained. "Francesca came to take my picture. I invited her out."

"And she brought you to this squalid house of torture," he said, still unconvinced. "Ah, well, each to his own form of misery."

"Francesca said you're a famous journalist. How famous are you?"

"Is a celebrity," Francesca said. "He write for all the papers and magazines. Always is something new. Last week he do a series on America about religious fantastics."

"Fantastics?"

"Fanatics," Scarponi corrected her. "It was a series in *Mezzanotte*. It make a sensation."

"He write about the giant neon statue of Gesù—"

"Jesus Christ," Scarponi translated.

"—in Times Square."

"There is no giant neon statue of Jesus in Times Square," I said.

"No," Scarponi agreed, "but there should be one, no?"

"You're a creative journalist," I said. "Is that it?"

"Yes, I write the real truth about things. That is why people like to read me."

"Have you ever been sued?"

He laughed. "In Italy it is all creative journalism," he said. "We don't all sue each other. In America you are crazy with lawyers."

"You're right about that. What have you been working on recently?"

He shrugged. "This and that."

"He write the story in *Mezzanotte* on the American model," Francesca said, "the one with my pictures."

"You are a friend of hers, yes?" he asked.

"No, I only met her once, at a party," I answered. "Do you think Adriano Barone killed her?"

He smiled. "Certainly, but he will not be arrested. He will not even be questioned very much. This is Italy, my friend. There will be much talk, there will be more articles written, much gossip, but then it will disappear and there will be the silence of the tomb. Adriano

Barone? Listen, the country is in the hands of these people. Not even the judges of Milano are strong enough for them."

"Interesting," I said. "What if they turn up some hard evidence in the investigation?"

Scarponi shook his head, smiled again, and rubbed the thumb and index finger of his right hand together. "In this country it is money that commands. You will see." He leaned across the table and gave Francesca a quick peck on the cheek. "*Ciao, bella,*" he said, and turned to shake my hand. "Good-bye. I hope to see you again." And he headed across the room toward the director's table.

"Is he going to interview that poor guy with the porn star?" I asked.

"Yes. I tell Tommaso about him."

"How'd you do, Fran?"

She laughed and opened her purse. A fat white envelope lay nestled at the bottom between wads of Kleenex and her house keys. "Two hundred thousand lire," she said. "Is not bad, no?"

"And what's Tommaso going to do? Up the ante?"

"*Cosa?*"

"Make him pay more?"

"Ah, no. He is a friend. He just go over to have a drink with him. He knows Lucia, too."

"Tommaso gets around."

"Ah, yes." She leaned across the table and took my hand. "Later, Shifty, when we know more things, then we talk to Scarponi. He write big story."

"Why talk to him?"

"You understand nothing," she said. "You wait. You see. I show you how. We go now, no?"

"Sure," I said, looking around for our waiter, "we go now, yes."

My second night in Francesca's loft proved to be far more tumultuous than my first one. Francesca turned out to be an adventurous lover. She liked to play games. We made up the rules as we went along, but they were never less than inventive. She had a collection of masks and props that proved to be entertaining and useful. We cavorted through her space like demented gibbons, swinging wildly from one scenario to another. Sexual aerobics with highly theatrical overtones. Deprived of conventions, making love to her had little to do with sentiment. Pure lust replaced affection. She was a circus act to be caught only in mid flight, pleasure seized on the wing. We ended the night not in fulfillment but in exhaustion and lay still in each other's arms until dawn. In the morning we hardly spoke. I gave her my address in Rome and she said she would call me there. I left her without even a kiss on the cheek.

When I walked into my hotel a little after nine o'clock, I was greeted by two men who, the concierge informed me, had been waiting for an hour. Neither of them spoke English. They were in their thirties, short and swarthy, with small brush mustaches, and they wore dark, ill-fitting business suits and somber neckties. They both possessed badges that identified them as police officers, and it was made clear to me that they expected me to come along with them. "The magistrate wishes to speak with you," the concierge explained to me. "These men are from her office."

I was not allowed to go up to my room to shave or brush my teeth, but was whisked away in an unmarked police sedan across the city. Twenty minutes later, I found myself once again seated in Angela Tedeschi's office. She was not pleased to see me. "Mr. Anderson," she said from behind her cluttered desk, "I have had a difficult time finding you."

"I haven't been home much recently."

"So I gather," she said dryly, glancing out the window as if she found my very presence in her office distasteful. "You're meeting a great many people, I understand."

"Are you tailing me?"

"I'm sorry?"

"Following me."

"No, but I have information. Lavenante and Gianpaolo Caruso. The latter is very upset. He came to see me in person."

"And what did he tell you?"

"That you had threatened him."

"I did not threaten him, Miss Tedeschi. I only wanted to find out what happened that night. You haven't been a mine of information on the subject. It's lucky Jake Dawson hasn't called me, because I have nothing to tell him."

"I cannot share information on this investigation with you," she said. "You must know that we are doing everything we can to find the murderer."

"Then she *was* killed. How did she die?"

"I am not at liberty to divulge that information either at this time." Again she looked out the window, as if her attention had been caught by something unexpected—a cry in the street, the sudden noise of an accident.

"Is this what you want me to tell the girl's father?"

"He has called me directly," she said, refocusing her gaze on me. "I have tried to explain the situation to him." She leaned forward across her desk and looked sternly at me. "I simply cannot have you meddling in this matter. What you don't seem to understand, Mr. Anderson, is that there is far more at stake in this investigation than a banal killing."

"Oh, really? Like what?"

"What you must believe is that I am more dedicated to bringing these people to justice than you can imagine. Your going around the city stirring up trouble is making things more difficult."

"Excuse me," I said, "I'm not going around stirring up trouble. I'm interested in finding out who killed Bobby Jo and in getting her body back to her father in the States. And what exactly do you mean by 'these people'? Have you even questioned Adriano Barone?"

"I will not discuss the case with you, Mr. Anderson. There are issues at stake you do not understand and which are none of your business or Mr. Dawson's either. The question of who killed this girl is not as important as you might think in the large scheme of things."

"Oh, really? I thought that was the point of the investigation," I said. "What is the point? Is justice involved at all?"

"Justice in a higher sense, yes," she said. "All I can tell you is that this Bobby Jo is merely one of many victims. The person or persons who killed her are part of a large conspiracy, a larger problem. In a case of this kind the fate of a single individual cannot be the paramount concern. Justice is also an ideal to which the individual is sometimes sacrificed. Do I make myself clear?"

"I'm aware, Miss Tedeschi, that 'justice' is one of those big abstract words that often have no basis in reality," I said. "But all this girl's father wants is to find out what happened to his daughter and to see her killer brought to trial and condemned. The larger picture is not his worry."

"But it is mine," Angela Tedeschi said. "I live in this society. I have to abide by and to enforce its rules and respect its priorities."

"You know what?" I said. "I think all these fine abstract concepts you're spouting are basically bullshit."

"What?"

"Turds of the bull," I continued, "designed to shield and distort the truth. It's the kind of talk that serves the interests of people like Adriano Barone and his friends and of people like you."

"Like me?"

"People connected to power and privilege."

Angela Tedeschi did not immediately answer me. She seemed to be thinking things over, her hands quietly folded in her lap, her dark piercing eyes focused on my face, as if seeing me clearly for the first time. Curiously, I felt that nothing I had said had offended her, that she had even enjoyed my outburst. I had been assigned a part to play, and evidently I was playing it with panache and fervor. I wouldn't have been surprised if she had smiled. Instead she suddenly stood up and held out her hand. "Thank you for coming," she said, as if I had had a choice in the matter. "Think over what I said. Do what you must, but stay in touch with me. Good day."

I shook her hand, feeling somehow a little foolish. What did I know about law and order and police investigations, especially in Italy? "I don't know why," I said, "but I have a feeling you're not really upset with me."

"I have said what I felt I must say," Angela Tedeschi answered. "I think you understand. Good-bye." And she gestured politely for me to leave, which I did, more confused than when I'd arrived.

12

PARKER

The *portiere* at the Portoghesi in Rome greeted me like a long-lost friend. "Signor Anderson, how have you been?" he said. "It is pleasant to see you again. You have been in America?"

"No, Milan," I said, as I handed him my passport.

"Ah, Milan," he said, shaking his head. "A cold city. Welcome back to Rome."

"I'm very happy to be here," I said.

"And how long is your stay with us this time?"

"At least a few days."

"Marvelous," he answered, as I signed the registration form. "We have the room for you on the fourth floor, very quiet, off the street."

"Thanks." I finished signing in and picked up my suitcases.

"Ah, one moment," he said. "There is a message for you." He handed me a slip of paper. "A Signor Ravelli. There is his number. But he said not to call unless there is a change in plans. He will pick you up here at seven o'clock."

I thanked him, stuffed the note into my pocket, and went upstairs. My room was small but comfortable and cheerful, with a window that looked out on a narrow courtyard festooned with drying laundry. I unpacked, took a shower, dried off, and looked at my watch. It was nearly one o'clock, which made it about five in the morning back in Kentucky. I picked up the phone and dialed Jake Dawson's number.

"Hell no, I'm not asleep," he said. "We already delivered two foals this morning, couple of nice little colts. What the hell's going on, Anderson?"

I filled him in on my recent activities in Milan, though I left out any mention of my carnal involvement with Francesca Pirro, and concluded with an account of my most recent conversation with Angela Tedeschi. "She told me you'd called her directly," I said.

"Yeah, I did," he said. "I hadn't heard from you, so I thought I'd find out what I could. She gave me the old runaround, nothing new."

"There's something she's not telling us," I said.

"There's a hell of a lot she's not telling us," Jake Dawson said. "It's the same old bullshit."

"That's what I told her. Jake, she's on to something here, but she's got an agenda of her own that we know nothing about. Everything points to this guy Adriano Barone as Bobby Jo's killer, but so far as I can tell she isn't doing anything about him. I'm not sure he's even been questioned by the police, incredible as that sounds."

"I asked her when I could expect my daughter's body to be sent home and she gave me the same old stuff about when the investigation is over and all like that," Dawson said. "Goddamn woman, no telling what she's up to."

"Anyway, Jake, I'm in Rome for a few days," I said. "I'm going to meet this guy Adriano while I'm here. He's got a horse in the Italian Derby, which is being run this Sunday. I'll let you know what I can find out."

"Yeah, Anderson, hang in there. I got another couple of weeks here, then I can come back, if I have to."

"If we can't get any action before then, it might be a good idea to get the story played up in the press again," I suggested. "It's quiet now, but I met a couple of journalists and I could feed them a good story about Bobby Jo and about how no one's doing anything about solving the case. You want me to try that?"

"Hell of a good idea, Anderson," Jake Dawson said. "Get on it, fella."

"We could stir up a hornet's nest, Jake."

"That's the idea, ain't it?"

"I'll see what happens over the weekend and I'll get back to you." I gave him the number of the Portoghesi and hung up.

I spent the rest of the afternoon wandering around the city. It was a perfect spring day, with a deep blue sky above and a warm sun beating down over the ancient stones of the old capital. Once again I had this strong feeling that I had been here before, in some remote past of my life. The very smell of the place, a musty blend of dust, ancient vegetation, cooking, and exhaust fumes, seemed familiar to me, as if I had grown up with this odor in my nostrils from the first day of my life. I walked everywhere and spent the last hour of the afternoon perched halfway up the Spanish Steps, looking down on the swarm of passersby below me, on their way to and from the shops of the Via Frattina and the Via Condotti, or simply milling aimlessly around the strange stone fountain in the shape of a boat at the foot of the steps. Swallows were doing their evening dance overhead, in pursuit of insects, and in the distance church bells rang above the clamor of traffic along the main avenues. I could have stayed there forever, I thought, and found myself contemplating the possibility of spending future time, every year, in this place. I felt warmed by it, nourished, as I had never felt anywhere in L.A., which is not a city at all but a sprawling collection of towns and neighborhoods criss-crossed by freeways and boulevards. Only in Del Mar, where I spent every summer playing the horses at the seaside racetrack's summer meet, had I ever felt equally at home, though Del Mar is mostly beaches and the outdoor life and the horses. Rome was something else, a way of living rooted in history and food and wine and beauty and an overwhelming sense of time not meaning all that much.

A few minutes after six, I walked down the steps and threaded my way through the crowd in the piazza toward my hotel. As I started down the Via Condotti, Parker Williams suddenly stepped out of a bar entrance to my right. She was in a hurry and didn't notice me. I called out and caught up to her a few doorways down the street. "Oh, Shifty," she said, startled. "What are you doing here? I didn't see you."

"I came down for the Italian Derby," I said. "What are *you* doing here? I thought you were in Monte Carlo."

"I was and I'm going back in a couple of days," she said. "They flew me down here for a special showing. I've got a job at the Excelsior tomorrow morning. It's a private showing for some German buyers and I'm one of two models. The Grizzutis. Do you know who they are?"

"No."

"Alfredo Grizzuti and his mother, Elena. Big designers, but very exclusive, mostly aimed at slightly older people. They don't do shows, but their clientele is private and very tony. I picked up the job in Monaco, but I have to go back for three more days there."

"Where are you rushing off to? Want to have a drink?"

"Can't do it, Shifty. I'm late for an appointment."

"Where are you staying?"

"At the Inghilterra. It's just down the street here, but I'm flying back tomorrow night."

"Back to Monaco?"

"Yeah. I have two more showings and then I'm going home."

"Back to Milan?"

"No way. I'm through here, Shifty. I want out."

"I'll walk you to your hotel."

"Okay, but I can't linger."

We set off at a brisk pace for the Inghilterra, one of the city's fancier hostelries, I'd been told. It was located on a side street off the Condotti, a couple of blocks away. Parker had her track shoes on and I had a hard time keeping up with her. She didn't seem eager to talk to me and she asked no questions about Bobby Jo or the progress of the investigation. I pumped her about her activities in Monaco, but she spoke only vaguely about her time there, depicting the period merely as one of very hard work for not enough money. "It's been a bitch," she said, summing it all up as we reached the hotel entrance. "A bunch of rich Eurotrash assholes, Shifty. They bought nothing, but partied a lot. I didn't give a shit. At least they're paying me for my time. And I got this added gig because of it. Alfredo was there, and his mom likes me because I don't screw the customers."

"You didn't ask me about Bobby Jo," I said, as she leaned over to give me a parting peck on the cheek.

"I'm trying to forget it, Shifty," she said. "I just want to get my work done and go home. And this is it. I'm not coming back, never."

"I could forget about Milan, but Rome . . ."

"That's because you haven't lived here," she said. "You don't know how corrupt it is. You don't know what they can do. I got to go, babe." She whirled away from me and hurried inside.

I lingered for a moment or two, then walked back to the Via Condotti. Instead of turning left toward my hotel, I headed up the street toward the doorway Parker had come out of. The bar was called the Greco. A plaque on the wall outside informed me that the establishment had been around for well over a century and a half and that it had been declared a national monument, a traditional gathering place for artists and writers. The outer room consisted of a bar serving drinks, hors d'oeuvres, and pastries to a clientele of purposeful, well-dressed shoppers and wide-eyed tourists. The inner rooms were dark, with old canvases adorning the walls, and the customers sat at small, round marble-topped tables being waited on by elderly men in tails. None of these customers looked like artists or writers either, and I guessed that the Bohemian types had long since fled the premises for less commercialized surroundings, leaving the scene to rich local bourgeois types and tourists. I saw no one who looked familiar to me and I was about to leave when Adriano Barone emerged from the rest rooms at the rear of the establishment. He was wearing gray slacks, an open-necked shirt, and a blue cashmere jacket slung over his shoulders like a cape. He walked straight to a corner table, scanned his bill, dropped a wad of lire notes on the small silver tray left by the waiter, and headed for the door. There were two empty glasses on the table.

I followed him out into the street. He turned left toward the Piazza di Spagna and headed for a nearby bank of taxis, to the right of the Spanish Steps. He also was clearly in a hurry. I found myself wondering what he and Parker Williams had found to talk about.

*   *   *

I'm not much of a party guy, but every now and then, usually in periods of frustration or stress, I'll let myself go and turn my night into a surreal landscape blurred by alcohol and nonsense. Maybe it had something to do this time with Parker's reappearance and my fear that she knew more about Bobby Jo's death than she had so far revealed. I was in Rome, a city I had fallen in love with, I was alone, and I wanted to have a good time. I didn't want to have to think about Bobby Jo and what had happened to her. I decided, long before I got back to the Portoghesi, that I was going to hang loose that night and just enjoy myself, go with the flow of events, and not worry anymore about Bobby Jo, an obvious loser, and her overbearing old man. Okay, so he was paying me five thousand dollars to act on his behalf; that didn't mean I had to spend every waking moment of every day working for him. Let Angela Tedeschi and the cops do their stuff. I was in Rome, it was spring, and it was party time.

I was standing in front of the hotel when Carlo Ravelli swooped into view in his cream-colored Ferrari a few minutes after seven o'clock. His car was a two-seater and he already had a passenger, a leggy blonde of about twenty-two who was wearing a white miniskirt and sequined blouse through the fabric of which her nipples were clearly visible, tiny spikes aimed like pistols at the world at large. "*Ciao*, Luigi, this is Claudia," Ravelli said. "Get in."

"Where?"

"Claudia, *tesoro, muoviti*," he said to the girl, then waved me on. "You sit and Claudia sit on you."

"I like the arrangement," I said, as Claudia giggled and stepped out of the car. I climbed in and Claudia lowered herself into my lap.

"Is okay?" she asked, favoring me with a dimpled smile.

"It's more than okay," I said. "It's a delight."

"Claudia speaks little English," Ravelli said, as we roared away up the narrow street, scattering pedestrians in our path, "but who needs to talk?"

"What does Claudia do?" I asked, my arms now around her waist to keep her from going through the windshield as Ravelli maneuvered through the crowded streets.

"Do? She do nothing," he said. "You look like Claudia, what is it necessary to do?"

"Good point," I agreed, my eyes fixed on those golden knees. "Carlo, you have a genius for life's minor pleasures."

"Minor? In what way minor?" Ravelli said, as he spun the car around and shot backward up a one-way street.

Claudia screamed. "Carlo, *che fai? Stronzo!*"

"She call me a shithead," Ravelli said, as we came to the end of the block and he made a sharp left turn. He mumbled something to Claudia in Italian. We cut off a slice of sidewalk, then sped out into the avenue leading toward the Piazza Venezia and a huge white monument that looked like a typewriter. "Women know nothing about driving," Ravelli said cheerfully. "I tell her to shut her eyes and be calm. We must make the first race, no?"

"Makes sense to me."

We swung around two buses and picked up speed on the wrong side of the road to get past them. Claudia screamed again. Ravelli swooped in front of the second bus just in time to avoid a head-on collision with an oncoming camion, whose driver leaned out his window to shout at us as we passed. "*Cretino!*" Ravelli shouted back. "*Stronzo!*"

Ravelli and Francesca had evidently attended the same driving school. I buried my face in Claudia's back. A half hour or so later, the car screeched to a halt and Ravelli said, "We are here. Come on, we are late."

I remember little about the Tor di Valle harness track except that it reminded me of a giant ice cream parlor, with rows of seats and tables overlooking what looked like a mile-long racing surface. As we were ushered to a reserved table directly over the finish line, the horses for the first race appeared on the track and began warming up, trotting past like animals in a circus parade. Claudia squealed and clapped her hands together. "*Che bello!*" she said. "*Adorabili! Guarda come sono carini!*"

"They are adorable," I said, "until you bet on them."

Ravelli disappeared toward the wagering windows. I signaled a waiter over and looked at Claudia. "Want a drink?"

She nodded and laughed. "*Sì, un* gin *e* tonic."

"Scotch and a splash of soda," I said.

The waiter left and I looked at Claudia. The little spiky nipples jabbed relentlessly at the fabric of her blouse. I wondered how she managed to keep them fixed there like tiny spears. She caught me looking at them. "*Ti piacio?*" she asked.

"I'm sorry."

"You like?"

"I like very much."

"*Bene.* I like you, too. Your name is Luigi?"

"Yeah, that'll do."

"You cute. *Adorabile.*"

"Thank you. Same to you."

Our drinks arrived as Ravelli returned from his foray to the windows. He dropped a betting slip into Claudia's lap and handed another one to me. "What are you doing, Carlo?" I asked. "I didn't want to bet here."

"A small gift," he said. "The number two is winning, you'll see."

I glanced at my ticket. It was a hundred-thousand-lire betting slip to win on the two at odds of five to one. Claudia jumped up and kissed Ravelli on the mouth. "Carlino," she said, "*come sei adorabile!*" Clearly it was her favorite word.

The horses lined up behind the moving barrier of the starting gate and broke as one. The two horse tucked in on the rail behind the leader and was still second as they reached the backstretch. He remained second around the turn, but never made a move and came in fifth. "Better luck next time," Ravelli said.

"*Che è successo?*" Claudia asked. Ravelli didn't answer, but got up and left the table. Claudia looked at me in dismay.

"He didn't win," I said. "We lost."

"Oh, *che peccato,*" she said, looking at her ticket. "*Era così bellino.*"

The rest of the evening went pretty much according to the form set by our opening venture. Ravelli would disappear between races and return just before post time for the next one with betting slips he'd bought for all of us on various animals, none of whom did much running. I entertained Claudia with magic, mostly simple stuff, coins and cards, but she ate it up, clapping her hands together and squealing after every move. I wondered what the evening was costing Ravelli, who didn't seem to mind losing and persisted in dropping what amounted to several hundred dollars a race. To him, I suppose, the money meant very little; he was rich, or at least his father was.

Just before the last race, however, he reappeared looking triumphant. He handed Claudia and me betting slips of two hundred thousand lire each on a horse breaking from the seventh hole. "This one win for sure," he announced. "You'll see. Mario tells me about him."

"Who's Mario?" I asked.

"He's here every night," Ravelli said. "Mario knows everybody. This animal wins."

I was happy to learn that the business of touting is an international profession. I glanced at the tote board. The number seven was six to one, but Ravelli had bought tickets on him from one of the legal bookies on the premises at odds of eight to one, so we stood to make a bundle if this beast ran according to Mario's prediction. I picked up my binoculars and focused on the seven, a dark brown gelding being driven by a fat old man at least in his sixties. It did not reassure me, but then I knew enough about harness racing to know that the age or weight of the driver seemed to make little difference. Trotters and pacers competed in a world of racing that was a mystery to me and would always remain so. I didn't even like the look of harness races, with all the horses clip-clopping along with ridiculous-looking little buggies dragging along behind them.

Claudia clutched her ticket in both hands and rose to her feet as the race went off. The seven, whose name was Terra Incognita, broke quickly and swung over to the inside, going only two wide around the first turn. The old man driving our champion was proving to be a skillful operator, since being fanned on turns is the surest way to lose a harness race. On the backstretch Terra Incognita moved up to fourth, still only two wide. On the turn for home he suddenly spurted to the lead, got it, and tucked in on the rail. He gradually began to pull away from the field. At the sixteenth pole, he was four lengths in front and there was no way he could lose. Claudia began to jump up and down and squeal. I kept my binoculars trained on the race. I saw the old man driving our horse glance behind him and then, for no apparent reason, Terra Incognita broke stride. The old man grabbed the reins and pulled his horse to the outside as the field swept past him.

I haven't been to that many harness races, but I had never seen a more flagrant piece of skulduggery at a racetrack anywhere. I waited for the public to rise up in rightful wrath and burn down the grandstand. Failing that, I expected at least vociferous protestations of outrage. Nothing happened. A few angry bettors shouted imprecations and insults at our driver as he came back toward the winner's circle, but most people in the crowd seemed to accept what had happened as merely a bit of bad luck.

"Carlo, we were robbed," I said.

Claudia was still on her feet, clutching her betting slip. "*Che è successo?*" she asked. "What happen, Luigi?"

"Our driver cheated," I told her. "He threw the race."

"*Cosa?*"

"No, no, Luigi, you do not understand," Ravelli said. "It was not his turn. Next time, maybe."

"I hope you didn't buy a ticket for Mario," I said.

"No, Luigi. When I win, I give him something."

We drove back into town to a restaurant a couple of blocks behind the Via Veneto and ate a gourmet late supper. Ravelli ordered champagne and toasted our lack of success. "On Sunday, at Le Capannelle, we win, Luigi," he said, as we touched glasses.

"I come, too," Claudia said. "You like, Luigi?"

"Sure I like," I said.

She giggled, kissed me on the cheek, and dashed off to the ladies' room. Ravelli smiled. "You like Claudia?"

"What's not to like, Carlo?" I said. "Who is she?"

He shrugged. "A girl. She is a *stellina di* film, a starlet, you say, I think."

"She's very pretty."

"She's for you, Luigi. Enjoy."

"Does she know that?"

"Oh, yes," he said, "it's all arranged. I want you to have a good time, Luigi."

"How do you know her?"

He shrugged again. "I know many girls, Luigi. You don't worry about it, okay?"

I'm a horseplayer, and being a horseplayer teaches you a lot about life. One of the lessons I learned early from horses is that no one in life gives anything away. Somehow down the line there's a payoff to someone and a price to pay. I decided to keep my distance from Claudia. When the evening ended and Ravelli had dropped us off in front of my hotel, I went inside the lobby with her and called a taxi. Claudia looked astonished. "You no like me?" she asked.

"I like you very much, Claudia," I said. "You're very beautiful. But I'm with someone."

"Oh. Here?"

"No."

"Then why you no like?"

"I'll explain it to you sometime, Claudia, but not tonight."

"Okay," she said, laughing. She kissed me on the mouth. "You stupid, but nice."

A couple of minutes later the taxi pulled up and I gave the driver twenty thousand lire. Claudia waved cheerfully to me as she sped off into the night.

13

LE CAPANNELLE

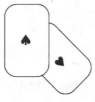

The next morning, a Saturday, the day before the running of the Derby, I rented a small Fiat and drove out to Le Capannelle by myself for a day of racing. The track is located in open country along the ancient Appian Way, about eight miles south of the city and halfway to the Alban Hills. Ravelli had told me that the Italians had been racing horses there since the middle of the nineteenth century, after the reigning pope banned the city's nobles from racing their animals in the middle of town, down the Corso from the Piazza del Popolo to the Piazza Venezia. The first official meet was held in 1881 and the track was named after *le capanne*, a couple of huts on the premises where a local entrepreneur had sold refreshments to travelers.

The grounds are huge, about three hundred acres, containing two major turf courses known as the Pista Grande and the Pista Piccola, a couple of training tracks, a steeplechase layout, and an inner dirt course, used, I was told, only for cheaper animals. Sprint races are run out of a chute on the straightaway, and the stretch run of the Pista Grande seemed endless. I figured out that the circumference of the Pista Grande, where the Derby was to be run, was a little over a mile and a half, the distance of the race. The infield contained stands of umbrella pines and fragments of ancient Roman aqueducts behind which horses would sometimes disappear.

I spent an hour or so wandering around and checking the layout. The grandstand consisted of three large sandstone blocks that looked like small palaces. There were betting windows, terraced grandstand seats, several restaurants, an appropriate number of TV monitors, and, of course, a tote board flashing the odds. Between the grandstand and the racing surface lay a long strip of lawn over which families had spread picnic lunches and children gamboled. Behind the palazzi were the kiosks of the accredited bookmakers, cold-eyed men who chalked up on blackboards the odds they were willing to offer to suit their own narrow perspectives. Peddlers at portable stands hawked olives, fresh coconut slices, beans, dried seeds, nuts, and candy. There were no more than three or four thousand people on hand, a smaller crowd than I'd seen at Tor di Valle, but then someone, maybe Ravelli, had told me that harness racing was more popular in Italy than the Thoroughbreds, a fact I found inexplicable.

I had bought the local racing form, a tabloid called *Il Cavallo*, and I sat in the sun on a bench by the paddock an hour or so before the first race trying to make sense of it. It wasn't too hard to decipher, but what appalled me was the lack of information in this rag. It listed the horses in post position order, the colors of their silks, the names of the owners, trainers, and jockeys, the weights they carried, and the results of their previous four or five races. It explained what sort of races they had been—the class, the distance, the number of competitors, the condition of the course—and where the horse had finished and at what price. Missing, however, was just about everything an experienced handicapper would want to know. There were no charts, no fractional times, no speed ratings, no trouble lines, and no listed workouts. I decided to use maximum caution and to make no wager larger than ten dollars on anything that afternoon.

The first race was for maiden three-year-old fillies at about a mile on the Pista Piccola. An animal named Franchina was being sent off as the odds-on favorite in a field of ten, and I went out to watch the contest from a perch in the grandstand, near the finish line. Franchina broke well, went immediately to the front, dropped back to the middle of the pack, then swung to the outside for the long run down the stretch. She made up some ground, but came in a well-beaten third, eight or nine lengths behind the easy winner. It had looked much like every other European race I'd ever seen on TV, with the horses just galloping easily along for most of the race until the stretch, when at last they were asked to put out their best effort.

As Franchina came trotting back toward the finish line, a chorus of raucous shouts, boos, whistles, and insults arose from the crowd. The target of this discontent was obviously her jockey, a sallow-faced, lanky rider named Ottavio Catti. I went down to the winner's circle to watch the ceremony and to see the riders weigh in. As Catti stepped on the scales, another howl of protest greeted him from the watchers packed along the rails. When he left to go back to the jockeys' room, he was escorted by a half dozen armed carabinieri and followed by a knot of ten or twelve protesters shouting insults and imprecations. I laughed and the man next to me, a short, swarthy citizen in his mid-forties, looked up. "You American?" he asked.

"Yes," I said. "What are they shouting at the jockey?"

"That he is very *cattivo*," the man said. "His name is *catti*. *Cattivo* means bad, you understand? They are also calling him *pessimo*, which mean very bad. And they are saying that his mother slept with many men for money and that his father is a *cornuto*." He held up his index fingers and placed them at the top of his temples. "His father is wearing the horns."

"He's a cuckold."

The man shrugged. "Is nothing new," he said. "Catti is famous for losing races he should win."

"We have jockeys like that in the States."

"Where you from?"

"Los Angeles, California."

"Ah, I have been there," the man said. "To Santa Anita. Is very beautiful. Is not like here."

"This is a beautiful track, too."

The man shook his head. "The racing is not good." He stuck out his right hand and I shook it. "My name is Pippo," he said. "I see you like horses."

"I like racing."

"Once, in Italy, we have very good racing, very good horses," he said, "but then the English and the French buy all our good stallions and *femmine* and now we have bad racing. It take many years to make good horses."

We strolled over to the paddock together to have a look at the entries in the second race, while Pippo continued to fill me in on the realities and vagaries of the Italian racing scene. "No one care," he said at one point, as we leaned over the paddock railing and watched the animals being saddled. "No one do nothing for the people. Is all for the rich."

"But the purses are fairly big," I said. "How do they pay these purses, when so few people come to the races?"

"Is the Ministero dell'Agricoltura," he explained. "The government, you understand? They pay for these rich people for to run their horses. That is why the big races is won by so few stables, you understand?"

"We call that socialism for the rich," I said. "The taxpayer foots the bills, right?"

"Yes, that is it," he said, nodding.

"I presume you'll be here tomorrow," I said. "Do you think Tiberio can win the Derby?"

He shrugged gloomily. "Is nice animal, very good in Italy," he said, "but the French and the English, they will send good horses. They always win. And anyway Tiberio is English, too, you know."

"You mean bred in England."

"Yes. So if he win, is English, too. Luca Barone, he buy his horses in England and France. He win many races in Italy."

"You know him?"

Pippo grinned and shook his head. "Know Luca Barone? He is big *papagallo*, I am only small *uccelleto*." He held his thumb and forefinger an inch apart to demonstrate how insignificant he was. "A little bird, you see. I like to bet his horses because they win many races, but tomorrow no. I bet the English and the French, my friend."

A couple of minutes later, he excused himself and left me to talk to some friends he had spotted. I hung around the paddock until the horses and riders moved out toward the racing surface. I strolled past the nearest bookie stand and saw that the favorite was quoted at even money. I went back to the stands to watch the race and the favorite won easily this time, paying nearly two to one in the tote, an outcome that gave me a clue on how to bet. After that, I began to risk a few thousand lire each race, always on the favorite as quoted by the bookies, but betting them only in the tote. It didn't work. By the seventh and last race on the card I had yet to cash a ticket.

I studied my racing form closely this time and came up at last with a horse I thought might be a winner. The bookies were quoting the animal at nine to five, so I bought a thirty-thousand-lire win ticket on him through the pari-mutuel machines, then went to the paddock to have a look at my selection. His name was Blue Top and he clearly had more speed than anyone else in the race, which was being run at seven furlongs on the straightaway. He was dropping a notch in class and his trainer was listed among the top ten winners of the year. I was suddenly feeling confident as I stepped up to the paddock rail.

I arrived just in time to witness a large woman being hoisted into the saddle of my selection. "What the hell is this?" I asked aloud, wondering if I could sell my ticket. Pippo, who was standing a few feet away from me, smiled and waved. I walked over to him. "What is this?" I asked. "I have a lady who looks like an opera singer on my horse. Can she ride?"

"No," Pippo said, "but is all bad. *Amazzoni*. The jockeys are all *amazzoni*."

"Amazons?"

"*Sì*, women jockeys, you understand?"

I checked the rest of the field. Sure enough, every rider was a woman, several of them heavier and stouter than my own. It was a condition of the race I had failed to pick up during my study of *Il Cavallo*.

"Who you bet?" Pippo asked.

"Blue Top."

"You don't worry," Pippo said. "Blue Top, he win this time."

Pippo was right. Blue Top led every step of the way and paid better than five to two in the tote. I had bailed myself out for the day. Pippo and I walked out to the parking lot together. "Luigi, remember," he said, as we parted to go to our cars, "if you bet tomorrow, you find me first. I explain things to you. And you don't bet against the English and the French, *amico*. They do not send their horses here to lose."

Francesca was waiting for me in the hotel lobby when I returned. "*Ciao*," she said, bouncing to her feet to give me a hug. "Is all right I come here? I call, but I miss you. So I stop here."

"It's great," I said. "Where are you staying?"

"With a friend near Piazza Navona. You know where is that?"

"Sure. It's my favorite piazza in the world."

"Is nice, only noisy. Is full of *turisti* and at night is like a party there."

"Who's your friend?"

"Mercurio Fredi. You hear of him?"

"No, can't say I have."

"Is designer for theater, very sweet." She giggled and touched my cheek. "You don't worry," she said. "He like only boys. You take me to dinner?"

"I can't, Fran," I said. "I'm invited to a party. Adriano Barone is giving a dinner at the Osteria Greca, wherever that is."

"Is very elegant, on the Tiber," Francesca said. "I know about this party. I come, too."

"I thought you said you hated Adriano?"

"I do. Is disgusting man. But I come with you. Is big party and Mercurio has invitation, too. We make Adriano to dropping shit in his pants. You want, no?"

"I'll let you handle that part of it," I said. "I'll be the naive American tourist."

She laughed and kissed me on the cheek. "*Bravo*," she said. "I meet you at the middle fountain in Piazza Navona at eight, *va bene?*"

"*Va bene.*"

"We walk from there."

She bounced out the door and I went up to my room to shave and change clothes. I left the hotel a little before eight and walked the few blocks to the Piazza Novona. It was a balmy spring night and all of Rome seemed to be out in the open. The great square, with its three spectacular fountains, was crowded with strollers, tourists, vendors, and children. Rock music was blaring from somebody's boom box, but it was all but submerged by the friendlier sound of people enjoying the night and one another's company. Francesca was sitting on the edge of the middle fountain next to a tall, thin, bald man in his early forties who was dressed in a magenta suit with a large daisy in the buttonhole of his lapel. "Is Mercurio," Francesca said, introducing us. "He is coming, too."

"We'll make quite an entrance," I said.

"Oh, Adriano's parties are all appallingly vulgar," Mercurio said, in a flawless English accent. "He would be so beautiful, if he did not have the soul of a butcher. We will hardly be noticed, as there will be a mob. *Le tout trendy*. I will try to find myself a beautiful person to converse with and retire to a corner, leaving you and Francesca to cavort with the roughnecks. Shall we go?"

The Osteria Greca was a small Renaissance palazzo on the near bank of the Tiber, a five-minute walk from the piazza. It was reported to be one of the more elegant and overpriced restaurants and nightclubs in the city, catering to the very rich on the international scene. The Barone party had taken it over for the night and we were stopped at the entrance by a couple of security men in civilian clothes. Mercurio produced a large engraved invitation that served to admit him and Francesca, but I was forced to wait outside until Carlo Ravelli appeared to rescue me. "Luigi," he said, shaking my hand and ushering me inside, "come in. I was not certain you were coming."

"I came with Mercurio and Francesca," I told him.

Ravelli grinned. "That disgusting *froscio*," he said. "He is at every party everywhere. He brought the paparazza?"

"Yes. She told me Adriano once raped her."

"She lies so much, she should have a nose like Pinocchio. Come on, forget about her. We have the good time now. Like with Claudia. You like Claudia?"

"She was very sweet," I said. "What did you pay her?"

"Luigi, I am ashamed of you," he said, smiling. "You don't ask. It was a gift."

"I sent her home."

"You send her home? Oh, Luigi, I am sorry. She's very nice."

"Carlo, I'm not into working girls."

"Ah, Luigi, you Americans, with your Puritan thoughts."

He led the way up to the second floor where the Derby party was in full progress. A small but loud rock band was playing at the far end of the room and couples were dancing. At the tables surrounding the dance floor an older crowd was eating and drinking. At a buffet table against a side wall, people were lined up two and three deep for food. A large banner had been strung overhead from wall to wall proclaiming the imminent victory of Tiberio. "You want to eat now?" Ravelli asked.

"No, I'll have a drink first," I answered.

"Over there." Ravelli pointed toward the corner to my left, where a bar had been set up. "I see you in a few minutes, okay?"

"Fine."

Ravelli headed off toward the buffet. Out on the floor, I spotted Adriano Barone. He had taken off his jacket, rolled up his shirt-sleeves, and was dancing wildly with a tall, serene-looking blonde I was sure I had seen on the cover of some magazine. I couldn't see Francesca, so I pushed on toward the bar. No sooner had I acquired a glass of red wine and turned around than I spotted her. She was dancing with Mercurio, who turned out to be as graceful as a gazelle. A couple of times they swooped past Adriano and his cover girl and I noticed him looking at Francesca. He did not seem pleased to see her, but went on dancing.

I found a relatively isolated spot at a table to the left of the bandstand, where Francesca and Mercurio eventually found me. "A splendid band," Mercurio said. "Quite jolly, really."

"You're quite a dancer," I said.

"Is fantastical," Francesca said. She was glistening with sweat and her dark curls lay tumbled around her face. "Mercurio is like Fred Astaire."

"Better," I said. "He's alive. I think Adriano saw you out there and I don't think he's pleased."

"I do that for purpose," she said. "I make him *furioso*."

"Maybe they'll throw us out of here," I said.

"Why would they do that?" Mercurio said. "I brought Francesca. Adriano would hardly want a scene on this festive occasion, especially with his father present."

"Where's he?" I asked.

"Over there," Mercurio said, indicating a corner table to the right of the entrance. A tall, elegant, white-haired man in a dinner jacket presided over a gathering of older couples, among whom I recognized Franco Bellinzona, the banker, and his wife. "Luca Barone is the very handsome one with the white hair. You can see where Adriano got his looks."

"Is there a Mrs. Luca Barone?"

"Oh, yes, but she never attends these functions. She remains a recluse, spends most of her time abroad. They have flats in London and New York. She's very social, but not in Italy."

"Why not? Isn't she a Milanese aristocrat?"

"Oh, yes, but that's the reason. She despises her husband's friends, people like Bellinzona and Tommaso Cataldi. She considers them vulgar *arrivistes*. She's a patroness of the arts. It was she who assembled the collection on the island. What she likes to do is attend auctions. Which is fine with him, because all he cares about is business and making money. And horse racing. He's mad about horse racing. The Barone have the biggest stable in Italy."

"And Adriano takes after his father in that respect."

"Well, perhaps. What he likes to do is gamble. He's a very heavy gambler at the races and in the casinos, too. He loses a great deal of money. His father has tried to interest him in the horses. He gave him Tiberio. But Adriano is essentially a wastrel. Gambling and women are his two passions, when he isn't doing something to himself with drugs."

"I've met that banker," I said.

"A dreadful man. Where did you meet him?"

"At a party, a very unusual party."

"Ah, one of those," Mercurio said. "I hear they are entertaining."

"Not really. Are the Pelagras here?"

"No, they always go to Thailand at this time of year. Although now, I don't know. The Bangkok baths reek with disease, I'm told. Someone said the Dominican Republic now, but I don't know for certain. They will have found someplace suitable for their peculiar tastes, I'm sure."

As we sat there talking, I saw Adriano Barone escort his partner back to their table, then look around the room. He spotted us and came over, smiling but with eyes as cold as ice. *"Ciao, froscio,"* he said to Mercurio, who blushed, *"come vanno le inculate?"*

Mercurio seemed to be at a loss for words. I had no idea what Adriano Barone had said to him, but I knew it was insulting.

"Adriano, *smettila,*" Francesca said.

"E tu, mia bella lesbica, con chi vai a letto adesso?" Adriano Barone said to her, still smiling, his eyes as mirthless as before.

"Adriano," Mercurio said hesitantly, "this is a friend of ours, Lou Anderson. He's American."

I guessed that Mercurio was trying to use me, a stranger, to fend off Adriano's insults, so I stood up, smiling brightly, and stuck out my hand. Adriano Barone looked at it with distaste, then at Mercurio again. "An American bugger boy?" he said. "I thought you liked them much younger, Mercurio." He looked back at me. "Does he fuck you or does he suck your cock?" he asked.

"Actually, neither possibility had occurred to me," I said, "but somebody clearly ought to wash your mouth out with detergent."

"When you travel with pederasts and Lesbians, you must expect to be insulted," Adriano Barone said. "You mustn't take it personally."

"A little oblique irony would improve your style," I said. "Outright boorishness is not cool."

Francesca tugged at my sleeve. "Shifty," she said, "please. Is all right."

"Cretino!" Adriano said. "I break you in half."

Mercurio stood up and backed nervously away from the table. "Adriano, please, calm yourself," he said. "We'll go."

"No, no," Adriano Barone said, "I teach this stupid American a lesson." He lunged at me, grabbed my shirtfront, and pulled me up to him. "I break your face."

I brought both arms up inside his and broke his grip, then brought my heel down hard on his instep. He howled in pain, leaned over, then lunged forward again, swinging wildly. I stepped aside and pushed him over my outstretched leg. He fell over an adjacent table, scattering an outraged party of four. A woman screamed. Somebody grabbed me by the arm and pulled me away. Francesca was standing on the table, hitting a man over the head with her handbag. Ravelli's face, looking dismayed, loomed up briefly. Somebody else grabbed my other arm and I was hustled toward an exit, down the stairs, and out into the street.

The two men holding me threw me against a parked car. I doubled over, gasping for air. When I looked up, I found myself alone in the street with Mercurio, who came up and put an arm around my shoulders. "Are you all right?" he asked.

"Fine," I gasped. "Lost my breath. Francesca?"

Before he could answer, she came rushing out the front entrance to join us. "Shifty, you okay?"

"Yes. How are you?"

"Is okay. My God, you get us killed. Adriano is screaming."

"It was most impressive," Mercurio said. "Shall we go home now?"

"We haven't eaten," I said.

"I'll cook some pasta," Mercurio suggested.

"He's marvelous cook," Francesca said. "Shifty, you are *incredibile*. Where you learn to fight?"

"A woman friend of mine named Mary Conroy, back in L.A. She teaches a women's defense class."

"Is marvelous."

"Most impressive," Mercurio said.

"Come on, let's eat," I said, linking arms with my two new friends and feeling suddenly very pleased with myself. "I don't know why, but I'm starving."

"You kick so good," Francesca said.

"I was inspired," I admitted. "I've never met a man I disliked more."

14

MERCURIO

Mercurio cooked up a simple gourmet feast—*penne all'arrabbiata*, veal chops, a green salad, cheeses, fruit—and we ate outside on his terrace overlooking the piazza. It was nearly midnight when we finished, but down below there seemed to be no slackening of activity. The vendors were still vending, the tourists were still touring, the young were still milling about the fountains in restless pursuit of one another. "Rome lives by night," I commented, looking down on the scene.

"When the warm weather arrives, the Romans empty out into their streets and piazzas," Mercurio said. "I was born in Turin, a dark and dismal place. When I first arrived in Rome twenty years ago in June, I thought I had moved to paradise."

"I can understand that," I said, sipping at my third glass of dark red Chianti. "Do you think we should go back to the party?"

Mercurio stared at me in astonishment. "Are you mad?" he said. "Adriano's thugs will beat us to a pulp."

"Just kidding," I said, laughing. I looked at Francesca. She was sitting slumped into her chair, her face half-hidden in shadow. "What about it, Fran? Want to give it a try?"

"Mercurio is right," she said. "You crazy. He kill us. He's no good, Shifty. He's bad peoples."

"Why did he call you a Lesbian?" I asked. "Is that his ultimate form of insult?"

"He can't believe he isn't the most attractive man in the universe," Mercurio said. "So when a woman refuses him, it has to be because she's gay."

"Makes sense." I stood up and stretched. "I suppose I should go home."

"Why? You can stay here, if you like," Mercurio said. "I have four bedrooms."

"We only need one," Francesca said. "Shifty, you stay, no?"

"I stay, *sì*," I said, "but I'd like to call in for messages. May I use the phone?"

"Of course," Mercurio said. "In there."

I went into the living room, found the phone on a table near the entrance hall, and called the hotel. There was one message, from Ravelli, asking me to call him most urgently at his flat. I dialed the number and he picked up on the second ring. "Luigi," he said the moment he recognized my voice, "what happened? Why do you make such a scene?"

"I didn't start it, Carlo," I said. "He was behaving like a boor."

"Adriano get like that sometimes," he said. "He don't like that paparazza you bring."

"I didn't bring her. Mercurio did."

"He don't like Mercurio either."

"Mercurio had an invitation."

Ravelli snorted derisively into my ear. "Luigi, that *froscio*—"

"What does *froscio* mean?"

"Is good word for pederast, but stronger, you understand?"

"So why did he send him an invitation?"

"He didn't. That *froscio* invite himself. Somebody gave him the ticket, you understand?"

"But why all this hostility, Carlo? So they crashed his big Derby party, so what? Why make a big scene?"

"Is you who make the big scene, no?"

"No. I protested his rudeness and he grabbed me. He was going to hit me, if I let him."

"Ah, Luigi. Is big misunderstanding. I'm so sorry. Adriano can be so nice. It's too bad."

"I guess I haven't seen the nice side. I'm not sure I'll be that patient."

"I'll explain to him, Luigi, when he's calm. He get so excited. But if Adriano win the Derby tomorrow, he is very happy and I talk to him, you understand? But you keep the paparazza away from him."

"What's she ever done to him, Carlo? She says he raped her. So what's he so angry about? She's the one who should be angry, right?"

"She don't like men, Luigi. Adriano hates pederasts and Lesbians."

"How do you know she doesn't like men?"

"Everybody know. For two years she live with that actress, Dora Mendes."

"The movie star?"

"Yes, she only like women. They live together a long time."

"So she's bisexual, so what?"

"I don't care, but Adriano does."

"That's his problem," I said. "It doesn't give him a license to behave like a pig."

"No, Luigi, of course not. But listen, you are coming to the Derby?"

"I wouldn't miss it for anything. I'm going to be rooting very hard against Tiberio."

"I see you there," Ravelli said. "Maybe it is better you don't come near Adriano."

"I don't intend to. Good-bye, Carlo."

We sat out on the terrace for another hour or so, enjoying the night with its sounds of muted revelry from the piazza below. Mercurio kept us entertained with chatter about doings in Rome's movie and TV colony, which turned out to be fairly similar to happenings in Hollywood and show biz in general. "What's Dora Mendes up to these days?" I asked at one point.

"Ah, darling Dora," Mercurio said. "My God, she hasn't made a good movie in two years. I adore her. I think she's in Spain shooting a series based on the Spanish Civil War. She plays an older guerrilla fighter for the Republic, one of those Katina Paxinou parts. You know, like in *For Whom the Bell Tolls*. Didn't you just adore that movie? A classic. Ingrid Bergman looked so much like a boy, I could have fallen in love with her myself."

"Ingrid Bergman has never looked like a boy to me," I said.

"Why you ask about Dora?" Francesca said.

"I like her movies," I said. "She used to be big news in the States, when she made that first movie of hers based on some big French novel."

"*C'est Toujours Demain*," Mercurio said. "*It's Always Tomorrow.*"

"That's the one," I said. "I was just curious."

"She's such a darling," Mercurio said. "I've seen all of her films. Strange, isn't it? She's so feminine on-screen, but really very butch in life."

"So I heard," I said.

Mercurio glanced suddenly at Francesca, then switched topics. He began to talk about a backstage scandal at the Rome Opera House involving two coloratura sopranos who loathed each other and had fought openly during an unfortunate production of an Offenbach opera earlier in the season. I listened with only half an ear. When it was over, I stood up and stretched. "Mercurio, this has been terrific, but I can't keep my eyes open," I said. "Please forgive me."

"No, no, we're all departing into the arms of Morpheus," he said. "Just help me bring everything into the kitchen, if you don't mind. We don't have to clean up, my maid comes tomorrow."

Later that night, as Francesca and I lay in each other's arms in the darkness, she said, "Who tell you about Dora and me?"

"Carlo Ravelli," I said. "I don't care, Fran."

"She always nice to me. I love her very much. I leave her because I like men."

"Hey, you don't have to explain anything."

"So why you ask about her?"

"To see what you would say. If you'd denied it, I might have been suspicious about you. Stupid, right?"

"You funny, Shifty." She leaned up on one elbow and kissed me. "You funny guy, don't you?"

"In addition to being a superb *mago*, I'm definitely one of the world's funniest guys."

"Keep still now. Kiss me."

I did, but we didn't make love that night. We were both too tired or drained by the events of the day. Francesca curled up into a ball and lay on her side with her back to me. I cradled her in my arms until we both fell asleep.

I slept until well after nine o'clock. Francesca and Mercurio were out on the terrace sipping *caffè latte* when I joined them. It was another perfect day and the piazza below was already alive with vendors and tourists. "*Buon giorno*," Mercurio said, smiling. "Would you like some breakfast?"

"Just coffee and milk, please," I said.

"I'll go heat up the milk," Mercurio said, bounding to his feet and heading for the kitchen. He was dressed in a striped blue and white jersey and white shorts out of which his long, skinny legs stuck like pretzels. "I hope you slept well."

"Like a stone," I said. "How long have you been up?"

"Oh, I always wake up very early," Mercurio said. "I go down and buy the newspapers, then make coffee. I'm usually on the phone by this time or at my atelier, but today I don't work." He disappeared toward the kitchen.

I leaned over to kiss Francesca, who was stretched out in a lounge chair with a pile of newspapers on her lap. She was wearing her usual blue jeans and a white shirt with the sleeves rolled up to just below her elbows. "Is big story in the papers," she said. "About Barone and his friends."

"About last night?"

"No, no. Here." She dug into her pile of papers and handed me a copy of the *London Times*. "Mercurio buy this for you. Is story there, too. Is about Luca and his friends." She pointed to the headlines in the Italian daily on her lap. "Big investigation of Luca's money."

The story in the *Times* was not on the front page, but under a headline on page three. A Milanese magistrate named Paolo Montserrat had revealed in a press conference that he and his fellow judges were investigating possible links between the Banca dei Due Mondi and one of the big holding companies owned by the Barone family. It was suspected that funds had been routed from this company through the bank to buy favors from several political parties, most prominently the Socialists. Tommaso Cataldi, a high-ranking Socialist party official and ex-cabinet minister, was known to be an intimate friend of both Luca Barone and Franco Bellinzona, the director of the Banca dei Due Mondi. Possible currency violations were also suspected regarding the illegal export of billions of lire through the bank to foreign institutions in Luxembourg and Switzerland. "Who's Paolo Montserrat?" I asked, as Mercurio reappeared from the kitchen with a pitcher of steaming hot milk.

"Another of those incorruptible Milanese magistrates," he said, setting the tray down on a small glass-topped table next to my chair. "They are forever tilting like tireless Don Quixotes against the windmills of Italian malfeasance. Ultimately a hopeless task, but they are nothing if not persistent. You know, Mussolini was once told it must be very hard to govern the Italians, and he answered, 'No, it is not hard, but it is useless.'"

"I'm told a lot of people have gone to jail," I said. "It's been going on for some time, hasn't it?"

"Oh, for centuries," Mercurio answered. "Italy has been going downhill for a thousand years."

"No, I mean this particular investigation."

"Oh, yes, but only the smaller fry have been scooped into the net," he said, as he poured coffee and milk into a cup and handed it to me. "The brothers, the nephews, the cousins, the friends—they go to jail. The real culprits, the prime movers behind the scenes, are always untouchable. Let me tell you what will happen in the long run. The magistrates will find irregularities. Luca Barone will deny an involvement, saying that he himself cannot be responsible for the actions of some misguided employees. Some people will be arrested and charged and sent to prison. The bank will be fined. The Socialist party has already ceased to exist, the victim, like all the other prescandal political parties, of previous investigations. It's conceivable that Cataldi himself could be arrested. He has been denounced before as the recipient of funds from many other sources. The head of his own party is a condemned criminal. But Bellinzona is probably beyond reach. He has connections with the Vatican. As for Luca Barone, he is one of the untouchables. You will see, Shifty. It is much like the opera. Many people screaming, but in the end everyone goes home."

I sipped my *caffè latte* and stared out over the piazza to the ornate baroque facade of a church almost directly across from us, where people were gathered on the steps. In the distance church bells rang, the hum of traffic and the bleating of car horns punctuated the morning.

"Paolo Montserrat is very good friend of *la* Tedeschi," Francesca said.

"You think she's involved in this investigation, too?" I asked.

"Most certainly," Mercurio said, turning to Francesca. "Have you spoken to Angela about this?"

Francesca shook her head. "No, no. Not at all."

I looked at Francesca. She seemed suddenly uncomfortable, as if Mercurio had asked her an unexpected question. "You know Angela Tedeschi?" I asked.

She nodded. "Yes, I know her. We go to university together in Bologna," she said, "but I don't see her for many months."

"I thought you might have heard from her," Mercurio said.

"No, why?"

Mercurio shrugged. "Just wondering." He stood up and stretched. "Well, my beauties, I have to go and confront the world now. You'll excuse me, I'm sure."

"If you know Angela Tedeschi," I said, after Mercurio had gone, "why haven't you asked her about Bobby Jo, or have you?"

"I ask her," Francesca said. "She tell me what you know, nothing more. Is not like when we know each other in school. Is different. She's a judge, I'm a photographer." She held her hands apart. "Is two worlds, Shifty."

15

TIBERIO

Francesca and I drove out to Le Capannelle together that after-noon in her tiny Fiat. The traffic on the Appian Way was heavy, but Francesca maneuvered recklessly through it, several times resort-ing to the shoulders of the road to keep moving. Again I braced myself against the dashboard. "Don't tell me you drove this death machine down from Milan," I said.

"Sì, I make good time, six hours," she said, as we swooped past a lorry and cut in front of a bus, whose driver began to scream curses at us out of his side window. Francesca ignored him. When we arrived at the track parking lot, she managed to gun past the guard at the entrance to the special section reserved for press and staff and swung in beside a dark blue Jaguar belonging, she informed me, to Luca Barone himself. Then, festooned with two cameras hanging off her shoulders, she talked us past the ticket booths and into the grounds.

"What did you tell them?" I asked, as we headed for the padlock area.

"That you are famous American journalist," she said, "and I am taking pictures for you. They don't care. Is all for publicity, no?"

We were still an hour away from post time for the first race, but the crowd on hand was already much bigger than Saturday's. People milled about between the betting kiosks and the ring, while the stands were more than half full. A pick up soccer game was in progress on the lawn next to the stretch and a small band was playing martial airs on a stand next to the winner's circle. "I leave you now," Francesca said. "I take pictures. I see you later at the, how you say, *recinto?*"

"Paddock? Where they saddle the horses?"

"*Bravo.* I see you there after *il* Derby, okay?"

"Okay."

She hurried away toward the main grandstand, where she intended to circulate in order to photograph the rich and trendy. I took the copy of *Il Cavallo* I'd bought that morning out of my pocket, found a bench near the paddock, and sat down in the warm spring sun to do a little handicapping. I'd barely finished studying the second race when Pippo showed up and joined me. "Eh, American, how are you?" he said. "You come for the big day, eh?"

"Pippo, how could I not come?"

He tapped my racing form and scowled. "Throw away this paper, it is full of lies. I tell you who win today, okay?"

"Okay."

He took my program and scanned the entries. "The first two races is shit," he said. "You don't bet, okay? Now look, in this third one there is a horse, Famiglia, she win easy." He took a black felt-tip pen out of his breast pocket and circled the animal. "You don't bet the next one," he continued. "Then after that one you bet this horse, Carlo Buti. He win, too."

"How can you be sure?"

Pippo looked up at me and grinned. "In horses nothing is sure, eh? But I tell you these two is going to run real good, believe me."

"And in the Derby?"

"Not Tiberio."

"You said the English and the French horses. Which ones, Pippo? There are five of them in the race."

"This one," he said, tapping his felt-tip against the name Winged Joy. "Or maybe this one, eh?" This time the pen singled out an animal called Freeloader. "Both English. They run good there, no? And then there is this one." He pointed to Mont Joyeux, one of the two French contestants.

"None of these animals has ever competed in a graded race back where they come from," I said. "What makes you so sure one of them will win?"

"Ah, because the Italian horses is shit," Pippo explained, a sour look on his swarthy face. "The English and the French, they come here to win all our big races. They don't need to send the best ones, you understand?"

I looked at Tiberio's statistics and found them impressive. He had never raced outside of Italy, but he had only been beaten once, the first start of his life, in six attempts. And the longer the races, the more easily he seemed to win. He was by Blushing Groom out of a Damascus mare, so I figured he'd love the distance and he'd already won two mile-and-a-quarter contests at San Siro, the track in Milan. I mentioned all this to Pippo, who responded by spitting at the ground and snorting in contempt. "You want to throw away money, American, you do it," he said. "I tell you it's either the English or the French."

I decided I could do a lot worse than pay attention to Pippo, especially after Famiglia won the third race by ten lengths and enriched me by thirty thousand lire. When Carlo Buti also won, this time putting a hundred thousand lire into my pocket, I became a confirmed Pippo fan. I stuck close to him throughout the afternoon. Mostly, we'd hang around the paddock, make our bets as soon as the horses had left for the post parade, then scramble to seats high up in the grandstand and near the finish line. Pippo had established territorial rights up there and no one contested his spot. He knew a lot of people and everyone seemed to know him. He was obviously respected by his fellow players and he indulged in a good deal of banter back and forth with a handful of other knowledgeable punters in the seats around us.

I estimated the crowd at about ten thousand. Inside the paddock before every race a throng of well-dressed burghers milled about, chatting and laughing and checking one another out. Everyone was dressed to kill, the men in expensive tailored suits or flashy sport coats, the women featuring ruthless materialistic displays of jewelry, hats, and slaughtered animals. Twice I spotted Francesca inside the paddock, scurrying from group to group snapping pictures. Once she waved to me and I waved back, but otherwise I had no contact with her. She was working and I was doing what I do best at racetracks anywhere, just having myself a terrific time.

The Derby was the next to the last race on the card. By that time, thanks to Pippo, I was ahead a couple of hundred thousand lire, only about a hundred and twenty dollars at the current rate of exchange, but I felt like a millionaire and invincible. Pippo and I stood at the paddock rail and checked out the scene.

The horses, like stakes horses anywhere, looked magnificent, with gleaming coats and muscles that rippled impressively as they were paraded around the walking ring. Winged Joy, a chunky colt, looked more like a sprinter to me and had never run at more than a mile, so I decided to throw him out. Freeloader and Mont Joyeux both looked the part, big rangy colts built for distance, and two or three others in the field of thirteen looked possible as well. Tiberio was a roan, not outstanding physically, but impressive nevertheless; he had an intelligent-looking head and seemed to be casing the scene as he bounced around the ring, full of himself, feeling good, anxious to get out there and strut his stuff. I mentioned this to Pippo. "You wait," Pippo said. "The English and the French, they break him in two."

Tiberio's entourage was huge, consisting of a couple of dozen fancily attired citizens, including Luca Barone, Bellinzona, and a half dozen magnificent-looking women. Adriano Barone was casually dressed in gray slacks, black loafers, a foulard, and a navy blue cashmere jacket. His face was flushed and excited, his long black hair tumbling down over his forehead as he moved nervously about his horse. I was happy to see that he was limping slightly. Ravelli was there, too, with Claudia in tow, and they came over to speak to me. Claudia was wearing a tight red mini skirt, a purple blouse, and several pounds of gold jewelry, including huge hoop earrings. "Shifty," she said, "you come?" She indicated I should come into the paddock with them.

"No, it's better you stay there," Ravelli said. "Adriano is very nervous now. He is betting much money on Tiberio. I did speak to him about you, Luigi. I tell him is all big misunderstanding and that you don't come there with Mercurio and the paparazza. I don't tell him you are friends with the model, you understand?"

"I don't care what you tell him, Carlo. You think Tiberio can win this?"

"Oh, yes, he win, Luigi," Carlo said. "This is a good horse, believe me. You bet on him. If he win, I call you and leave a message at your hotel. Adriano wants to meet you. You join us for the party, but don't bring the paparazza, you understand?" He squeezed my shoulder affectionately, then grabbed Claudia by the arm and pulled her back into the middle of the paddock. The horses, led by their grooms, began to circle about the ring as they waited for their riders.

"You know those people?" Pippo asked.

"What people? Ravelli and the girl?"

"No, the Barone. You know them?"

"Not really."

"They are dirty people," he said, "not even honest robbers."

"You read about the investigation going on?"

"Is shit, *amico*. Nothing will happen. You remember that *modella* who die?"

"I knew her."

Pippo turned to look at me in surprise. "You know her?"

"Yes, I met her at a party in Milan. I went out with her. And I know her father. What about her?"

Pippo grunted and nodded toward the Barone group. "They kill her," he said. "Is clear, no? But nothing will happen. They are saying it was robbers who stop her car and kill her."

"Where did you hear this, Pippo?"

"I hear things," he said. "I have friends."

"I'd like to talk to your friends."

"Yes? You care about this girl?"

"Her father in Kentucky has asked me to act for him here. We can't seem to find out anything. I'm not a cop, Pippo, I'm just a friend."

Pippo looked around, then leaned on the rail and indicated with a nod of his head for me to come in close to him. I joined him, close enough to his face so I could pick up a strong whiff of garlic and cheese on his breath. "Is very serious, this business," he said. "You don't go to the police, all right?"

"The police haven't come to me," I said. "Why should I go to them?"

"Good. Tomorrow my friend Bisanza come to my store in the morning," he said. "You come and I introduce you to him, okay?"

"Who's Bisanza?"

"Never mind. Is good friend from Milano," Pippo explained. "I do much business with him. They call him La Zanzara."

"There was a horse by that name, a big gray mare who used to run in California. *Zanzara*, that's a mosquito, isn't it?"

Pippo nodded and grinned, revealing a pair of gold teeth that flashed in the sunlight. He made a little closing motion with the tips of the fingers of his right hand. "La Zanzara, he bites good," he said. "He take a little blood, but never too much. That's why I do business with him, okay? You come to my store at twelve tomorrow, okay?"

"Okay. Where is your store?"

"You know Campo dei Fiori?"

"Yes, near Piazza Navona."

"Good. On the corner by the Palazzo della Cancelleria is my store," he said. "La Cancelleria is big palazzo, you can't miss it. My store say '*Elettronici.*' You come in, I'm there."

"Electronics? What do you sell? Radios, stereos?"

Pippo smiled again. "You see, *amico*. This and that, this and that. You don't ask too many questions, okay? You come, I introduce you, you talk to Bisanza. He talk to you, if I tell him is okay, you understand? Maybe you give a little present, he talk a little more."

"How expensive?"

"Oh, maybe two hundred thousand lire, three hundred thousand. Is not expensive."

"I'll be there."

The jockeys had mounted and the horses now began to move out toward the track. The crowd along the rails stirred restlessly in excitement and voices began to call out here and there. Quite a few of them shouted Tiberio's name and that of his jockey, a bowlegged gnome named Domenico Lipatti, his regular rider from Milan. Tiberio was the only Italian entry anyone gave much of a chance to, and he was clearly the crowd favorite. Pippo and I began to push our way through the mob to get back to our seats. "You bet, *amico?*"

"No," I said, "I'm going to pass, Pippo. I don't want to bet against Italy, but I can't bet on Tiberio."

Pippo grunted his disapproval. "One of the English or the French," he said. "I bet on Winged Joy."

"He looks like a speed horse to me," I said. "Can he go this far?"

"He go all the way. You'll see, *amico*. If he don't, I also have Freeloader."

By the time we reached our seats the horses were halfway around the stretch turn, warming up before heading for the starting gate. I focused my glasses on Tiberio, who was cantering easily along, relaxed, not fighting his rider, but with his ears pricked alertly forward, obviously all business. He looked terrific to me and I was feeling foolish for not having bet at least a few thousand lire on him. He was the third choice in the race at three to one, just the kind of animal I would ordinarily have taken a plunge on back home.

He broke alertly from the gate, but Lipatti took a hold on him and dropped him back to midpack as the field of twelve neared the first turn. As expected, Winged Joy opened up about two lengths, but he was not being rushed either. I could see that his rider also had a strong hold on him and I guessed that the early fractions in the race were slow, although there was no way to be sure, as the tote board did not supply that information.

Winged Joy continued to gallop along in front around that first turn with the field strung out behind him. From time to time the horses would disappear from view behind the fragments of ruined aqueducts or small groves of umbrella pines. When they reached the backstretch my sight of the leaders was blocked by a TV camera crew speeding along the inside course on a flatbed truck. Not until the horses neared the final turn was I fully able to figure out what was going on. Winged Joy was still in the lead, four or five lengths in front and not shortening stride. Pippo grunted in satisfaction. "I tell you, *amico*, the French and the English, they don't come here for nothing. You see who is running second?"

Freeloader, a big, rangy chestnut, had emerged from the pack to be second and seemed to be eating up the ground with every stride, even though he wasn't gaining much on Winged Joy. Tiberio was next to last, still under a stranglehold from his rider. But then, as the field swung toward the head of the long stretch, Lipatti began to ask his mount for speed and Tiberio responded. He picked up one horse after another, moving through the field with the agility of a ballet dancer. "Here comes Tiberio," I said.

"No chance, *amico*," Pippo responded. "He run third, maybe."

At the end of the lane, Winged Joy still had plenty left, but Freeloader was wearing him down stride by stride. It looked as if they would hit the wire together. The crowd rose to its feet with a roar of excitement, but not because it figured to be a photo finish. Tiberio, now on the extreme outside and in the clear at last, was uncorking an explosive run that electrified the watchers. Fifty feet from the finish Freeloader had caught Winged Joy, but Tiberio, running along the outside hedge, swooped past them both and won the race by an easy length, with his two rivals nose to nose in his wake. Despite myself, I cheered along with the rest. No matter who his owners were or what they had done, the animal was innocent and talent had to be acknowledged. Out of regard for my new friend Pippo, I managed not to overdo it, but I couldn't entirely conceal my appreciation of Tiberio's marvelous effort. "I'm sorry, Pippo," I said, "I'm sorry you lost, but Tiberio ran one hell of a race."

Pippo grunted, tore up his losing tickets, and shrugged. "*Beh*, is good Italy win for a change, no?"

"That's a real good horse, Pippo," I said. "Even if the owners are pigs."

"You say that right, *amico*." He shook my hand. "Okay, I go now. You come tomorrow."

"At twelve o'clock. I'll be there."

We pushed our way down from the stands to ground level, after which Pippo waved and took off. I walked over to the winner's circle, where a large silver trophy was being presented to Adriano Barone and his entourage, and wedged myself up against the rail. Luca Barone was standing off to one side, gazing with satisfaction at his son's horse, as a TV camera crew filmed the ceremony and cameras clicked and whirred all around me. People in the crowd called out congratulations and bravos. Domenico Lipatti, his weathered features wrinkled in delight, waved to the crowd from his perch in the saddle, all but submerged by a huge wreath of flowers draped over his mount's neck. Tiberio, cool and elegant, not even sweating from his major effort, eyed the mob with disinterest and calmly allowed himself to be led about in a small circle by his groom, then stood totally still, like a statue of equine perfection, for the formal pictures in the winner's circle.

Francesca detached herself from the mob scene around the horse and came over to me. "Shifty, is nearly ended here," she said. "We go then?"

"Whenever you wish."

"Adriano is crazy," she said. "He bet ten million lire on Tiberio."

"Good bet," I said. "This is a nice horse, Fran."

"Too good maybe for Adriano."

"A donkey would be too good for Adriano."

Lipatti had dismounted and was now being carried around the ring on the shoulders of several admirers. He was waving and laughing as the crowd shouted its approval. "Wait here, Shifty," Francesca said. "Two more pictures and then we go." She rushed off after the jockey.

I looked for Ravelli, but couldn't spot him in the crush around the Barones. Luca and Adriano were now standing arm in arm, being interviewed by a swarm of reporters. Tiberio, the protagonist of this small drama, was being led away toward the barn area. I was feeling stupid for not having bet on him to win the race, because my golden rule in wagering on horses is to follow my own deepest instincts; I had felt, from the moment I first saw him, that the animal was a true competitor. On the other hand, I had not been able to make myself bet on the Barones, and perhaps that was just as well for my peace of mind; it would have been like betting on Hitler when he invaded France.

*   *   *

With my modest winnings I took Francesca and Mercurio out to dinner that night. Ravelli had left word at my hotel for me to join the victory party at some big nightclub up around the Via Veneto, but I wasn't in the mood for it. I certainly had nothing to celebrate and I had no plans to congratulate Adriano Barone on his victory. Mercurio suggested a small trattoria between his house and the Pantheon, halfway to my hotel, and we met there at about nine o'clock. Francesca came a half hour late, having had to spend a couple of hours at the Rome offices of *Mezzanotte* to process her photographs. "They take the one of Lipatti on the horse," she said, sinking into the chair beside me and reaching for the wine. "So boring. I have good photos of everything and they choose the boring one. *Detesto gli editori!*"

"Editors are much the same in every profession," Mercurio said. "They can help a great deal or they can mangle your best work. It's not predictable."

"So, Shifty, you win much money?" Francesca asked.

"Enough for dinner."

"You bid on Tiberio?"

"Bet, not bid. No, but I wish I had."

"So who you bid?"

"Bet. I had help." I told her and Mercurio about Pippo and his winning selections. "Usually I don't listen to so-called information at racetracks, but in Italy I'm a stranger in a strange land. Anyway, all tracks are a great mine of information and gossip. Pippo also has information on Bobby Jo. He has friends in Milan."

"What does this Pippo do?" Mercurio asked.

"Electronics, whatever that means," I said. "He has a shop. He says the Barones did it, but that they're trying to pin the murder on other people."

"What peoples?" Francesca asked.

"I don't know. Robbers, hijackers? Anyway, I'm going to talk to somebody he knows tomorrow." I told them about my appointment with The Mosquito for the next day in the Campo dei Fiori.

"You be careful there, Shifty," Mercurio said. "That's the thieves' quarter of Rome. It's famous. Your man Pippo sounds like a dubious character to me."

"I come with you," Francesca said.

"No, I don't think that's a good idea," I said. "The man won't talk to me if I bring anyone else."

"Why he talk to you alone?"

"Because we're horseplayers. And because I'm paying him."

"How much you pay?"

"Two, three hundred thousand lire maybe."

"This Pippo," Francesca said, "why he trust you?"

"He knows I'm not a cop. And let me tell you something about the world of horse racing," I explained. "It's like a conspiracy. It's a big international confraternity of people in all walks of life who love the horses. It doesn't matter who you are, what you do, where you come from, or where you're going. If you love the game, then you're part of it, one among equals. The only thing that matters is who's going to win the next race, that's all. Nothing else. Pippo and I are both charter members. He knows it and so do I. Maybe he'd stiff his own mother—"

"Stiff? What is stiff?"

"Betray. But he's not going to stiff me. If he says The Mosquito will talk to me, then The Mosquito will talk. Maybe he's a horse-player, too."

"What is mosquito?" Francesca asked.

"*Una zanzara,*" Mercurio said. "Is that what they call him?"

"Yes, because he only takes a little blood at a time."

Francesca seemed uneasy. She sat quietly twirling her wineglass and drumming the fingertips of her left hand on the tabletop. "I don't like," she said at last.

"Don't worry, I'll be careful," I said. "Listen, Fran, it's probably nothing but rumors. But what the hell? Nobody else is telling us anything."

Francesca remained subdued for the rest of the evening, which Mercurio filled with more of his seemingly endless flow of gossip from the entertainment world. We parted at about midnight outside in the street. "Shifty, I no see you tonight," she said. "I go to sleep, okay? I leave very early for Milano. You come?"

"In a couple of days. But maybe I'll call you tomorrow night. I'll tell you what The Mosquito has to say."

"You be careful, Shifty," she said, kissing me on the cheek.

She and Mercurio went off together and I headed back to my hotel. I was tired, too, but I hadn't expected Francesca to brush me off so decisively. We could have just gone to sleep in each other's arms, as we had the night before, and I wondered if I had said or done something to put her off. But then I've long since abandoned any hope of understanding women. I've had a long string of failures to my credit in that department. All I've ever been able to do is to be as straightforward as I can with them and hope for the best. As my old racetrack crony Angles Beltrami once put it, "Women? They're from another planet, man. Don't try to understand them. Enjoy them."

16

THE MOSQUITO

The Campo dei Fiori turned out to be a revelation. It's a large, rectangular piazza in the heart of medieval Rome that is the site of a daily open-air market. Under a sea of large canvas umbrellas vendors hawk their merchandise, everything from fresh fruit and vegetables, fish, meat, and cheeses to sandals and T-shirts. One end of the piazza is dominated by the brooding statue of Giordano Bruno, a philosopher and freethinker who was burned at the stake there by the Inquisition in 1600. In fact, I had learned from a guidebook I had bought, the whole piazza had for a time been the scene of executions and tortures, as well as a main artery through which travelers passed on their way to and from the Vatican across the nearby Tiber. At the time I arrived the market was in full action, with merchants hustling their goods, buyers pushing their way up and down the aisles, and children scampering underfoot. People were moving in and out through the narrow side streets that fed this frenzy, and I guessed that living in this part of town had to be terminally noisy, what with all the uproar of the market underlying the din of traffic. The ancient buildings that surrounded the Campo seemed to be leaning cheerfully against one another like gawking tourists, their windows unshuttered and open at midday to the full-throated roar of the bazaar at their doorsteps.

I entered the Campo dei Fiori from a street that led directly into the heart of it, and it took me a few minutes to locate Pippo's store. It was at the end of the piazza where Bruno's statue brooded over the proceedings and on the corner directly across from a huge gray palazzo that occupied one whole side of an adjacent square. This was the Cancelleria, once the Vatican treasury, an austere, forbidding structure containing a small church within its walls. I stared at it for a few minutes, then spotted Pippo's window. The sign *Elettronici* indicated its presence, but it didn't seem much of a store. The window looking out on the piazza displayed a single piece of merchandise, a small refrigerator, while the one facing the Cancelleria was empty. No attempt was being made to lure the casual customer inside. Access was further discouraged by the presence near the doorway of a couple of surly-looking youths, unshaven and unsmiling, who stood leaning against the wall of the building with cigarettes dangling from their lips. Just up the street from the shop, a small panel truck was parked with its back door open, revealing a pile of shoe boxes. As I approached the entrance, one of the two men casually barred my way. "*Sì? Chi vuole?*" he asked.

"I'm looking for Pippo," I said. "I'm a friend, *amico.*"

The youth grunted. "*Un momento,*" he said, vanishing inside. I waited, as his companion continued to look at me with suspicion. I ignored him and gazed out over the piazza.

Pippo appeared in the doorway. "Eh, American, how are you?" he said, shaking my hand heartily and tugging me inside. "You come in now."

"Pippo, these guys in the doorway, they don't exactly encourage commerce," I said. "How's business?"

"Business is good, *amico,*" Pippo said. "We don't sell to everyone, you know. This is special store."

"You have a private clientele, is that it?"

Pippo smiled. "Yes, that is it. Very private. You must be known, you understand?"

I looked around his main showroom. It was a white room with bare walls that housed two more large refrigerators, a pile of cartons apparently containing transistor radios, a shelf of small electric clocks, a rack hung with men's clothes, mostly sport coats and slacks, and a stack of shoe boxes rising from floor to ceiling. It looked less like a store than a small warehouse. "This is where you sell your stuff?"

Pippo shrugged. "Sometime," he said. "We have regular people who know us."

"What do clothes and shoes have to do with electronics?" I asked.

Pippo grinned. "We sell, *amico*, we sell many things. You don't ask too many questions, okay? Come."

I followed him through a door at the rear into a small, dark inner office furnished with two desks, several straight-backed wooden chairs, and four or five metal cabinets. A thin, unshaven man of about forty rose from behind the desk facing us as we entered. He had a long, pointed nose, thin lips, and a wary air, as if he were afraid of being surprised in the open. He was wearing a baggy gray suit that looked a size too large for him, and his thin, graying hair was combed straight back and slicked down. "Bisanza," he said, with a little nod of the head.

The Mosquito could not speak English, so we talked through Pippo, who translated for both of us. I sat down in one of the wooden chairs, as Pippo and Bisanza chatted, presumably laying down the ground rules for our conversation, after which Pippo stuck his head out into the other room and shouted for one of the young men outside the front door. "*Tre espressi!*" he said, then glanced at me. "Is good?"

"Fine," I said. "Thanks."

Pippo leaned against the wall. "I tell Bisanza about you," he said. "He don't want to talk to you, but I tell him is okay, eh? You don't go to the police, eh?"

"No, no, of course not. Did you tell him I'm just a family friend? That I knew the girl?"

"Yes."

"And that I'm acting for her father?"

"Yes, yes. And I tell him you pay something." I reached into my jacket and handed Pippo an envelope containing three hundred-thousand lire notes. Pippo stuffed the envelope into his back pocket.

"*Grazie*," he said. "Now you ask Bisanza what you want. He trust me. Me and Bisanza, we go back many years, you understand?"

I looked at The Mosquito. "Pippo tells me you think you know who killed my friend Bobby Jo," I said.

The Mosquito nodded. "Yes," Pippo said, translating. "It was Adriano Barone."

"But you say the police are trying to pin it on other people."

"My friends in Milan tell me that," Pippo translated. "The police have arrested two men and they have seized a car."

"Who are they?"

The Mosquito looked at Pippo, who then turned to me. "Is better you don't ask their names," Pippo said.

"Okay, no names. But why did they arrest them?"

"They find them with the car the girl was driving when she left the villa. The car was missing. Only the girl's body was found. The police are saying the two men stole the car, after they stop the girl on the road and kill her. That is what the police say."

"What do these men say?"

"They say Adriano Barone was driving the car. He was alone in the car. They stop him and they steal the car. They know nothing about this girl."

"In other words, Barone drove Bobby Jo away from the villa that night, beat her up, maybe raped her, dropped her dying by the lake, and started to drive back to the villa," I said. "The two men are robbers, car thieves, who hijacked the car that night after Bobby Jo was dropped off. Is that it?"

The Mosquito listened attentively to Pippo's translation, then nodded. "Yes, that is right. These men are robbers, not rapists and murderers."

"They work with a group that steals cars," Pippo explained. "They take them apart into many pieces and sell them. Some they take across the borders and sell them there, you understand?"

"Where are these two men now?" I asked.

"They are in jail outside Milan, near Lodi."

"Have they been formally charged?" Pippo didn't understand

what I meant, so I tried again. "Are they going to be put on trial for this crime?"

"No one knows," The Mosquito said. "Probably, but that is up to the judges."

One of the youths outside the store now returned with a small metal tray holding tiny white cups of coffee and a sugar bowl. He set it down on the desk in front of Pippo and left. We sipped the hot, bitter *espressi* in silence for a minute or two. "I've seen nothing in the papers about this," I said, draining the last of the liquid and setting my cup back on the tray.

"No, it is strange," The Mosquito said. "Nothing. The lawyer for the two men does not know what is happening either. He says it is most unusual."

"I'm going back to Milan in a couple of days," I said. "I'd like to talk to this lawyer. Does he speak English?"

The Mosquito looked at Pippo, who said something to him in Italian, then fished a card out of his wallet and handed it to me. The lawyer's name was Alberto Dente and his office was in a part of Milan not far from where Francesca lived. I recognized the name of the street as one I'd passed two blocks from her house. "He's American. Bisanza will telephone and tell him you are coming to see him," Pippo said. "I think he will talk to you."

I looked at The Mosquito. "What do you think happened?" I asked.

The Mosquito seemed to shift uneasily inside his baggy suit, as if recomposing himself before risking an answer. "Who knows? Only one thing is sure to me. These men did not kill the girl. I know them. They are not assassins. They are only very good robbers. Maybe they steal the car from the villa, not on the road. That part is not entirely clear. What is clear is that there is another investigation or inquiry going on that is against this one. Maybe someone very high up, some large bird somewhere, is protecting the murderers of the girl."

"That would have to be Luca Barone, wouldn't it?"

"Who knows? It is the talk of certain circles in Milan, but these are not the circles of polite society. Perhaps Dente can fill you in."

"I like his name," I said. "It's how I like my pasta cooked."

The Mosquito looked puzzled. "What?"

"Al Dente," I said.

Pippo laughed. "Is true," he said. "I never think of that. Alberto is Al, no?" He laughed again. "You are very funny man, *amico*."

The Mosquito was not laughing, but he did permit himself the tiniest hint of a smile, though his eyes remained dark and lifeless. He was not, I could tell, a citizen whose life was blessed with merriment. He mumbled something to Pippo, who nodded and turned back to me. "Bisanza and I have to talk, *amico*," he said. "Why do you not walk about the piazza for a few minutes, maybe twenty minutes, then come back here and we have lunch, okay?"

"Sounds good," I said, getting up and shaking The Mosquito's hand. "Thanks. I appreciate your help." I started for the door.

"Tell Mario to show you some good shoes," Pippo said. "He is the boy who bring the espresso. He have some very good shoes outside, in the truck. Very cheap. You like Italian shoes?"

"They're the best," I said. "I could use a pair of black loafers."

"You ask Mario. He show you, *amico*. Then you come back in twenty minutes, eh? We eat. I know a very good trattoria around the corner from here, okay?" He walked me out into the street, where Mario and his friend were still lounging against the wall by the front door. He spoke briefly to them in Italian, shook my hand, and returned to his inner office.

Without saying a word, Mario walked me over to the back of the panel truck. He rummaged about inside and produced three shoe boxes labeled Ferragamo, one of Italy's best brands of footwear. He gestured for me to have a look. I opened them and found three pairs of brand-new loafers, two black and one dark brown. I leaned against the truck, took off my shoes, and tried on the loafers. The second pair, one of the black ones, fitted me perfectly. I walked about in them to be sure, then looked at Mario. "How much?" I asked. "*Quanto?*"

"*Trentamila*," he said.

"Thirty thousand lire?" I asked, astonished. The sum he had mentioned came to about twenty dollars, a fraction of what I'd have had to pay in a store and probably less than it had cost the manufacturer to make them. "*Poco,*" I said.

Mario shrugged unsmilingly and looked away from me, as if to make sure no one was observing this negotiation. "*Trentamila,*" he said again.

I reached into my pocket, fished the sum out of my wallet, and handed it to him. "*Grazie,*" I said. "It's a bargain."

Again Mario glanced quickly around, then thrust the bills into his pocket, stuffed the loafers back into their box, and handed it to me. He looked at his companion, still at his post by the front door of the shop, nodded, and left me to rejoin him. I stuck the box under my arm and strolled out into the piazza to check out the scene.

When I came back, about half an hour later, Pippo was standing in the doorway. Mario was with him, but the other young hood and the panel truck had both disappeared. So, apparently, had The Mosquito. As he saw me approaching, Pippo pulled out a mass of keys and began to lock up his shop, a procedure that took several minutes, with a great rattling of chains and the grinding sound of a large bolt being slid ponderously into place. "This is not a safe *quartiere, amico,*" Pippo explained, with a sardonic glance back over his shoulder at me. "There are many bad people."

"I don't imagine you'd have any trouble," I said. "You seem to be well known here."

Pippo grunted as he turned the last key in its lock. "You know good Roman proverb? *Bene fidarsi, meglio non fidarsi.*"

"Which means?"

"Is good to trust, but is better not to trust." He turned to look at me. "You like the shoes?"

"They're great," I said. "How can you afford to sell them so cheap?"

"We have direct source of supply, *amico,* okay? You don't ask anymore, okay?"

"Okay. thanks. I needed a new pair of loafers."

"You need something, *amico,* you come to Pippo, okay? I take care of you. Not always I have what you need, but many times I can find it. TV, radios, watches, everything. I sell cheap."

"You're a discount store."

He nodded vigorously. "Ah, yes," he said. "I discount. That is good word, very American, no?"

"Yes."

"But you don't ask me more, okay? Now we go eat. Mario stay here. He work for me."

"He doesn't seem very happy with his work."

"Well, what can you do, American? Is not like the States here, *amico*. People come, people go. People disappear for a time to places that are not comfortable, not *simpatico*, you understand? Mario, he become careless three years ago and they send him to a bad place in a bad section. Not a nice atmosphere. Very closed in and dark. Mario is from Naples. He like very much the sun. In a place where there is no sun, he become very low in his spirits. It is sad. And he lose his girlfriend, too. She don't wait for him, she go with another man, a *capo*. Not nice for Mario. He is sad now, but everything work out in the end, I tell him. He don't believe me, but that is because he don't know the world. The world is like the horses, *amico*. One day you are down, the next one you are up. Mario do not understand this and so he remain sad, like Bisanza. He is sad, too. If I am sad, I go to the horses. You understand, *amico*?"

"Perfectly," I said. "At the racetrack it's always tomorrow."

He linked an arm through mine and we headed away from the Campo up a narrow, cobblestoned street behind the Cancelleria. "Food and horses, what else is there?" he asked.

"Women?"

"No," Pippo said, "that is serious. That is something else, *amico*. Now we eat and talk horses and we laugh and have a good time, okay? Women, that is something we talk about another time, okay? There is much sadness in women for a man of the world. We don't talk women now, *amico*. We do not have regrets and we do not suffer, not today."

17

THE TOOTH

After Rome, Milan was like a splash of cold water in the face, but at least it had stopped raining. The light was pale and misty, with the sun trying valiantly to warm up the scene. I checked into the Piccolo and found a message from Francesca. I called her first at home, then at another number she had left me, which turned out to be the editorial number for *Mezzanotte*, but she wasn't at either location. I was getting dressed to go out for lunch when the phone rang. "Ah, Luigi, you are back! Good," Ravelli said. "Did you enjoy yourself?"

"I think I like Rome better than any city I've ever been in," I told him.

"Ah, that is because you do not know it," Ravelli said. "I hate Rome. Everything is so old there."

"That's why I like it, Carlo," I said. "Also the sun shines there."

"That is all that shines there," he said. "Rome is a city of Medusas. You stay there long enough, you turn to stone, like all the old monuments. It is depressing, no?"

"No, but then I haven't been there enough."

"Listen, Luigi, tonight we go to the Circolo dell'Aquila, all right?"

"What is it?"

"It is my club. It's very nice, Luigi. After dinner. Adriano will be there, we play cards and we have a good time, all right?"

"Okay, when?"

"I pick you up at ten o'clock. I have to have dinner with my parents tonight, but then I come and get you. Where do you eat?"

"I know a place, don't worry."

"And remember, just you, Luigi."

"I understand, Carlo. Don't worry."

When I returned from lunch, I found a message to call Francesca at home, but decided temporarily to ignore it. I went back to my room to read the *Paris Tribune*, which carried another account of the Banca dei Due Mondi scandal. This time, there was only a passing mention of Luca Barone. The bank, according to the *Tribune*, was under investigation not only for being used to funnel illegal payments to political parties and individuals, but for carrying out illegal currency transactions on a truly massive scale. Bellinzona had disappeared, last seen in Rome at the running of the Italian Derby, and the authorities had seized his bank, halting all transactions until such time as a full investigation could be completed. "I'm appalled at this news," Milan's *Corriere della Sera* quoted Luca Barone as saying. "Franco Bellinzona has been an intimate friend for twenty years. I find it impossible to believe these charges will be found to have any merit." He declined to discuss the matter further with reporters.

Alberto Dente's office was on the top floor of a seedy-looking six-story palazzo at the corner of a broad avenue lined by commercial establishments of one sort or another. Half the store windows flaunted banners proclaiming special sales or discounts. Street peddlers with pushcarts were carrying on a brisk trade in secondhand books and magazines, transistor radios, CDs, cassettes, plastic goods, shoes, neckties, cast-off clothing, junk jewelry. It was not a joyous market scene such as the one in Rome's Campo dei Fiori, but a fairly grim one, as the people who swarmed on the sidewalks were poorly dressed and looked dismayed by their own poverty. There was something almost Dickensian in the scene, a squalor so profound that it hung over the neighborhood.

The elevator was out of order, so I climbed six flights of worn, steep stairs to the top landing. Dente's office was one of four, in a corner to the right of the elevator shaft. His name appeared on a printed card over the doorbell, which I pushed. Almost at once the door opened a crack and the wrinkled face of a very old woman peered at me over the links of a chain lock. "Signor Dente, *per favore*," I said.

"*Chi è lei, scusi?*"

"*Il* Signor Anderson, *amico del* Signor Bisanza."

"*Un momento.*" The door shut on me. Two minutes later, it reopened and swung wide enough to admit me. "*Di là,*" the old woman said, pointing back along a short hallway to an inner room. She was dressed in black, with a black shawl over her head, and standing on two rags she apparently used to clean the tiled floor. No sooner had I walked past her than she shut the door behind her and shuffled along in my wake. "*Ecco, entra,*" she said, as I reached the inner door.

Before I could knock, the door opened and Alberto Dente presented himself to me. He was a short, stocky man in his fifties with a heavy-jawed, square face under a formidable jet-black toupee that looked as if it had fallen on him from above and stuck there, slightly askew. He had a large brush mustache, also dead black, and immense-looking dark eyes behind the thick lenses of a heavy pair of rimless spectacles. He was wearing a wrinkled shiny green suit and a pink necktie stained by drops of tomato sauce. "You're Bisanza's friend?" he asked.

"Lou Anderson," I said. "I met him in Rome."

Dente's English was remarkable. He spoke it like an American from some East Coast city slum, without a trace of an Italian accent. He smiled when I asked him about it. "I was born in Philly," he said. "I was raised there until I was about ten. I didn't speak a word of Italian, except maybe for some dialect phrases, until I came over here. That was right after the war. Sit down." He pointed to a leather armchair facing his desk.

The office was small, mostly taken up by a huge wooden desk facing a window that looked out on the street. The window was open and the noise of traffic and voices from below invaded the room. The desk was piled high with papers and folders. The wall behind me was taken up by shelves of law books and more piles of papers. To the right of the door were two metal filing cabinets and a floor lamp. Behind Alberto Dente's desk a small sea of framed photographs occupied all the space, mostly pictures of family gatherings—men and women of all ages in dark, formal attire, children in frilly party clothes, all posing solemnly for the camera. Only one photograph displayed a single head, that of a bald man of about forty who was staring at the camera as if it had caught him unawares; his mouth was open and his eyes looked startled. It was a vaguely familiar face, but I couldn't quite place it. "Nice pictures," I said. "Your family?"

"Yeah. Oldies, taken a long time ago back in the States," he explained. "I'm the youngest kid in most of them."

"And the man? That your father?"

"Yeah, that's him. He didn't like to have his picture taken. You'll notice he ain't in most of the family shots. Actually, a cop took that picture of him. It made the papers and we got hold of a copy, I don't know how."

"Should I know who he is?"

"I don't know, maybe. He was in the rackets back in Philly. You remember, during the war the government used some guys who were connected to help with the invasion of Sicily, guys who knew how the system worked there. You remember Lucky Luciano?"

"I read about him."

"Yeah, well, my pop worked for him in Philly. Nothing bad. No drugs. Just hookers and gambling, small potatoes. Well, when the war was over they deported back to Italy a whole bunch of guys who'd been doing time or were in the rackets with the big boys. In those days most of the Italians who came in and were connected didn't have no papers. I mean, they wasn't immigrants. They were just brought over and stayed. That was the case with Pop. So he got shipped back along with the others. That was the payoff for the Sicilian caper. No hard time, you didn't have to go back to jail, but you had to leave. So all the boys got shipped back to wherever they came from back in the old country. Luciano was lucky, like his name. He got sent to Naples. Most of the wiseguys had it worse. I mean, they had to go back to little villages, Podunks nobody ever heard of, up in the hills in Calabria, Sicily, wherever. In those days there was no TV even, maybe not even a movie. And the Italian government wouldn't let 'em go anywhere. They had to stay where they was born. Some of them would have chosen to remain in the slammer, if they could have stayed in the States once they done their time, but there wasn't no choice, see? Pop was one of them."

"He got sent to Milan? That's not so bad."

"Are you kidding? Bergamo. That's a town between here and Venice. It's big now, but then it was nothing. There was nothing to do. A village on a mountaintop. Pop tried to open a nightclub, they shut it down. Anything he tried to do, they stopped it. And they kept arresting him. Every week they'd arrest him for something. They kept trying to pin something on him. If he was selling bananas, they'd arrest him because some guy slipped on a banana peel and broke his arm. Finally, he just stayed home and went into the wine business."

"The wine business? He made wine at home?"

"Sort of." Dente permitted himself a tight little smile. "He'd buy this cheap local white wine and put some bubbles in it, bottle it, and sell it for champagne. That's how we stayed alive for ten years. Then things lightened up. We got permission to move to Milan, which is where Pop was selling the champagne to. He opened a club here with two other guys from the old days. It did all right for a while. He had nice clean girls in there, a good band, dancing, a floor show. He did okay till he dropped dead one day. He put me through law school."

"And your mother?"

"You met her. She opened the door for you. She likes to take care of me, so I let her." He rubbed a hand over his jaw and gave his mustache a brisk stroke. "She ain't all there anymore, but she's happy. She takes care of the house and me. But you didn't come here for the family history, right?"

"No, but it's a great story."

"Yeah, well, maybe they'll make a movie someday. What do you want to know, pal?"

"I gather The Mosquito called you."

"Bisanza? That creep, yeah. He said you wanted to know about two of my clients, is that right?"

"Yes. According to Bisanza, they were arrested for the possible murder of Bobby Jo Dawson, the girl whose body was found by the lake."

"I know who she is," the lawyer said. "They didn't kill her. They can prove they didn't kill her."

"Then why are they holding them?"

"They're trying to pin it on them."

"They must have something."

"What they got is the car, and the cops can't even prove they stole it. They raided this garage out here in Monza, which is a suburb a few miles east of here, and they found the car."

"Your clients own the garage?"

"They work there. It's a legit operation. The car just happened to be there."

"How did it just happen to be there?"

"A guy brought it in and sold it to them. My clients buy and sell cars all the time. That's what they do."

"Do they know who sold it to them?"

"No. Some guy comes in, he's got the papers and the car and he sells it to them. The guy disappears. They don't ask no questions. It's not in the nature of the business to ask too many questions."

"How can they prove they didn't steal the car themselves? Maybe hijack it with Bobby Jo in it, get rid of her, and take the vehicle?"

"They both got alibis, good alibis. They was home with their girlfriends. This is a bunch of bullshit."

"Can we talk turkey here, as they say back in the States?"

"Jesus, I ain't heard that phrase in years. Yeah, go ahead, shoot." He leaned back in his chair, folded his hands behind his head, and eyed me with mild curiosity.

"Here's the picture I get," I said. "It may not be accurate, but let me try it on you."

The lawyer nodded. "Shoot."

"You represent a couple of career criminals who work for a gang whose specialty is stealing automobiles and shipping them across borders or dismantling them and selling them for parts," I said. "A lot of cars are being stolen every day around here, especially in the wealthy suburbs. Maybe they also do a little breaking and entering into villas and homes, too, pick up TVs, stereos, tape recorders, radios, electronic goodies of one sort or another. But cars are probably the lucrative part of the business. One nice Alfa Romeo or Ferrari is worth a whole bunch of TV sets and transistor radios, right?"

Alberto Dente did not answer me at first, but gazed impassively at me, as if I'd said something so unexpectedly bizarre that I couldn't possibly have meant it. "You a cop?" he finally asked.

"No, I told you."

"You didn't tell me nothing."

"Well, I'm sure somebody did. No, I'm a friend of Bobby Jo's and I'm acting for her old man, that's all. He wants to know who killed his daughter and why, and he wants his daughter's body sent home so he can give her a proper burial. I have nothing to do with the police. The police don't even want to talk to me. I'm just trying to get a picture of what really happened here. The judge in charge of the case is not being helpful. Now you're telling me, in effect, that they're trying to pin the murder on your clients. Have they been formally charged or indicted?"

"No, but you're right, that's what they're doing. It's a cover-up."

"How long can they hold your guys?"

"Are you kidding? As long as they want to. They don't have habeas corpus in this country. They can let them sit in jail and rot for months, years even. I'm doing what I can to get them out, or at least get the formal charges made against them so I know what we're dealing with."

"They stole the car, didn't they?"

"No comment. They'll have to prove that. At worst they bought a hot car, that's all, from whoever did steal it. That could be some jail time. But murder? They didn't kill nobody."

"You mind telling me their names?"

"Why? What for?"

"So I can confront this Angela Tedeschi with them. Maybe she'll tell me something."

"Which you'll then tell me, right?"

"It's a deal."

Alberto Dente grabbed a small pad of paper, hastily scribbled two names on it, and handed the sheet to me. "Tonio Ruffo and Tito Scotti."

"Innocent young men?" I asked, as I took the paper from him.

"Not exactly," the lawyer said. "They got records, all right? They've done time. But murderers, they ain't."

"How long have you represented them?"

"I'm on a retainer from the garage where they work. You don't need to know more than that, all right? Where are you staying, in case I need to talk to you?"

I gave him the number of the Piccolo. He wrote it down, then looked up at me. "What do you do, by the way?"

"I'm a magician."

"You're kidding."

"No. Want to see?" I took out my wallet, removed a ten-thousand-lire bill, and crumpled it into a ball. Then I rubbed it very hard between the palms of my hands until I'd reduced it to the size of a marble. I tossed it to him. "Open it up," I said.

Dente took the little ball and painstakingly unfolded it. It turned out to be a blank sheet of paper. He looked up at me and grinned. "Pretty good," he said. "Where'd you learn that?"

"From a lawyer," I said, getting up to go. "You guys are the best at making money disappear."

"I know this man Dente," Francesca said. "He is lawyer for bad peoples."

"Well, his father was a mafioso, so I guess he went into the branch of the law he understood from childhood," I said. "But his story is interesting."

"Very," she said. "I think he's right. They trying to make guilty the hudlums for the car."

"Hudlums, I like that."

"Is not right?"

"It's fine. It's perfect."

"Oh, you always make the fun of me," she said. "Why you don't speak Italian? Then I make the fun of you."

"Why don't you kiss me instead?"

"Is good idea." She leaned over and did so, this time on the mouth.

"You want to make the beast with two backs?"

"What beast?"

"Make love? Remember? I kiss you, you kiss me, one small move leads to another and the earth trembles."

"You crazy. I understand nothing you say."

"Here, let me show you." I kissed her this time and began to unbutton her shirt.

"Wait," she said, fending me off. "I'm dirty. I wash first, okay?" She stood up and headed for the bathroom.

"I'll join you."

"You crazy," she called back over her shoulder. "Is very small space."

"An added inducement."

"*Cosa?*"

"Temptation."

I had walked over from Dente's office and found Francesca at home. She'd been working in her darkroom and sorting through contact prints of the pictures she'd shot in Rome, hoping to pick out some additional shots she could peddle to newspapers and magazines. It was about five o'clock and I had plenty of time to kill before meeting Ravelli for my soiree at the Circolo dell'Aquila. She had been glad to see me and we'd spent the past half hour catching up, which essentially meant my telling her about my adventures with Pippo, The Mosquito, and now Alberto Dente, who had assumed the permanent nickname in my head of The Tooth. "You talking to very bad peoples," Francesca had said. "It's periculous."

"It's what?"

"*Pericoloso.* Periculous."

"You mean 'dangerous'?"

Sì. Is wrong?"

"I like periculous, a terrific new word."

"You shut up, Shifty. You always make the fun of me."

In her bathroom, we sat together in her tiny tub and allowed the warm shower water to cascade over us while we washed each other. Then I took her, right there, with water spilling over us. She laughed when she came, as if I'd just told her a funny story. Afterward, we gently dried each other, wrapped ourselves in bath towels, and went back to the studio for wine. I think I was as happy at that moment as I had been in many months. The memory of a recent failure with a woman I had really cared about had faded at last in someone else's arms, though I'd always bear the scars of that one. We collect scars as we stumble through life, but then how does the old song go? "When lovely Venus lies beside her lord and master Mars, they mutually profit by their scars." Cole Porter? Who else could it have been?

18

COLD DECK

The Circolo dell'Aquila was located on the second floor of an old palazzo on the Via Brera, a street that wound through the ancient quarter of the city behind La Scala. The building, like most of the older structures in this part of town, looked cold and forbidding from the street, its facade stained black and corroded by decades of pollution, but inside it proved to be an elegant haven for the rich. Ravelli took me in through a massive front portal that led into a garden, then we turned right and walked up a broad flight of worn marble stairs to the club, which occupied the entire floor. Great dark nineteenth-century canvases—romantic landscapes, battle scenes, mythological figures in allegorical groupings—adorned the walls of the outer rooms. One hall was hung exclusively with tattered medieval tapestries. Here and there great bronze statues of Roman gods and goddesses loomed out of the shadows. One huge room contained an exhibition of medieval armor, another a collection of Louis XV French furniture, mostly roped off. "It's a museum, not a club," I said to Ravelli, as we strolled through it.

"Wait, Luigi," he said, "This is all for show. Originally it was the apartment of one of the Dukes of Milan, you understand? In Italy we destroy nothing, but build on top. These rooms are to remind us of the last duke. The club is back here."

Behind these outer rooms, where I hadn't spotted a living soul, and around to the far side of the building were the club rooms, where the members of the Circolo met to eat, drink, and presumably carouse. The halls had been chopped up into smaller, more convivial spaces. There was a dining room, a bar, a lounge with an immense television screen, several small sitting rooms, comfortably furnished with modern pieces, and several game rooms. Ravelli led me straight to the bar, where three well-dressed older men were sipping cognacs. "We have a drink first," he said, "and then we find Adriano. I think he is playing cards." He greeted the men at the bar, who did not seem enthusiastic to see him, but did not bother to introduce me. "Old farts," he said, after we had been handed our Sambucas and moved away. "Very snobbish. Most of the people who are in this club are very, how you say, tight up."

"Uptight," I corrected him. "Who are the members here?"

"First it was only the old families of Milan. It was very boring, but now we are all members. You need to have money, that is all."

"If it's so boring, why be a member? Why not just find a club that isn't boring?"

"Tradition. And it's quiet. Adriano likes to gamble here."

"No women?"

"Of course not, Luigi. That is why men like to come here."

He led me to the game area, which consisted of two pool tables, Ping-Pong tables, video games, and several cardrooms. In one of them Adriano Barone was playing poker with five men of about his own age. One was Gianpaolo Caruso, the jeweler, who sat directly across from Adriano. He looked up at me, but gave no hint of recognition. Ravelli introduced me and Caruso nodded warily. Adriano Barone smiled. "Ah, Carlo's famous magician again," he said. "He says it was a misunderstanding about the other night."

"I guess it was."

"Well, it is a good thing we are not outside then," he said, still smiling but not really. "I would have been forced to break your face."

"That would have been unpleasant," I said.

"Anyway, it is all forgotten," he said, "but I must finish the hand. You wish to play?"

"I might."

"Then perhaps you will join us." He smiled at Ravelli. "Carlo, of course, must play. He always loses, so we invite him always to play. Carlo, you will join us?"

"When I finish my drink, Adriano."

"*Bene. Bravo.*"

Adriano Barone picked up his cards, scanned them, then set them down on the table. "A *chi tocca?*" he asked. The man to his right dropped two blue chips into the pot. Adriano matched him, as did the other four players, after which they all discarded cards and the dealer picked up the deck. They were playing five-card draw, but I didn't know for what stakes until Ravelli whispered to me that each blue chip was worth fifty thousand lire and the red ones a hundred thousand. I estimated that the pot already contained close to a million lire. After the draw, the dealer dropped out and Adriano opened the bidding, but the pot went to Caruso, who was holding three sevens.

Ravelli and I sipped our Sambucas and watched the game. It only took me three hands to figure out that Adriano was cheating. He and Caruso were playing as a team, shooting each other signals by the way they placed their cards down on the table after looking at them, a stunt any experienced casino operator would have picked up within ten minutes. I finished my drink, chewed on the little coffee bean at the bottom, and set off for the bar. "Carlo?" I asked, raising my empty glass as I headed for the door.

"I come with you," he said.

"Your pal is cheating," I told Ravelli, as we walked down the hall.

"You are sure, Luigi? How does he cheat?"

"He and Caruso are working as a team. They're giving each other signals."

Ravelli didn't say anything more until we had replenished our drinks and started back toward the game rooms. "I wonder how Adriano always win," he said. "One time he always lost, but for one year now he always win. He and Gianpaolo."

"You want me to put a stop to it?"

"How you do that?"

"Let's get into the game. It's a little heavy for me, though. You can have whatever you win, but if I lose, you have to repay me. Is that a deal?"

"A deal?"

"Agreed."

Ravelli thought it over, then nodded. "Okay."

"What have you told Adriano about me?"

"That you are a *mago*, that's all."

"Does he know what I do?"

"No, only that you are a *mago*. He thinks magic is stupid, for children. He thinks you saw woman in half, stick swords in them, find rabbits in hats, things like that."

"Good. Let's go play poker."

Ravelli laughed nervously. "My God, Adriano will be furious," he said.

"I hope he doesn't take a swing at me again."

The rules of the game were simple enough. The ante was fifty thousand lire, paid by the dealer, table stakes, with each player putting up a minimum of three million lire. It was straight five-card draw, no wild cards or jokers. Ravelli guaranteed my financial participation and I was given a seat to the left of Caruso, who was also the banker. He shoved a stack of blue and red chips my way. Ravelli was on Adriano's left. I was introduced to the other four players again. They all looked like clones of Ravelli and Barone, good-looking young studs in expensive clothes, smooth-shaven, with long hair and that air of quiet arrogance that inherited money seems to impart.

I dropped out of the first two hands, one of which Ravelli won, taking a small pot with two pairs, kings high. Adriano laughed. "That is the first time Carlo win anything in three months, right, Carlo?" Ravelli didn't answer, but smiled as he pulled in his chips.

It was an honest game for about half an hour, with no one doing much of anything, until Caruso laid down his hand after my second deal. The corner of his packet was aimed at an angle toward Adriano. I had a pair of queens and stayed in through the first round of bidding until Caruso and Adriano had whipsawed the pot up to over a million, bumping one another back and forth while one other player and I lingered. Unfortunately for me, I drew a third queen.

When the bidding resumed, Adriano and Caruso slammed me back and forth like a Ping-Pong ball. The other player had dropped out, but I hung on. At five million lire, Adriano folded and I was left to confront Caruso. Instead of trying to frighten me off with a huge bet, he checked. I saw him. He had three aces and raked in the pot. I pretended to be only mildly dismayed and drew another three million lire in chips from the bank. "Ah, Giancarlo is lucky tonight," Adriano said to me. "Too bad."

"Yeah, nothing like holding second hand high," I said. "I could go bankrupt that way."

"Don't worry, Carlo will wind up paying for all of us," Adriano said, smiling. "Right, Carlo?"

"Not tonight, Adriano," Ravelli said. "I feel lucky."

Twice more over the next hour and a half I watched Adriano Barone and Caruso bid up winning pots. I looked around the table. No one seemed to suspect anything, even though there was some mild grumbling from two of the other players, both big losers for the evening. I had managed to win a couple of small hands, but I was still down two million lire. Ravelli was about even now. During one break, when both he and I folded early and went to the bathroom, I whispered to him, "On my next deal, Carlo, stay in the hand."

"They are still cheating?"

"Oh, yes. Caruso's getting the cards tonight. Adriano's just helping him out, making sure the pots are big enough to ensure a nice profit."

"I see them lose sometimes."

"Never when the pots are big, Carlo."

"You are right, Luigi. Teach them a lesson."

"I'd better, or I won't get my money back."

Ravelli grabbed my arm as we headed back toward the game. "I want to win," he whispered. "They have been cheating me for many months, Luigi."

When at last it was my turn to deal again, I shuffled the cards and waited for Caruso to cut them. He gave me a three-way cut for the first time that night, but it took me only a few seconds to make the fix. I had all the cards I needed exactly where I wanted them, at the bottom of the deck. After I finished dealing the hand, I looked across the table. Adriano was doing his best not to betray any emotion, but his hands trembled slightly as he set his cards down, one end aimed straight at Caruso.

When the bidding began, everyone stayed in, just as I had planned they would. The pot began to grow until the bidding finally stopped only because two of the players ran out of chips. They were planning to play out their hands, but would participate only in an allotted portion of the final pot, which threatened to be a huge one. Adriano was holding a cold full house, kings over tens. Ravelli had three aces, a deuce, and a three. The four other players all had strong hands, nothing less than three of a kind, and one had a flush. Caruso and I, of course, had nothing, but it was our task to remain in the bidding and keep the betting going at a fever pitch.

Which is exactly what happened. Everyone stayed in through two more rounds of betting. Ravelli was now holding an aces-high full house. One of the other players had a smaller full house, jacks over treys. The remaining three had three of a kind. The latter had all dropped out by the third round, leaving three men holding full houses, Caruso and me to fatten the pot. By the time the betting was over and there was no more money to put on the table, Adriano Barone had become wild-eyed with anticipation. He was a bad player, because a good one would have realized earlier that his full house wouldn't stand up. He would have had to assume from the cards drawn and the strength of the betting that someone could have four of a kind. I was going to have Ravelli beat him, however, with an aces-high full house to make him look like the fool he was.

On the last round of betting, Caruso and I folded, as did the third full house, leaving Adriano and Ravelli to confront one another. "Carlo, *sei un idiota*," Adriano Barone told him. *Sei fregato.* You are fucked."

"What do you think, Luigi?" Ravelli asked me. He slipped me his cards and I pretended to look at them as if I had no idea what I might find, then passed them back to him across the table.

"I like your chances," I said.

Adriano Barone dropped his hand faceup on the table. "There, Carlo," he said. "How do you like that?"

"It's very nice, Adriano," Ravelli said, "but I like my cards better." He slapped his aces-high full house down and began raking in the pot, a great mountain of chips totalling about twelve million lire.

It caused a sensation. The other players at the table began to chatter animatedly in Italian, commenting on the action. Caruso looked stunned and sat silently in place. I pretended to be impressed and congratulated Ravelli. "It's not very often you have a hand like this one," I said. "Congratulations, Carlo."

Adriano Barone rose to his feet in a fury. He stared at me, his eyes bulging with rage, his hands trembling. "You cheat," he said. "You fix for this to happen."

"No, I didn't," I said. "What makes you think I did? It was just luck."

"You are a liar," he said. "Carlo told me you are a magician. You do this on purpose."

"I think I'd better go," I said, pushing my chair back and rising to my feet.

Adriano Barone whirled on Carlo and began berating him in Italian. Ravelli protested his innocence, but Adriano would have none of it. He grabbed Ravelli by his lapels and raised him out of his seat, then began pushing him backward, jabbing at him with both hands. Two of the other men came up behind Adriano and grabbed him, as they tried simultaneously to calm him. Adriano broke free and whirled on me again. "You!" he said, and lunged for me.

I stepped aside and prepared to defend myself, but Adriano's friends pulled him away. Caruso joined them and they managed to get Barone out of the room. I could hear him cursing and shouting as they maneuvered him down the hall toward the bar. Ravelli was leaning against the wall, looking pale. "*Dio mio*," he said, "what do we do?"

"Do? You cash in your chips and we leave. That's usually what happens at the end of a poker game."

"Adriano is furious. He will never forgive me."

"With friends like Adriano," I said, "you don't need enemies.

He's a bad loser, that's all. I don't know about you, Carlo, but I'm leaving."

Caruso, looking shaken, came back into the room. Ravelli said something to him and pushed all of his chips toward him. Without a word, the jeweler began to count the chips, then handed Ravelli a fat wad of lire notes, while I waited. I had no chips to cash in, of course, but I wasn't about to walk alone out of the club. After Ravelli had pocketed his money, we all shook hands, except for Caruso, who merely sat in place, looking sullen. I wouldn't let him get away with it. "Good night, Signor Caruso," I said. "It's been a most entertaining evening. I have to confess I'm not sorry you and Barone lost."

He didn't answer. Ravelli and I walked out of the room toward the exit. I could hear Adriano Barone shouting from behind a closed door somewhere, but we ignored it and kept going. As we neared the front entrance, an older man, perhaps the manager of the Circolo, came hurrying up to us. He spoke rapidly to Ravelli, who answered him in some detail. The man nodded and looked distressed. "*Sempre cosi,*" he said. "*È impossibile. Bisogna parlare all'Architetto. Qui protestano tutti.*"

"What did he say?" I asked, as we headed out toward the street.

"It is the manager," Ravelli explained. "He ask what happened and I tell him. He say it is impossible, that Adriano is always making scenes. Other people are protesting. He must speak to L'Architetto."

"Who's that?"

"Oh, his father. They call him The Architect sometimes, because he was one and he build so many things. Come, Luigi, I drive you home."

"I'll walk, Carlo, thanks. It's a nice night. I'm only sorry about one thing."

"What is that?"

"I guess Adriano and I are never going to be friends."

"You are joking."

"You bet."

Before driving away, Ravelli handed me my part of the loot, about six million lire, roughly four thousand dollars. It wasn't the best cooler I'd ever dealt, but by far the most satisfying one.

*   *   *

Francesca's telephone call woke me up the next morning. "Shifty, it is me," she said. "You are waking now?"

"Barely. What time is it?" I groped around in the dark for my watch. "Is something wrong?"

"Parker," she said. "They kill her."

"What?" I sat up. "Where are you? What's going on?"

The story was in the morning newspapers. On her last night in Monaco, Parker Williams had gone to a party given by the Cherise brothers, the designers who had hired her, in a villa they shared high up above the coastline. She had stayed at the party for about an hour and a half, then left to drive back to her hotel in the blue Peugeot she had rented during her stay. She had not drunk very much and she was known as a careful driver who had often been overheard lamenting the driving habits of the Italian men she knew. "An Italian man behind the wheel of his car is a goofball mesmerized by his sense of sexual grandeur," she had once commented to a friend. The chances were that she was not speeding during the long descent down from the Grand Corniche to her hotel in Monte Carlo.

The roads along that part of the French Riviera are known to be dangerous. When Parker started out that night from the Cherise villa, the descent for the first five kilometers was precipitous and full of curves. There was no moon and it was very dark. The account Francesca read to me about what happened surmised that Parker's brakes must have failed, causing her car to plunge through the low retaining wall. A second account, however, a more detailed one in the *Corriere della Sera* that we read later, stated that investigators had found that Parker's car had been struck from behind by another vehicle, causing her to lose control. A French policeman, who arrived on the spot within twenty minutes of the accident, declared that the added force of such a blow would have caused Parker's car to break through the retaining wall more easily. The left rear fender of the Peugeot was badly dented, indicating that it had received a blow of some sort. It was a rented car, and it wasn't likely that Parker Williams would have accepted a damaged vehicle from the leasing company. An employee of the company stated that the car had been in excellent order when it had been leased to her and that it had been driven less than twelve thousand kilometers.

The Peugeot broke through the wall and hurtled down a long, steep slope below the road. Before hitting anything, it rolled over several times. The farmer who owned the orchard through which the car fell heard the noise of the accident and thought he had also heard a high-pitched scream of terror. The Peugeot finally slammed into an ancient olive tree uphill from the farmer's house and burst into flames. Parker Williams, strapped into the driver's seat, had no chance. Her body was burned beyond recognition, but she was identified by the silver charm bracelet she wore on her left wrist and by the contents of her purse, found on the floor behind the front passenger seat.

"They kill her," Francesca said to me over the phone.

"Why?" I asked. I told Francesca about having seen Parker in Rome and that I was fairly sure she had been having a drink with Adriano Barone at the Greco.

"She know something," Francesca said. "They kill her."

"Adriano must have tried to buy her off," I guessed. "She was scared, Fran. She was going to leave Italy for good as soon as the Monaco gig was over."

"Those peoples do anything, Shifty, anything. You be careful."

19

SCARPONI

"Yes, we are investigating the involvement of these two men in the possible abduction and killing of this girl," Angela Tedeschi said. "You are quite right, Mr. Anderson. But may I ask, how did you learn of these arrests?"

"Through a friend of a friend of mine, in Rome," I said. "And then I talked to their lawyer, a Signor Dente."

"A dubious source, I must say."

"But the information seems to be accurate," I observed. "You admit these men are considered suspects."

"I am not denying it. They were in possession of the car the girl is said to have been driving at the time of her disappearance from the villa."

"How do you know she was driving the car? Couldn't someone else have been driving it?"

"Who?"

"Adriano Barone, of course,"

"We have investigated that possibility," she said. "Two witnesses, who were at the villa that night, say that Adriano definitely did not leave, not to drive Bobby Jo home, nor for any other reason. She apparently left on her own in this borrowed car sometime around one or one-thirty A.M."

"Are you telling me that Adriano Barone is no longer a suspect in this business?"

"He seems to have a strong alibi, Mr. Anderson."

I sank back in my chair and gazed at Angela Tedeschi in disbelief. "Am I right in believing that you have no plans even to question him further?"

"Oh, we have questioned him and we will again, if we need to," she said. "Informally, at least. There is no reason at the moment to charge him with the crime."

"These people who provided such a convenient alibi," I said, "don't they have a strong interest in providing Barone with one?"

"Pure speculation, isn't it? We can't act on pure speculation," Angela Tedeschi said.

"What about Parker Williams?"

"What about her?"

"You think her death was an accident?"

"So far we have no reason to think otherwise."

"The mark on her car's rear fender indicating she may have been forced off the road?"

"Not conclusive, Mr. Anderson. That is still being investigated by the French authorities, and we are in close touch with them." She leaned back in her seat, her hands together beneath her chin, finger-tips touching lightly. She looked thoughtfully at me, as if sizing me up, perhaps estimating the extent of my skepticism regarding her efforts to catch Bobby Jo's murderer. The pale morning light came through the window blinds of her office, casting shadows across her face. "Even if it is established that some other vehicle did contribute to Miss Williams' unfortunate demise, it would still be difficult to prove that the accident was caused on purpose," she continued. "She might have been the victim of a hit-and-run driver. The road there is very steep, full of curves, very dangerous. Miss Williams was not familiar with it. Every year there are bad accidents on that stretch above Monaco. It is notorious. Parker Williams may have died of foul play, but it seems equally likely that she was merely the victim of a bad accident. And why would anyone want to kill her?"

"Isn't it possible that she may have known something about

Bobby Jo's activities the night she was killed that would undercut the alibis being provided for Adriano Barone by his friends?" I asked. "Isn't that why Adriano may have approached her in Rome, to buy her silence? When the Barones decided she couldn't be trusted or posed some sort of continuing threat, perhaps blackmail, wouldn't they have arranged to eliminate her?"

Angela Tedeschi smiled. "You have a vivid imagination, Mr. Anderson. This is all pure speculation. We don't go about accusing and arresting people unless we have a strong foundation in the form of hard evidence or eyewitness testimony to act on. You do see our dilemma, don't you? Especially as we now have two suspects in hand who could very easily be the culprits."

"According to my sources, Miss Tedeschi, neither of these men is a killer. They are car thieves, possibly hijackers, but not killers."

"One of them, Ruffo, has a long history with the law," Angela Tedeschi said. "He is a convicted rapist. He has also served prison sentences for assaults on women, primarily his ex-wife, whom he beat nearly to death four years ago. He is the older of the two suspects. Scotti is only in his early twenties, Ruffo is thirty-five. He was the one in charge. We know him well."

"Has he admitted guilt?"

"No, but the investigation continues. We are hoping that Scotti, who has much to lose by remaining silent, will eventually talk. We can perhaps arrange what I believe you in America refer to as a plea bargain."

"And that will, of course, take Adriano Barone off the hook."

"Really, Mr. Anderson, why do you involve yourself in this matter? You are not qualified nor authorized to do so," Angela Tedeschi said. "Why don't you go home?"

"I promised Jake Dawson I'd act for him in his absence," I reminded her. "I expect to leave in a week or so at most, when Dawson returns."

"He is coming back?"

"Yes. He wants his daughter's body."

"By that time we hope the investigation will be complete," Angela Tedeschi said. "We will be able to turn over his daughter's remains to him. Now you must excuse me." She rose to her feet and extended her hand.

I shook it and said, "By the way, I know an old friend of yours, Francesca Pirro."

"Oh, Francesca? Yes, we knew each other at university," she said. "How is she?"

"Fine. She's the one who took the pictures of the crime scene."

"Yes, I'm aware of that. She was a wild thing, I remember. Very amusing."

"You don't see each other anymore?"

"No, it's too bad, really. I miss her. She used to make me laugh."

I glanced up at the large painting of old Armore Tedeschi, whose hawklike gaze seemed to transfix me. "I love that portrait," I said. "I'll bet he'd have known how to make a criminal confess."

"Other times," Angela Tedeschi said. "He was a wicked man."

I started for the door, then turned back. "I forgot to ask you," I said. "Was Bobby Jo raped?"

Angela Tedeschi nodded. "Yes," she said, "and brutally beaten."

"By one man or two?"

"We don't know."

"Do you do DNA testing?"

"Of course. Do you think we are in the Third World, Mr. Anderson?"

"And?"

"The killer used a condom, Mr. Anderson. You see, even in Italy criminals take precautions. Ruffo is very smart."

"Fingerprints, hair?"

"No hairs. Many fingerprints, including Adriano's. It was his car."

"Adriano is also a rapist who likes to beat up women."

"We'd have to be able to prove that in court, not always possible."

"Why do I have the feeling you've already made your mind up about this case?"

"I don't know. Perhaps tomorrow, if we have new evidence, I could act differently," Angela Tedeschi said. "I have to conduct my affairs based on factual evidence, Mr. Anderson. Adriano Barone may be a rapist, a brutal thug, as you say he is, but I cannot arrest him for murder unless I can prove his guilt. Good-bye now. Go back home, be a magician again. Let us do our jobs here. When Mr. Dawson returns, I will be happy to see him and bring him up-to-date. This is an unpleasant business."

"I was sure you would come to me," Tommaso Scarponi said. "You were a friend of this girl, yes? Maybe her boyfriend?"

"No, I wasn't involved with her," I replied. "I met her at a party. I took her out once, that's all."

"You fook her?" Francesca asked.

"No. We could have one night, but nothing happened," I said. "She was a sad, unhappy girl."

"A loser," the journalist said. "I know the type. Milano is full of these sad young people with their pathetic dreams. It is like Hollywood here."

Tommaso Scarponi's apartment looked like an Antonioni movie set, all whites and blacks. It was on the twenty-second floor of a skyscraper halfway between the historic center of the city and the main railroad station, with a magnificent view directly over a large public park and extending miles out into the suburbs and countryside. The rooms were furnished with sleek, highly functional pieces— spare-looking sofas and chairs, metal lamps that looked like praying mantises, glass-topped metal tables, ashtrays everywhere. The only wall decoration was a huge blowup of Scarponi himself wearing a trench coat, with a cigarette dangling from his mouth, and standing outside the Galleria facing La Scala. It was the sort of shot Humphrey Bogart might have posed for to advertise a romantic thriller. No books or magazines or newspapers anywhere. In one corner a large Sony television set; against one whole wall a long worktable supporting a computer, a printer, and a stereo with a CD player and a tape deck. It was hard to imagine a human being actually living in this room. The atmosphere was impersonal, cold, supremely functional, dominated by the photograph, as if only the image of the man counted.

"I take that picture," Francesca said.

"I should have guessed."

Scarponi adjusted the portable tape recorder he had set down on the table between us and fiddled with the volume control. He was wearing sandals, a pair of black slacks, and a white shirt. He hadn't shaved and his red hair was uncombed, as if he had just gotten out of bed. It was four o'clock in the afternoon. "Good, that should be right," he said, looking up. "Now, before we start, we have some coffee. Francesca?"

"Sì, grazie," she said. "Is breakfast for you, Tommaso, no?"

"Yes. I am a night person." He left the room and I could hear him rattling around in the kitchen.

"This is a little risky, Fran," I said. "What's to stop Miss Angela Tedeschi from arresting me and having me thrown out of the country?"

"Nothing," she said cheerfully, "but it is Tommaso who write the story. You don't worry, all right?"

I decided I had nothing to worry about, even though I had no idea what laws, if any, applied to my status in the country as a tourist. It had been Francesca who had suggested contacting Scarponi. "He write big story, it make big splash, many questions is asked," she had said to me at lunch, just before she had called him. "Is only way anyone pay attention, Shifty. Luckily, Luca Barone not own *Mezza-notte*. Maybe after this story he buy it, but for now is good."

I wasn't sure what Francesca meant by all this, but I knew the value at this point of publicity. "Your pal Angela is convinced that Adriano did not murder Bobby Jo," I had said. "She has a vested interest, I think, in believing that."

"We call Scarponi now," Francesca had declared, bouncing to her feet to do so. "We make the big stink."

Scarponi returned from the kitchen with three cups of steaming *caffè latte*, which he set down in front of us. He lit a cigarette, sucked the smoke into his lungs, and made one last check of the tape recorder. He glanced up at me. "Ready?"

I nodded and Scarponi turned on the machine. "Now," he said, "we begin at the beginning. My name is Tommaso Scarponi, it is late afternoon on Wednesday, May 31, and I am interviewing Signor Lou

Anderson, a famous American magician who has a remarkable story to tell. . . ."

The interview lasted about an hour and a half, with me doing most of the talking. I provided a detailed, blow-by-blow account of everything that had happened to me since I had first set eyes on Bobby Jo Dawson. When I had finished, Scarponi turned off the machine, sighed, and leaned back in his seat. He stuck another cigarette in his mouth, lit it, and blew smoke out into the air above our heads. He had not stopped smoking since we had begun, and a blue bank of contaminated air had risen to the ceiling. My eyes were itchy and my throat was sore. "Those things are going to kill you," I said.

"What does it matter what kills me?" the journalist answered. "Something kill everyone, no? This way I die happy."

"I guess you haven't met anyone who has emphysema," I said. "It's not much fun not being able to breathe."

"Oh, you Americans," he said, "with your gift for turning every human pleasure into a sin-filled torture. I live when I live, I die when I die."

"When are you going to write your story?" I asked, anxious to get out of there.

"Now," he said, "as soon as you go."

"Then it will be out in a day or two?"

"Why? You think I am lazy? Tonight."

"*Mezzanotte* is a night paper," Francesca explained. "It come out before midnight. Is very popular."

"You come by the office at ten o'clock," Scarponi said. "I give you personally a copy. Now you go. I have to write the story. I type it into the computer, it goes directly to the *redazione*, the editors, you understand? Modern technology is miraculous, no?"

I went back with Francesca to her studio, where we sipped wine and then made love. Or rather she allowed me to make love to her. When we had finished and were getting dressed, I said, "What's wrong, Fran?"

"Wrong? Is nothing wrong."

"You don't seem very interested."

"Oofah, you Americans!" she answered. "You think all love is like one miracle? No, sometimes it's like starnuting."

"Star-what?"

She made a sneezing sound. "Like that."

"Oh, sneezing."

"Sì, *starnutire*."

"A nice image."

"You no like fooking?"

"I like very much. That's why I asked. Never mind, it's probably just me. I want it to be right, Fran."

"Nothing is wrong. Now we go eat."

We had dinner at Peppino's, where again we were received with open arms and I gave another small demonstration of sleight of hand that delighted our hosts. It was after nine when we left the place and Francesca drove us to the *Mezzanotte* building, a modern four-story structure two blocks from the railroad station. We took the elevator up to the top floor and walked out into an open space containing a couple of dozen people working at desks and computer terminals. A sweating fat man in shirtsleeves stepped out of a small, glass-enclosed office to my left. "Ah, Francesca,"he said, "*che fai qui?*"

She answered him in Italian, then introduced me. "Giulio Camerini," she said. "He is editor."

"Ah, you are the magician," he said, shaking my hand. "Scarponi write a marvelous story. We make the sensation. Wait." He went back into his office and reemerged with a long tear sheet that he handed me. "We come out in twenty minutes, also with photographs— the girl, Adriano, Ruffo, Scotti, this model who die in Monte Carlo, others. We don't have the father or you, too bad. But later, maybe. He comes back, no, to take his daughter home? Good, we take his picture then. You, Francesca, you make sure we get a photo, yes? Now excuse me, I go downstairs." He walked away toward the elevators, leaving me holding Scarponi's story, which, of course, I couldn't read.

Francesca took the article from me and led me into Camerini's office. We leaned against the edge of his desk while she did her best to translate it for me. "Who Killed the American Model?" was the headline. The subhead, as I inferred it from Francesca's creative version, read: "The Investigation Leads Nowhere. The Judges Cover Up the Possible Real Killer, Adriano Barone, While Holding in Prison Two Men Found with the Playboy's Car. The Hand of the Architect Behind This Travesty of Justice."

"Wow," I said. "You couldn't write this back home."

"No?" she asked. "Why not?"

"We have libel laws."

"What is?"

"Never mind. Read on."

Scarponi's story was sensational, all right; it would have landed any American journalist and newspaper into a lawsuit involving millions of dollars in damage claims. Although I couldn't get an exact word-for-word translation, I had no trouble piecing together what Scarponi was saying. Based entirely on my account of events, the story outlined what had happened to Bobby Jo, gave an account of her background and a fevered portrait of the world of Milanese fashion models and the people—agents, art directors, designers, photographers, playboys, rich businessmen—who preyed on them. Adriano Barone was described as a ruthless seducer who moved, like all of his friends, in a fast lane of pretty girls, orgies, drugs, and gambling. Obsessed with the one woman he couldn't have, even though she had been bedded by dozens of others, he had lured her to his lakeside villa with gifts and flattery, then tried to rape her. When she had resisted, he had assaulted her, then driven her to a spot on the shoreline a few kilometers from his villa and dumped her, half-naked and unconscious, to die on the rocks at the water's edge. The two men, Ruffo and Scotti, who had been found with his car had either hijacked it from him on his way back to the villa or stolen it at some later date. They were now considered the chief suspects in the murder and were being held in secret at a prison near Lodi, well away from the city and the media. Why was Adriano Barone not considered the prime suspect? Why was he not even being interrogated? Who were the friends who were providing possibly false alibis for him that night? Had Italy reached such a state of corruption that the rich and powerful were above the law? If Luca Barone and his fellow plutocrats could buy the judiciary, what would become of the nation and its institutions? I was mentioned several times in the story and described as an intimate friend of the Dawson family entrusted with the task of finding out what had happened and with bringing Bobby Jo's body back to Kentucky. I was also hailed as the greatest magician since Houdini and a star of the Las Vegas casino scene.

"Is good, no?" Francesca asked, after we'd made our way together through the piece.

"I don't know if 'good' is the exact word," I said. "It's sensational."

"Come, we go downstairs and wait for the paper," she said. "Is on the stamp now."

"You mean the press?"

"Yes."

"If Luca Barone is as powerful as this story claims," I said, as we headed for the elevators, "maybe I ought to hire myself a bodyguard."

"No, you worry more about the police," Francesca said.

"I don't find that remark comforting," I said. "Maybe I ought to come and stay with you."

"Is good idea, Shifty. Nobody find you."

20

THE ARCHITECT

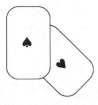

I was packing to move out of the hotel early the next morning when the *portiere* called me from the lobby. "There are two gentlemen here to see you," he said. "They ask that you come down when you are dressed."

"Are they police officers?" I asked.

"I don't know, *signore*. They don't tell me."

I considered briefly bolting out the back door, assuming there was a back door, but then I decided that would be foolish. They probably were police officers and had been sent to bring me in to see Angela Tedeschi, my least favorite judge. I didn't want to convert myself into a fugitive, so I dressed and went downstairs.

The two men were waiting for me in the lobby and rose smilingly to greet me as I emerged from the elevator. They were not the same two who had come to pick me up earlier; they were shaved and better dressed. They were also young and very polite. They introduced themselves and we shook hands. One of them, who looked about twenty-five and had a thick head of well-combed straw-colored hair, acted as official spokesman. He reached into his pocket, produced a sealed envelope, and handed it to me. "Please be kind to read it," he said, in careful English.

"Are you from the police?" I asked.

"No, no," the man replied, and said something in Italian to his sidekick, after which they both laughed. "Please read the letter."

I opened the envelope, which contained a typed message and a business card that read simply "Cavaliere Luca Barone." His name also appeared in solitary splendor on the letterhead, with no address or phone number. "Dear Mr. Anderson," the note read,

> Please do not be alarmed. It is important that we meet and discuss this difficult situation, now vastly exacerbated by the unfortunate article that has been published in *Mezzanotte*. You have every reason to be disturbed by the manner in which the investigation is being conducted into the tragic death of the young woman, the daughter of your friend, but you must believe me when I tell you that neither I nor my son are to blame in this matter. The sort of publicity that this disgusting article will generate can only delay a solution to the case. I would be very grateful if you would be kind enough to meet with me this morning at my house here in Milan. I have not telephoned you for obvious reasons, but have sent to you my personal assistant and my driver. If it is inconvenient or impossible for you to meet with me this morning, please so inform my assistant, Signor Gualtieri, and make an arrangement to meet with me at some future time, the sooner the better. It is extremely important that you do so.
>
> Yours sincerely, Luca Barone.

I looked at Gualtieri, who was standing there, beaming, as if he had conveyed an invitation to a party. "We can go now," I said, folding the note and tucking it into my pocket.

"Excellent. This way, sir," he said, ushering me out into the street.

The dark blue Jaguar I had seen in Rome on Derby day was parked up the block from the hotel. The driver preceded us up the street, opened the door for us and got behind the wheel, then whisked us out into the early-morning traffic as he telephoned ahead to announce our arrival. "Where does Signor Barone live?" I asked.

"Not far," Gualtieri said. "He has several apartments, here and in Rome. And then there is the villa in Lake Lugano. This apartment is on the Corso Magenta. A few minutes away, that is all."

It took less than twenty minutes to arrive at Luca Barone's town residence. It was located on the top floor of another one of those dark, elegant palazzi that grace the older sections of the city. Gualtieri escorted me through an archway, across a well-tended garden, and up a private elevator at the right rear of the building, which disgorged us directly into the foyer of Barone's apartment. A young maid in a black and white uniform appeared and nodded to Gualtieri, who shook my hand, excused himself, and left. The maid then led me into a large living room with French doors opening onto a terrace overlooking the garden. The room was airy, full of light, furnished comfortably and unpretentiously, with floor-to-ceiling bookshelves and a couple of very large abstract canvases occupying most of the wall space. I had never heard of either of the artists, but the works looked like those of Rothko or others of his ilk. I turned away from them just as Luca Barone walked into the room. "Ah, Mr. Anderson," he said, smiling and advancing with outstretched hand, "how kind of you to come right away. You like abstract art?"

"Not much," I said. "I'm pretty much of a square about art. I like to be able to recognize what I'm looking at."

We shook hands. "An odd thing for a magician to say. You specialize in illusions, do you not?"

"Maybe that's why I always feel abstract art is trying to put something over on me."

"An interesting point of view. Would you like to sit down?" He indicated the sofa. "Something to drink? An espresso?"

"That would be fine."

I sat down and Luca Barone sank into a chair across from me. He was dressed in a light gray custom-tailored suit, a dark red necktie, and a white shirt with large gold cuff links. His white hair framed his strong features, set off by thick dark eyebrows, like a halo. He pressed a button on the coffee table beside him and the maid appeared noiselessly in the doorway. "*Due espressi*, Maria," Luca Barone said. She disappeared again. "Now let us talk. I presume you have read this scurrilous article by this vermin Scarponi."

"Yes, I read it last night."

"And, of course, you know it is a pack of lies and half-truths."

"Well, he sensationalized much of what I told him, but essentially the piece strikes me as accurate."

"Do you mind if I smoke?" Luca Barone asked. I shook my head. "Thank you." He took a silver case out of his pocket, removed a thin, black cigarillo from it, and lit it, puffing a small cloud of acrid smoke into the air above us. "A vice, but, I'm afraid, an incurable one. Would you like to try one? Tuscan cigars, very strong."

"No, thanks. Don't use them."

"America is undoubtedly the healthiest country in the world," he said. "Another reason to be depressed about it. Let me speak frankly to you, Mr. Anderson, as a father. Do you have children?"

"No, I'm not married."

"You're fortunate. I have only one, my son, Adriano. As you must be aware, I've had a great deal of trouble with him. He has caused me a great heartache, Mr. Anderson. I am deeply disappointed in my own son. That is a difficult admission for a father to make."

"I can understand your disappointment."

"Adriano was a charming boy, gifted with many talents," Luca Barone continued. "I had the highest hopes for him, especially that he would come to work for me, eventually assume the responsibilities that come with running a very complex business empire. Unfortunately, by the time he was twenty Adriano had changed completely. Perhaps we spoiled him, I don't know. He became a gambler. He tried drugs, even heroin for a time. He began taking out beautiful women of very poor morals. When he got married, his mother and I had hopes he would settle down and change. But he didn't. He treated Gabriella abominably and she left him, taking the children. He resumed his former ways. I've tried everything to help him. I tried very hard to interest him in our horses. I gave him Tiberio and several other promising two-year-olds, but all he cares about is the gambling aspect of racing. I am in despair as to what to do about him. Basically, I have been hoping that he would outgrow these evils, that he would someday cease behaving like a spoiled boy and become a man."

"Have you tried tough love?"

"What is that?"

"It's a phrase we have in America for dealing with children and people we love who are hooked on drugs or alcohol," I explained. "You effectively shut your door to them. You make it impossible for them to exploit you, to count on you to bail them out every time they misbehave. You not only save yourself, but you force them to confront reality. I'm told it works some of the time."

Luca Barone thought that one over for a minute or so. He puffed on his cigarillo and blew more smoke into the air around him, then focused on me again. "Let me come to the point," he said. "I don't know about this tough love business. I will look into it, though I doubt that his mother will permit anything of the sort. But whatever we may do, I wish to stress one simple fact with you. Adriano did not kill this girl. Yes, he knew her. Yes, he wanted very much to know her better. Yes, he did give her an expensive present and invited her out to his villa the night she was murdered. But he did not kill her. The Barones are not murderers."

"What happened that night?"

"Adriano's friend Gianpaolo Caruso brought the girl to the party. Adriano paid court to her, but she would not give in to him. Adriano became angry. He told her to leave. She tried to get Caruso to drive her home, but he did not want to leave the party and refused. She made a scene and began to cry. Adriano gave her the keys to one of his cars, the little Alfa sports coupe, told her to leave it outside her hotel and to give the keys to the hotel porter so he could arrange to have the car picked up the following day. She left the villa at about one or one-fifteen that night. On the drive back she was ambushed by these two men, Ruffo and Scotti. They hijacked the car, they raped her, beat her nearly to death, and left her to die on the lakeshore. That is the simple truth of the story."

"And Adriano has witnesses, all friends of his, who say that he never left the villa that night and that Bobby Jo drove away alone in his car, right?" I asked.

"Yes. At least two people at the party have testified to that."

"How convenient. I don't see what the problem is."

"No?"

"No. This is exactly the same story Angela Tedeschi has obviously accepted," I said. "Isn't that where the investigation is leading?"

"You think so? Then tell me, why has there been no publicity regarding the arrest of these two men as the possible murderers?"

"Maybe because they're trying to find proof or get one of them to confess before making any announcement."

"They have the proof," Luca Barone said. "They know that Adriano did not kill this girl and that the two *bulloni* are guilty. But they do not wish the truth to come out."

"Why not?"

"*La* Tedeschi has quite another agenda, Mr. Anderson."

"To ruin you."

"Precisely. You know about our families? The past, I mean?"

"I've heard stories."

"What do you know?"

I told him what I had heard. "The essence of it is that you ruined Guido Tedeschi, that he tried to get even with you when he acquired political power, and that he died suddenly one night under mysterious circumstances. All of which accounts for Angela Tedeschi's hostility toward you."

"Quite correct in its essence," Luca Barone said, "but there was nothing mysterious about Guido's death. He died of a massive heart attack. Nor did I try to ruin him. We disagreed over business policies and I forced him out of the company I had founded and in which I was the senior partner."

"There are well-documented stories of corruption in high places," I said. "Payoffs to secure building permits, that sort of thing."

Luca Barone permitted himself a tiny smile. He waved a hand deprecatingly, as if shooing away a noisome insect. "There are always many such rumors regarding business ventures anywhere," he said. "You are not a businessman and you are not Italian, so you would not understand." He leaned forward in his seat to make certain he had my full attention. "Italy is a bureaucratic Kafkaesque jungle, Mr. Anderson, in which the politicians are in control of the machinery. To oil this machinery and make it work you have somehow to deal with them. Do I make myself clear?"

"I think so. In America we call it grease."

"A good term. Let us not go any further into it. Suffice it to say that nothing is possible in Italy without it. It has always been that way. It was so long before Fascism, all during Fascism, and ever since Fascism. Guido was of the old school. He was a brilliant engineer and builder, but an impractical man. He could not understand the necessity of dealing with power in a way that made it possible for us to do business, even to survive. He would not compromise. I was forced to separate myself and my affairs from him. He never forgave me. He became convinced I was a satanic figure, a peril to the future of the republic." Luca Barone laughed. "Mr. Anderson, I built Italy. I and other men like me. We are Italy, the modern, prosperous Italy of today. We took this backward nation of peasants and artisans and dragged her into the twentieth century. We are the true heroes of our time, not the misguided idealists like Guido Tedeschi, who was full of guilt because his father was a Fascist general who slaughtered helpless natives in Ethiopia and then surrendered ingloriously in North Africa to the English. The proof of what I am is what I have built and accomplished. My companies employ forty thousand people all over the world."

"You're a hero of our time," I said.

"You could say that. I do not believe in false modesty."

"No, I can tell."

Luca Barone stood up and began pacing about the room. "Forgive me," he said, "but when I become agitated, I must move about. Does it bother you?"

"No, not at all. Then I guess what you're saying is that Angela Tedeschi is trying to pin the murder of Bobby Jo on your son as part of her plan of revenge for her father."

"Precisely. She is a well-known Marxist, an ex-member of the Communist party, who has been hounding me and my family for years," Luca Barone said. "She is following in her father's footsteps and perpetuating an ancient feud. In her position with the judiciary, she has a weapon she can wield remorselessly against me and she does so. This investigation of my affairs and the Banca dei Due Mondi is a prime example. Paolo Montserrat, the investigating judge, is a crony of hers. This is a blood feud, not an impartial investigation of a crime or a criminal conspiracy. I am powerful and very wealthy, and this arouses much envy and hatred, but since when has it become a crime to be rich? You must realize, Mr. Anderson, that you are being used. Angela Tedeschi hates me, as she hates all men. You are in deep waters. She will use you and destroy you, too, if she can. You should try to secure the girl's remains and go home. I will know how to deal with all these unfounded charges."

"About these two guys being held in Lodi," I said, "and who you say should be the chief suspects, you know what's strange about that?"

"What, Mr. Anderson?"

"There are people connected to these two men, including their lawyer, who are convinced that the authorities are trying to protect your son by pinning this crime on them. And Angela Tedeschi tells me they are probably the real culprits. Now you tell me just the opposite, that the police and the investigating magistrate are trying to keep them under wraps until they can charge and convict your son. Ironic, wouldn't you say?"

"My version is the truthful one, Mr. Anderson." Luca Barone stopped pacing and turned to look at me. "You at least must understand the truth of the matter. You know the background of the story and what Tedeschi's motives are."

"I care about only one thing, Signor Barone," I said. "I want the truth to come out."

"You will not achieve that laudable goal by feeding inaccurate information to the scandalmongering press, to people like Scarponi, who are scum," Luca Barone said heatedly. "If you are interested in justice, you can do me a very great favor."

"What is it?"

"You can give an interview to a responsible reporter who will get the story right."

"A reporter for what newspaper?"

"*Le Notizie.*"

"Which you own, I presume."

"One of my companies, yes, but it is a highly respected publication with an independent editorial staff," Luca Barone said. "It does not lie or distort the truth. You could help undo some of the damage Scarponi has caused."

"I'll think about it."

"I would like you to talk to this reporter today, Mr. Anderson. I would consider it an invaluable favor on your part."

"I don't know," I said, rising to my feet. "I think I'd better go."

"Shall we say five o'clock, at your hotel?"

"Have him call me first." It seemed easier to pretend to agree.

"The reporter's name is Manuele Luccio. He will telephone you at four o'clock to confirm the appointment. You will tell him your story and he will write it as it should be written." He walked over and shook my hand. "Gualtieri and my driver will see you home."

"I'm curious about one other thing," I said, as we walked together toward the door.

"Yes?"

"Parker Williams. Why was she killed?"

"A banal accident at an unfortunate time," Luca Barone said. "I have this directly from the French police investigating the matter. She was struck from behind by a truck going too fast on that very dangerous curve of the Grand Corniche. The blow forced the woman's car through the stone wall. It was a tragic event, but not linked in any way to this business."

"Have they found the truck and its driver?"

"Not yet, but they think they will very soon."

"And perhaps you can explain to me what Parker Williams was doing at the Greco that afternoon in Rome having a drink with your son," I said. "She didn't like him and had warned Bobby Jo against him."

"Adriano believes that the girl telephoned Williams at her hotel that night before leaving the villa," Luca Barone said. "He was anxious to talk to her about that call. It would reinforce his story about what happened."

"How did he know she was in Rome? She was only in town for two days and going straight back to Monaco."

We had reached the door by this time, but Luca Barone stopped and put a hand on my arm. "Surely you must understand, Mr. Anderson, that it is not hard for me to find people when I need them."

"Right. Okay, what did Parker Williams tell Adriano that day in Rome?"

"Nothing of much significance. Adriano was disappointed. The girl telephoned Signorina Williams and asked her for help. She wished her to come out and get her at the villa, but that was over sixty kilometers away and so the girl took Adriano's car instead. That is all they talked about."

"Parker and Adriano had at least one drink together," I said. "What else do you suppose they talked about?"

"I don't know." Luca Barone opened the door and walked me out into the foyer. Gualtieri rose from a chair by the elevator and nodded deferentially. Luca Barone spoke to him in Italian, then turned to me and again shook my hand. "Thank you for coming. I am most grateful. I am concerned for my son. He may be many things, but he is not a murderer. Gualtieri will give you my business card with my private number, should you wish to contact me for any reason. I hope you will have a very pleasant trip home."

As I crossed the garden toward the archway, I glanced back and saw Luca Barone standing on the terrace outside his living room. He raised a hand in a parting salute, then turned and went back inside.

When the blue Jaguar pulled up in front of my hotel, the driver opened the door for me. Gualtieri accompanied me into the lobby. As I turned to say good-bye to him, he smiled and reached into an inside pocket of his jacket. I caught a glimpse of a shoulder holster and the butt end of a pistol. He produced a bulky white envelope and handed it to me. "From L'Architetto," he said. "For you personally. His card is inside. Thank you, sir, and a good day to you." He touched a hand to his forehead, bowed slightly, and walked back to the car.

I stuffed the missive into my pocket, picked up my key, and went to my room. I sat on the bed and opened the envelope. It contained a small business card and ten one-thousand-dollar bills. I put the money back in the envelope, stuffed it into my pocket, stood up, and began immediately to pack.

21

RAGE

Jake Dawson looked a lot better coming off the plane than when I'd last seen him, even though he hadn't had more than a couple of hours of sleep. He was carrying a garment bag and a small overnight case, so he hadn't had to wait for his luggage. Francesca took some photographs of him as he emerged from the customs area into the lobby at Malpensa. "Hello, Jake," I said, shaking his hand. "How was the trip?"

"Easy. I laid off the booze. What are the pictures for?"

"This is Francesca Pirro," I said. "She took the pictures of Bobby Jo's body. She's been a big help to us. Let me explain it to you on the way into town."

I didn't think we could all pile into Francesca's little Fiat, so I had hired a car and driver for the morning. It was waiting for us at the curb. Luckily, there were no other photographers or reporters present, so we were able to make a quick getaway. I asked the driver to roll up the inside window as we moved out into traffic. "So what's going on, Anderson?" Jake Dawson asked.

I filled him in on the events of the past few days. "A guy named Scarponi, a big-name journalist here, interviewed me and his story has stirred up a flap," I said. No sooner had I checked out of my hotel than a TV camera crew and a reporter from some news station had put in an appearance, having tracked me down, and others had followed. More newspapers had picked up the story. I had so far managed to avoid them all, mainly because I was afraid Angela Tedeschi might come after me and either throw me in jail or out of the country. "I'm staying at Francesca's place," I said, "but eventually they'll catch up to me. I wanted to lie low till you got here."

"I don't get it," Jake Dawson said. "All this cover-up business, for what? This guy Luca Barone, what is he? The pope?"

"Almost," I said. I proceeded to tell Dawson what else had been going on. "The Barone interests may be involved in this big bank scandal. There have been payoffs to political parties, illegal export of funds, all kinds of shady transactions going on, Jake. It's very complicated and I don't pretend to understand it, but this scandal and others like it have caused the fall of the Italian government and a whole restructuring of the country's political parties. The Socialists, the Christian Democrats, the Communists—they've all disbanded and become something else."

"What's Bobby Jo got to do with any of this?"

"Nothing, I guess. It just happened at a time when all this other stuff about the Barones was coming to a head," I said. "This Angela Tedeschi, the judge in charge of the case, has an agenda of her own. What's weird about it is that she seems to agree the cops have the right two guys responsible for Bobby Jo's death, but Luca Barone is convinced she's covering up for them and has some big dark plot hatching to pin the murder on his son and bring him down as well. I tend to believe Luca Barone on that count."

"You mean you don't think his son killed Bobby Jo?"

"I didn't say that, Jake. I only meant that I agree with him when he says she's playing a double game. He wanted me to give another interview to one of his own reporters, who works for a newspaper he owns. The idea was for me to refute Scarponi's story."

"You didn't do it?"

"No. He also paid me off. He had his bodyguard give me an envelope with ten thousand dollars in it."

"What'd you do with it?"

I took the envelope out of my pocket and handed it to him.

"Here. Do what you want with it. Maybe we should turn it over to Angela Tedeschi and tell her how we got it."

He stuffed the envelope into his pocket. "We got an appointment?"

"We'll call from the hotel. She'll want to see you. She's probably pissed off about Scarponi's story, and there'll be another one about your arrival here in *Mezzanotte* tonight."

"What's that?"

"Scarponi's scandal sheet. I just hope to God I don't get arrested."

"What would they arrest you for?"

"I don't know, but they don't have habeas corpus in this country," I said. "I could sit in an Italian jail for a while."

"This goddamn place is a nuthouse," Jake Dawson said. "I'll tell you, Anderson, I don't give a shit about any of this other stuff. I don't care if this guy Luca Barone stole the world or sells drugs to kids or uranium to Iraq. I want my daughter's killer brought to justice and I want to bring her body home and that's all I want."

"I'll be interested to hear what Angela has to tell you," I said. "I have a feeling she'll be more cooperative, now that the media is on to the story. You're going to be a celebrity here, Jake. I'm sorry, but I thought it was the best way to flush everybody out of the woodwork."

"We'll see soon enough, I guess," he said, looking at Francesca. "You speak English?"

"Yes, a little," Francesca said, flashing him a big smile.

Dawson looked at me. "You and the kid here getting it on or what?" he asked.

"We're pals," I said. "And she doesn't like Adriano Barone any better than you do."

"He rape me," Francesca said. "He's shit."

"You can speak English," Dawson said. "Where are we going?"

"I booked you into the Hilton. I figured that would be okay."

"Yeah, that's fine."

After the car pulled up in front of the hotel, I paid off the driver and Francesca and I accompanied Dawson inside to help get him settled. It didn't take long, and once we were up in his room I relaxed a little. I hadn't been outside in two days. "Now what's the plan?" Dawson asked.

"The plan is for us to go and see Angela Tedeschi this afternoon, if that's possible," I said. "The idea is to put as much heat on her as you can."

"That'll be easy," he said, sitting down on the bed and propping himself up against the pillows. "I ain't going home until I get some answers and they turn over Bobby's Jo's body to me."

"How long can you stay?"

"As long as I have to, Anderson."

"Things okay back home?"

"Yeah. We had eleven live foals and we got some more on the way, all nice and really good-looking," he said. "I hired a real sharp gal to come in and help me run things. It might be a good year, for a change. The sales figures at the recent yearling sales have been up, starting last fall. Maybe the breeding business is turning around. I sure hope so. So this Adriano guy has got himself a nice colt, huh?"

"Very nice, Jake. I don't know what kind of horses he beat here, but he sure did it impressively."

"Well, fuck him, buddy. If I get my hands on that son of a bitch, he won't be thinking horses for a long time," he said. "Let's give the judge a call."

Francesca dialed Angela Tedeschi's office and couldn't get through to her, but after a few minutes an assistant made an appointment for Dawson at three o'clock that afternoon. "You sleep now," Francesca said, after hanging up. "I bring Shifty here to get you at two-thirty, okay?"

We left Dawson lying there, his head resting on his hands, staring glumly out the window at a typically gray Milanese sky.

Jake Dawson burst into Angela Tedeschi's office like an exploding hand grenade. With her perfect command of the Queen's English, she found herself helpless at first to cope with his crudities. "I don't want to hear any more of your bullshit," was one of the first remarks she heard out of Dawson's mouth. "I want answers, lady.

What have you got to tell me about this son of a bitch Luca Barone and his scumbag son?"

At first, Angela Tedeschi tried to retreat behind her magisterial robes. She attempted to explain the complexities of Italian life to this Kentucky horseman, but he wasn't listening. "Just tell me what's going on here," he said. "Why aren't you doing anything about this Adriano kid? He's obviously the one who did it."

"We need evidence," Angela Tedeschi said. "I cannot charge Luca Barone's son for a murder he did not commit. It is true that we have been investigating the Barone interests, but we are dealing specifically here with the sordid little drama of a dead fashion model. We don't know if there is any other connection."

"I don't care about any of that," Dawson said. "If this Barone kid did it, I want him arrested. And I want my daughter's body. What are you covering up, lady?"

"What I'm covering up, Mr. Dawson, is the painful fact that your daughter may not even have been murdered."

"How can you say that?"

"Before I go on, I want your assurance that you will keep your temper and remain civil in my office," Angela Tedeschi said. "Otherwise I will have you forcibly removed. Is that clear?"

"Okay. I'm waiting."

"Your daughter was working for the police, Mr. Dawson."

"How's that again?"

"She was in this country illegally, without work papers," Angela Tedeschi said. "Every two or three years the police round up groups of these young people and send them home. Not the ones who come here only to work in season, with contracts, but the ones who linger on and on. Bobby Jo was one of those. Unfortunately for her, she was also apprehended with a small amount of cocaine in her possession. She could have been sent to jail. She was one of several young women who were interviewed at the time. When it was pointed out to her that she could be imprisoned on drug charges, she agreed to work as an informant. The police are always investigating the traffic in drugs. Adriano and his circle are suspected of being heavily involved, at least as users. That is why Bobby Jo went to Adriano's villa that night.

She wanted to refuse the jewelry and the invitation, but couldn't. She was not a useful informant, too naive and basically innocent. That's why I feel so badly now about what happened to her. If I could arrest Adriano Barone for her murder, I would do it at once. Your daughter was beaten and raped and left to die by the water's edge. She could have died accidentally by drowning, not as a result of the beating. The autopsy is inconclusive in this regard. We also don't know yet whether she was the victim of Adriano Barone or of the two men we arrested who were found with Adriano's car. We are hoping someone will talk very soon. Scotti, the younger of the two men, is under a great deal of pressure to confess. We think Ruffo, the other man, is the culprit. As for Adriano, at the moment we have no compelling reason to hold him or charge him with anything."

I remembered the phone call that night in Bobby Jo's hotel room, when we were making love. It had to have been the cops. I looked at Jake. He sat for a moment or two like a statue, then leaned forward in his chair.

"I'll tell you what I think, ma'am," he said. "I think you're using Bobby Jo now like you did when she was alive. I think you and the cops are responsible for her death, just as much as the man who killed her."

"I'm sorry you feel that way, Mr. Dawson," Angela Tedeschi said. "I do accept some of the blame. We miscalculated. But no one could have anticipated murder."

"What if they knew the police were using Bobby Jo as an informant? Wouldn't they have killed her? Maybe the two guys who you say killed her were working for the Barones. What about that?"

"Pure speculation. We think it very unlikely."

"You used Bobby Jo and you let her get chewed up like a piece of meat."

"I think this interview is over, Mr. Dawson," Angela Tedeschi said, standing up.

Dawson rose slowly to his feet. "You probably got the girl in France killed, too," he said.

"Come on, Jake, let's go," I said. "This isn't doing any good."

"I am not to blame for everything, Mr. Dawson," Angela Tedeschi said. "The accident to Parker Williams was just that, an accident. A lorry has been identified as the culprit and there is a warrant out for the arrest of the driver. We don't know the exact circumstances yet, but we expect to very soon. No connection to the Barones that we know of. As for your daughter, from everything we now know, she was a very lonely and unhappy young woman. I rather suspect that, as her father, you must share in the responsibility for what happened to her. She should never have come here at all."

"I guess I know that," Jake Dawson said, moving slowly for the door. "My mistakes were made out of carelessness, but I loved her. What's your excuse? Justice? Your investigation? You make me want to throw up on your fancy rug."

Angela Tedeschi's face went white and her lips compressed into a straight, tight line. "You will leave Italy within forty-eight hours," she said. "The order will be given to the police to arrest you after that time. Your daughter's remains will be sent home just as soon as I can arrange for their release, a matter of a few days now. Good-bye, Mr. Dawson."

At the door he turned for one last look at her. "You sorry bitch," he said. "You and all your fucking talk about justice. You're so uptight, lady, when you fart I'll bet only dogs can hear you."

Scarponi's second story on Bobby Jo broke that night in *Mezzanotte* under the headline "Father of the Slain Model Here Seeking Justice." There was a photograph of Jake Dawson arriving at the airport, and the impression given the reading public was that Scarponi himself had been on hand to greet him, that Dawson had granted an exclusive interview on the spot, in which he revealed a deep working knowledge of Italian justice and the political and economic scene. I didn't know Jake possessed such knowledge. And, of course, neither did he. "Scarponi gives creative journalism a new meaning," I said to Francesca, after she had guided me through the story.

"What do you mean?"

"I mean he should be a novelist," I said. "He makes Jake sound like an expert on Italy and the local scene."

"Is good, no?"

"I'm not sure 'good' is the word, Fran," I said. "I suppose it's effective."

This time, however, the Scarponi epic was relegated to one of the inside pages. Most of the issue was devoted to the discovery of Franco Bellinzona's dead body in a modest New York hotel room on Lexington Avenue. The banker had put a bullet through the roof of his mouth and blown his brains out against the wall. A maid, who had let herself in about noon to make up the room, found the corpse. No one knew exactly what Bellinzona was doing in New York, but there were rumors, so far unconfirmed, that he had spent time in Washington, D.C., as well. The *Mezzanotte* reporter, another creative type in the grand mold of Tommaso Scarponi, speculated that the banker had fled to the U.S. in order to raise the funds to prop up his crumbling financial empire. The CIA was supposedly involved in his affairs, although a spokesman for that agency had promptly denied any knowledge of the Banca dei Due Mondi and its operations. "This is a purely Italian business," the spokesman had said. "We have no knowledge of Mr. Bellinzona or of his dealings or his bank. We will, of course, cooperate with the Italian authorities in any way we can."

The rest of the piece dealt with the scandal involving the bank and its operations. Once again Luca Barone was prominently cited as one of the chief beneficiaries of the bank's overseas transactions, and the investigating magistrate in charge of the case, Paolo Montserrat, was quoted at length on the scope of the ongoing investigation. Luca Barone was described as in a state of shock over his friend's demise and unable to provide any clues regarding the reasons behind his suicide. "We have nothing to hide in this matter," the tycoon declared in a public statement released through his press office. "Whatever Franco Bellinzona may have been involved in and whatever his personal tragedy, we are not a part of any of it. I will, of course, cooperate fully with any investigation. We have nothing to hide and we will not yield to a political witch hunt conducted against us by interests with a long history of animosity to me and my family."

"What does all this crap mean?" Jake Dawson asked me later when Francesca and I went to see him that night at the Hilton.

I tried to explain the background to him, but I wasn't sure he made the connection. "It doesn't bear directly on Bobby Jo," I said, "but the cops using her the way they did may have something to do with it. They've been trying to pin something on Luca Barone ever since the kickback scandals began to break here a couple of years ago."

"You know what, Anderson?" Jake Dawson said. "I don't give a shit. I got forty-eight hours to get out of here or they're going to arrest me."

"They only deport you," Francesca said. "Is not jail."

He ignored her. "I'd like to get my hands on this Adriano bastard. I'd like to confront him just once before I go."

"Is good," Francesca said. "Is on the island, where they have the paintings. Is big show there Sunday."

"What's he doing there?"

"Is press showings for the paintings," Francesca said. "Is many new paintings of Canaletto. They show them Sunday before the public see them, okay?"

"And you think Adriano will be there?"

Francesca shrugged. "Maybe. All the Barone is there then."

"Let's find out," I said. "Maybe Ravelli knows." I dialed his number and luckily found him at home, about to go to bed. I asked him if he knew where Adriano might be.

"He is not in Milan, Luigi," Ravelli said. "I don't know. I don't see him since the other night."

"Could he be on the island?"

"It's possible, Luigi."

"Okay, thanks." I hung up and turned to Jake. "He might be there. You sure you want to do this?"

Jake nodded grimly. "I just want to talk to him, man to man," he said. "That way maybe I'll know if he did it or not."

"And then what, Jake?" I asked. "You going to kill him?"

"No, but I got to know, Anderson. It's important to me. If you don't see it, I can't explain it to you."

"Fran, how do we get to the island on Sunday?"

"Is easy," she said. "I get invitations through Camerini. I photograph. You come with me."

"Promise me you won't do anything stupid, Jake," I said. "You don't want to spend the rest of your life in an Italian jail."

"Don't worry about it, Shifty. It's my business, right? I want an answer from somebody before I leave this goddamn place." He got up, walked over to the desk by the window of his room, opened a drawer, and took out the envelope Gualtieri had handed me. "Here's your money, Anderson," he said. "I forgot to give it to her. Things kind of got out of control there." He tossed me the envelope.

"What the hell am I going to do with it?" I asked. "I can't take this money. It's a bribe."

"You figure it out, Anderson. It ain't none of my business. Buy yourself a horse. I got a nice yearling I can sell you cheap."

BOMBS

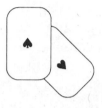

Early the next morning I rented a car and we drove out to the tiny fishing hamlet of San Lorenzo, a cluster of whitewashed stone houses less than half a mile from the Swiss border. The fishing boats were drawn up onshore, while out in the water pleasure craft of all sorts lay quietly at anchor. I parked in a public lot and we walked down to a curved jetty that shielded the harbor. At the tip of the jetty, a couple of dozen people were standing about, waiting to board a launch that was just then backing into place to pick them up. "That is it," Francesca said, as we hurried toward it. "Come."

Jake Dawson and I did our best to blend into the group of invited guests and journalists, most of whom knew Francesca. She bantered with several of the male reporters, while Dawson and I pasted benevolent smiles on our faces and pretended to understand what was going on. "You are friends of Francesca?" one man asked me, as we made our way on board the already crowded boat.

"Yes," I said. "We're covering this for the *New York Times*."

"The *New York Times*, that is impressive," the man said.

"The Arts and Leisure section."

"Ah, yes. Well, it is a big event," the man said. "Eight Canalettos few people have ever seen. Bought from the Russians, you know."

"So I heard."

"Tremendous work. I don't know how Luca does it," the man

said. "Every year he makes these coups. After London and the Louvre, this will be the finest collection of Canalettos anywhere. Too bad they are not all in Venice, where they belong."

As we chatted, the launch headed out into the lake. It was a warm, clear spring day and the water looked as blue and empty as the sky above. On the pier another group of invited guests had begun to gather, waiting for the launch to return for them. "I guess they're going to have quite a crowd," I said.

"Oh, yes," the man replied. "Every year this is a big event, but this year especially so."

"Why is that?"

The man shrugged. He was about forty, plump, with a round, cheerful pink face set off by a small goatee. "The troubles now with Luca's companies, all that arouses curiosity, you know," he said. "All the art critics are coming, of course, for this preview, but there are also people here from all the media."

"Do you think Luca will speak?"

"Oh, certainly. He will not answer any questions about the scandals, but he will be here. It would be, how do you say, a *brutta figura* if he did not attend such an important event that he is responsible for. The news of the Canalettos has been in the papers for months now."

"Yes, I know."

Jake Dawson tugged me aside. "Who's this Canaletti guy?" he asked in a stage whisper.

"An Italian painter," I said. "Try not to say anything, Jake."

Luca Barone's island home was a small, green emerald set in the blue waters of the lake. A long, gently sloping front lawn led up from a wooden dock at the water's edge to the massive white marble house, constructed in the Palladian style and sheltered by groves of trees and flowering bushes. We followed a young man up a gravel path flanked by tall cypresses to the front of the house, where about forty other guests were congregated. Several waiters were moving through the crowd with trays of soft drinks, wine, and champagne. Francesca had joined a group of other photographers and was gossiping with them, while Jake Dawson and I did our best to remain inconspicuous. I was wearing a white tennis hat I had bought for the occasion from one of the vendors on the avenue near Francesca's house and a pair of sunglasses, hoping I wouldn't be recognized by Gualtieri or Luca Barone's driver, who, I suspected, might be on hand. Dawson looked very American but presentable in pressed jeans, a pink shirt, and a gray sport jacket. So far nobody had recognized us. I sipped champagne and waited.

About forty minutes later, after the last boatload of guests and press had disembarked, Luca Barone appeared from inside the villa. He was flanked by a tall, trim, bespectacled young man in a dark formal suit and a handsome middle-aged woman in a plain black dress but with a triple strand of pearls around her long neck and large black pearl earrings dangling from her lobes. "Giovanna, his wife," Francesca whispered, as she rejoined us. "And *il direttore del museo*."

Francesca moved forward now with the other photographers and they all began taking pictures, as Luca Barone addressed the crowd in Italian. I gathered that it was a welcoming speech, during which he mentioned Canaletto's name and introduced his wife. She began to talk, also obviously about the opening of the new exhibit and its significance. Dawson and I remained toward the rear of the gathering. The curator then spoke for nearly twenty minutes, frequently mentioning Canaletto by name. One reporter toward the front asked Luca Barone something about Bellinzona that obviously had nothing to do with the occasion. Luca Barone frowned, but kept a smile on his face as he politely declined to answer directly. "*L'occasione è* Canaletto," he said, in conclusion. "*Oggi non si parla di cose triste.*" The remark was greeted with scattered applause.

The curator spoke again, then turned and led the way up to the villa. The Barones excused themselves and took a separate route leading around the left wing of the house toward what I assumed were their private quarters. The crowd, with Dawson and me bringing up the rear, surged forward toward the front entrance. I lost sight of Francesca, who was in the forefront with the other photographers.

Inside the front door of the villa was the entrance to the museum. Press releases about the exhibit and the history of the collection, as well as pamphlets about the various artists whose work was on display, were available at a counter next to a turnstile, through which we passed into a long series of large rooms containing the collection. The Canalettos were in a newly prepared hall on the ground floor, behind two rooms housing a dozen or so Flemish masterpieces. The brilliance of the Venetian paintings was dazzling, especially as we walked in on them from the cold gloom of the northern European canvases, with their dark landscapes and portraits of straitlaced burghers in somber clothes. I was so caught up in the splendor of the Venetian pictures that I didn't immediately notice Jake Dawson's disappearance.

I looked around for him, then walked out of the gallery onto a back patio area where a long table of refreshments had been set up. Francesca and a couple of other photographers were already sipping white wine and munching on small sandwiches. "Fran, where's Dawson?" I asked.

She shrugged and pointed toward the rear right wing of the house. "He say he go look for Adriano. There is big party inside for the other guests. This out here is only for the press."

"I better try to find him," I said. "He's liable to kill Adriano or get us all arrested."

Francesca pointed down across a long stretch of lawn toward the water where several small blue motorboats seemed to be circling the island. "Police," she said. "Maybe they look for someone."

I walked quickly around the rear of the house and found the private reception. Fifty or sixty people were gathered on a broad terrace outside the open French doors of the main living room, milling about and chatting with Luca and Giovanna Barone. A couple of white-jacketed waiters were moving through the crowd with drinks and hors d'oeuvres. Smiling and nodding, doing my best to look as if I belonged, I eased myself into the company.

Everyone around me was speaking Italian, and at first nobody paid any attention to me. Dawson, who would have been pretty conspicuous in this assembly, was nowhere to be seen. Somebody tugged at my sleeve and I turned around to find myself confronted by Branch Nevins. "You are Mr. Anderson, aren't you?" the assistant consul said. "Dawson's friend?"

"Yes, have you seen him?"

"He came walking in here from the house," Nevins said. "I don't know how he got in. He asked me where Adriano was."

"Where'd he go?"

"Back inside the house," Nevins said. "He may have gone upstairs. I told him Adriano might be up in his private apartment. I didn't want to tell him anything, but he said he had an appointment with him and threatened to make a scene. I suggest you go and find him and get him out of here. He said he was invited."

"He was, we both were."

"He was very determined and angry. I couldn't stop him. Luckily, the Barones didn't spot him in this crowd."

"Which way do I go?"

"Go through the living room. If anybody questions you, say you're going to the bathrooms. They're out in the hall. Once there, turn left. You'll see a big staircase facing the main entrance. The private apartments are all on the second floor. You can't miss the stairs. What does he want? Is he dangerous?"

"He wants to talk to Adriano. No, I don't think he's dangerous."

"Get him out of here, Anderson. This is not the occasion for a confrontation."

I made my way through the crowd to the living room, where a number of the older guests were seated, and out into a corridor leading to the entrance hall and a broad staircase. I stood at the foot of the stairs and looked up toward the second-floor landing. I heard nothing and was wondering whether to go up and look for Dawson when I became aware of some sort of commotion going on outside— voices shouting, people running.

I went out the front door as Gualtieri and two other men ran past me, with Francesca and a covey of journalists in their wake. She grabbed my hand and pulled me along with her. "Come," she said. "Something is happening."

We headed back to the party but stopped outside the terrace, where a number of the guests were talking loudly and pointing toward the dock area. Others were taking refuge inside the house. Francesca began taking pictures. A dozen or so men in dark blue uniforms and armed with automatic rifles were fanned out across the lawn and moving toward the house. Gualtieri and his cohorts walked down to confront them, but were immediately stopped and forced to lie facedown on the ground with their hands behind their heads. One of the invaders covered them, while the others approached the house.

Luca Barone, looking disheveled and wild-eyed with rage, now stepped out onto the lawn to face them. He was shouting and waving his arms about, but the men holding guns walked past him and began to move all of the guests away from the house onto the lawn. Barone continued to shout and one of the men now turned back to argue with him. The others seemed intent on calming the guests, who looked frightened and confused. Francesca pulled me to one side. "You don't be scared," she said. "Is police."

"What police? What's happening?"

"They say there is man with bomb inside the villa," Francesca said. "That is why everyone come outside."

There was a sound of shattering glass. Adriano Barone plunged through a window directly above us and fell to the ground, landing on his left arm. The sound of his arm breaking was like the pop of a dry piece of wood. Adriano screamed. I looked up and saw Jake Dawson looking down on us, his face battered and his nose bleeding. "*Eccolo!*" somebody shouted. "*L'assassino!*"

Two of the armed men outside ran into the house as Dawson disappeared from view. The rest of us were herded away from the scene to a presumably safer distance, while several people tended to Adriano Barone, who was lying on the ground clutching his shattered arm. Luca Barone and his wife were trying to reach him, but were prevented from doing so and forced to move away from the villa with the rest of us. One of the policemen began to speak to the crowd. "He say is not to worry," Francesca said. "They going into the villa to find bomb and the man."

"You mean Jake?"

"I don't know," Francesca said. "Maybe."

"But that's crazy."

"You wait, Shifty. Is all right, I tell you. You don't worry, okay?"

I was astonished by her unconcern, but more astonished to see Jake Dawson emerge from the house in handcuffs, flanked by two policemen. He was led away to the front of the building and disappeared from view.

Five or six men in plainclothes now showed up. Carrying empty boxes and canvas sacks, they walked silently and quickly past us into the villa. Luca Barone began shouting again, but he was led away, also around to the front of the house, and disappeared.

Francesca took my hand. "You wait, Shifty. Is all right."

I could hear something going on at the front of the building. Some ten minutes passed, during which half a dozen confused-looking servants and two terrified young women emerged from the villa to join us. One of the policemen said something, and we all began to move around the house, then were ushered along the gravel path toward the dock.

The launch with an initial load of passengers was pulling away from the shore toward the mainland. The cops urged us along, speaking quietly and authoritatively, gradually succeeding in tranquilizing the spectators to this bizarre drama. Francesca and I joined the others on the lawn and sat down to wait. She resumed taking pictures of the goings-on. I looked around for the Barones, but they were nowhere to be seen.

As we sat there waiting, a blue police boat pulled into the dock. Two men and a woman carrying black briefcases disembarked and began to walk briskly toward the villa. The woman, dressed in a severe-looking dark gray suit and carrying a large black handbag slung over her shoulder, was Angela Tedeschi. She was unsmiling, but looked triumphant.

23

COOLER

"I imagined you would wish to speak to me," Angela Tedeschi said, as I walked into her office at nine the following morning. "I'm sorry I couldn't accommodate you yesterday, but we were extremely busy. Please sit down."

"Where's Dawson?" I asked. "You aren't going to keep him in jail, are you? He didn't do anything."

"He threw a young man out of a window," Angela Tedeschi said. "We could keep him in custody for a while, I imagine."

"What's really going on here, Miss Tedeschi?" I asked. "You weren't after Jake Dawson yesterday."

"You haven't read the Italian papers or looked at a news program? I'd have guessed you would know what this is all about by now." She actually permitted herself a smile, more of a smirk than the real thing, but it startled me. I hadn't been able to imagine what could make this woman smile, much less laugh.

"I've read the papers, with a little help," I said. "The most imaginative and sensational coverage was in *Mezzanotte*, but then I gather that Scarponi is a master at this sort of thing. He wasn't there, of course. He doesn't get up before four in the afternoon."

"It was a brilliant article," she said, "one of his best. I enjoyed it very much. He is wrong on many of the particulars, but that is to be expected from Scarponi. What he is right about is the reason for the

227

event. We will be indicting and arresting Luca Barone and many of his associates for his involvement in the activities of the Banca dei Due Mondi, as well as for other crimes against the state. Before moving against him we will be evaluating and assembling our evidence in an orderly fashion. In the meantime, however, we have stripped him and his associates of their passports and they are under surveillance. They are not to leave their homes."

"What evidence are you talking about?"

"Files, bank records, correspondence, telexes, above all the computer records of all the Barone transactions," she explained. "There is a mountain of stuff. It will take us weeks, perhaps months, before we can act on all of it. But we already have enough to hold the Barone people. We will indict them swiftly on the easier charges. The others will follow."

"Why yesterday? Why couldn't you have raided the Barone villa before, if you knew the records were all there?"

"I needed the right moment, Mr. Anderson. You probably know that the island is in Swiss waters. We had to have the cooperation of the Swiss authorities, which is not easy to get, if you tell them it is a matter regarding money. The Swiss are very touchy about money. Their entire economy is based on the security of their banks and guaranteed secrecy for their major investors. It would have taken months to get them to agree and they would have insisted on controlling the investigation themselves. Luca Barone would have had plenty of time to protect himself by moving his documents and his operations to another site in some other foreign jurisdiction. We couldn't risk that, so we created an emergency."

"What emergency? A terrorist with a bomb?"

"Yes, we informed the Swiss at the last minute that we were pursuing a suspect and asked them to join us."

"Then not all those cops were Italian."

"The first ones, yes. The plainclothes officers who arrived with me were from Lugano. By that time my men were already inside the villa."

I leaned back in my chair and looked at her. She was positively radiant by her standards, which meant that her usually pale cheeks were slightly flushed with color. "And now you're going to tell me that Jake Dawson was your mad bomber," I said.

"We were mistaken, obviously. We have so informed the Swiss."

"Why Dawson?"

"We needed someone. He fit the role beautifully and we knew he would be there. When he threw Adriano out the window, it was perfect. We had an even stronger reason to go in. It was a successful operation."

"How did you know he would be there?"

"We knew. The occasion was perfect."

"What are you going to do about Dawson? Put him on trial?"

"No, no. He will be kept in custody for another twenty-four hours," Angela Tedeschi said. "Tomorrow he will be deported back to the United States."

"What about his daughter's body?"

"She will be going home with him. We have completed our investigation into her murder. Adriano Barone did not kill Bobby Jo. He is innocent."

"Who did? The car thieves?"

"Yes. Scotti has confessed and will testify against Ruffo, who was the actual perpetrator. We also have recovered the diamond pin. It was found in Rome."

"Do you mind telling me where?"

"It was recovered from a man named Bisanza, who traffics in such stolen goods. He was in Rome at the time, undoubtedly to sell it."

"To whom, do you know?"

"Why do you ask?"

"Just curious."

Angela Tedeschi shrugged. "There are establishments that buy stolen goods at a fraction of their worth and sell them clandestinely. Bisanza was en route to one of those places."

"But he didn't get there."

"No. He was arrested in his car as he was parking near the Campo dei Fiori. Perhaps the police should have waited and they could have arrested everyone involved, but it was more important to catch

Bisanza with the pin in his possession. He can confirm that he bought it from Scotti and Ruffo."

"I'm glad."

"About what?"

"Oh. That you found the murderer."

"Yes, we've known for quite some time, but it was difficult to prove. We needed Scotti's confession. He's young. He'll be out in ten or twelve years."

"And Ruffo? You don't have the death penalty in Italy, do you?"

"Unfortunately not. The presiding judge at his trial will decide."

"And what about Parker Williams?"

"That was an accident, nothing else. The French police were able to trace what trucks were on the road that night. They have now arrested the man who was responsible. He is an alcoholic who has been in accidents before and whose license had been revoked. The company he worked for in Nice has also been indicted, I understand. It was a tragic act of fate."

"What about the meeting between Parker and Adriano in Rome?"

"He wanted her to back up his story. Bobby Jo had called Williams from the villa. Adriano thought she might have heard Bobby Jo mention something about Adriano leaving her his car or some other statement that might have reinforced his alibi. Is there anything else I can tell you?"

"I'd like to see Dawson."

"Come to the airport tomorrow morning. Be there by eight o'clock. I'll be on hand, too. Meet me at the Alitalia information desk. Be prompt, please."

I stood up. "Well, it's been a fascinating and eventful trip." I reached into my pocket, took out the envelope Luca Barone had given me, and dropped it on her desk.

"What is this?" she asked.

"The ten thousand dollars Luca Barone gave me to give an interview to one of his hired hacks from some newspaper he owns," I explained. "I didn't give him the interview."

"That is no concern of mine," Angela Tedeschi said, handing the envelope back to me. "That is between you and Luca Barone. You can return it to him or spend it and worry about whether he'll ask for it back. I doubt that he will, as he'll have his hands full with other, far more pressing concerns for a very long time. I would spend some of the money in Italy before you leave. I understand there is a limit on the amount of currency you can import into the United States without declaring it."

"A good suggestion," I said, again pocketing the envelope. We shook hands. "I imagine your father would have been proud of you."

"There is another Italy, you know, Mr. Anderson," she said. "It is not the Italy of the Barones and their kind. It is the Italy of honest people like my father. It is the reason I became a judge, to defend that Italy. Good-bye, Mr. Anderson. I'll see you tomorrow morning."

The hawklike gaze of old General Armore Tedeschi followed me out the door.

I paid one of the scalpers standing around in front of La Scala that afternoon twelve hundred dollars for two tickets to the opening night of Verdi's *Il Trovatore* and took Francesca. She put on a black cocktail dress that hugged her slight frame like a silk glove. It was the first time I had seen her in anything but pants and a man's shirt and she looked sensational. "I don't like opera," she had said, when I told her about the tickets.

"You'll like this one," I said. "It's all about murder and revenge and blood feuds and ancient animosities. It's set in medieval Spain, but it's the most Italian opera I know. And it's full of great melodies. You'll love it."

Our seats were in the twelfth row, a little off to one side, but we had a great view of the stage. Behind me rose the cream and gold boxes in tiers soaring upward, as if challenging the singers to reach them with their best notes. The baritone who interpreted the villain of the piece was superb, with a great dark voice that flowed out of him like a flood, carrying us along on the tide of Verdi's tremendous score. The rest of the cast was more than adequate, and by the end of the evening I felt drained, at peace with myself, those glorious melodies still sounding in my head as we walked out into a chilly, breezy spring night. "What was about?" Francesca asked, as we walked away toward the Biffi Scala to eat a late supper. "I understand nothing."

"It was about life, Francesca," I said. "It was love, hatred, loyalty, despair, ambition, greed, vengeance, all the elements of the human condition."

"Buh," she said, "it only sound loud to me."

"Maybe you're tone-deaf," I suggested.

We ate at a corner table from where we had a good view of the other diners, mostly representatives of Milan's upper crust, the women dolled out in outfits that could have supported a working family for a month. I ordered a bottle of French champagne and a small mountain of Persian caviar, which I slopped up with a soup-spoon. "You spend much money," Francesca observed.

"I have much money to spend tonight," I said. "I want you to order the most expensive meal you've ever had. It's on Luca Barone."

She laughed. "I don't like caviar," she said, "but I eat anyway."

After we had finished an enormous meal that set me back well over five hundred dollars, I ordered two black Sambucas that arrived with a couple of raw coffee beans bobbing in each glass. I toasted Francesca. "To us," I said. "It's been a great month here."

"When you go, Shifty?"

"Tomorrow," I told her. "There's a flight out a half hour after Dawson's. I made a reservation on it. In first class, needless to say."

"Where you go?"

"Home, to Los Angeles."

She sipped her Sambuca slowly, then bit into one of the coffee beans and chewed it thoughtfully. She raised her glass to me and smiled. "*Salute*," she said. "Is nice to know you. You ever come back?"

"I don't know. I hope so. Tell me something, Fran."

"What?"

"It was you who told Angela Tedeschi that Dawson would be on the island, wasn't it?"

"Yes, I tell her."

"And she's more than just an old college friend, right?"

"What you mean?"

"I mean that you and Angela are close friends, ever since college days."

She nodded. "So?"

"So you've been keeping Angela informed of our doings all along, haven't you?"

"She ask me. I say yes."

"Angela set this whole caper up, didn't she? She needed an excuse to go in and seize Luca Barone's records. She used you and me and Jake to get what she wanted. But what do you get out of it, Fran? Are you and Angela lovers?"

"One time, long ago," she said. "But we stay friends. She don't like men. I do."

"I guess I know that." I raised my glass and toasted her this time. "*Salute*, Fran. You're quite a piece of work."

"What this means?"

"You're terrific, I guess that's what I mean. You're kind of a magician yourself, a mistress of the double deal."

We lay quietly in one another's arms that night and didn't make love. Whatever it was we'd had going there for a while was over and we both knew it. We had no future together, maybe that was it. If our paths ever crossed again, it would be only briefly and probably by pure chance.

Francesca drove me out to the airport the next morning, where I checked in with my airline and left my luggage. Angela Tedeschi was waiting for us at the Alitalia counter. She was dressed in one of her severe dark outfits that made her look, outside of her professional surroundings, like the warden of a correctional facility. She smiled at Francesca and shook my hand. "This way, Mr. Anderson," she said. "Mr. Dawson is being held in a private room."

She led us up a flight of stairs to a warren of administrative offices toward the rear of the terminal, away from the passenger gates. A uniformed young policeman armed with an Uzi was standing outside an unmarked door. Angela Tedeschi nodded to him and he opened the door for us. Jake Dawson rose out of his chair as we entered. He looked as if he hadn't slept for days and his face was still bruised from his encounter with Adriano Barone. "Hello, Anderson," he said. "They got you on this flight, too?"

"I'm leaving on another one, Jake, right after yours. I'm headed for L.A. You okay?"

"I'm all right," he said. He looked at Angela Tedeschi. "My daughter's body on the plane?"

Angela Tedeschi looked at her watch. "Any minute now," she said.

The door behind me opened and the young policeman stuck his head in the room. He spoke in Italian to Angela Tedeschi, who nodded, then turned to Dawson. "She is here," she announced.

Francesca began photographing as a man in a white uniform appeared in the doorway with his back to us. He pulled a wheelchair in over the sill, then slowly turned it to face the room. Bobby Jo Dawson, looking pale and much thinner than I remembered her, was sitting in the wheelchair holding a small overnight bag on her lap. Dawson stared at her in amazement. "Bobby Jo?" he said. "Honey, you—"

"Hello, Daddy," Bobby Jo said. "I'm okay, Daddy, I'm okay." She was smiling.

Dawson lumbered across the room to her, got down on his knees and took her in his arms. "Baby, you sure you're all right? Jesus Christ, baby, I can't believe this. What have they done to you?"

"They took real good care of me, Daddy," she said. "They told me everything would be all right and that we're going home. Is that right, Daddy?"

"Yeah, baby, that's right." He looked up at Angela Tedeschi. "That's right, ain't it?"

"Yes," Angela Tedeschi said. "We have booked seats for you in first class."

Dawson turned his attention back to Bobby Jo. "Are you okay, honey? Can you walk?"

"Yes, Daddy, I can. They made me sit in this wheelchair. It's the rules or something. I got to be careful for a while, but they said I'll be okay. I have my medical records in my suitcase."

Francesca had continued to photograph the scene from the

moment of Bobby Jo's arrival. Dawson turned on her. "Knock that off," he said. "I've had enough of that."

Angela Tedeschi nodded to Francesca, who stopped shooting and began to gather up her equipment. "Well now," Angela Tedeschi said, "have a safe journey home, Mr. Dawson. Your daughter will explain exactly what happened."

She and Francesca stepped out into the corridor, and I followed them. The policeman shut the door behind us. Angela Tedeschi turned to face me and held out her hand. "I think we might as well say good-bye here," she said. "I hope you've had an interesting time in Italy."

" 'Interesting' is hardly the word," I said, shaking her hand. "Why didn't you tell Dawson his daughter was alive? To keep the pressure on him and on everyone involved?"

"You're free to come to your own conclusions, Mr. Anderson."

"Do you play poker, Miss Tedeschi?" I asked.

"No."

"Too bad. You'd have made a great cardsharp."

"I'm sorry?"

"I thought I could deal a good cold deck, but this is the best cooler I've ever seen," I said. "You kept all of us in this fine Italian hand right to the very end, and it all came out just as you envisioned it. You should learn to play the game."

"If I ever have time," she said. "Good-bye, Mr. Anderson."

Francesca kissed me. "Good-bye, Shifty," she said. "You stay good."

"Maybe not good, but well. Who's going to write this story? Scarponi?"

She smiled. "Of course," she said. "Tonight, in *Mezzanotte*, with many wonderful pictures. I send you a copy."

"Another scoop. I'll write you, Fran."

"No, send me one postcard. I like pictures."

They walked away together out of my life. They were holding hands.

EASED UP

The man I bought my program from at Hollywood Park was amazed to see me. "Where you been?" he said. "We thought you was dead."

"Where'd you get that idea?" I asked.

"Somebody said so, I forget who. So where you been?"

"Italy."

"Italy? They got racing over there?"

"They've got everything."

"Well, it's good to see you back, Shifty. We missed you."

I'd been home two days, but I was still suffering from jet lag. I'd gotten out of bed late and spent an hour or so reading the *Racing Form*, after which I'd dozed off again until noon. I had already missed the first race, but it didn't matter. I'd soon catch up on the horses again. I was back in action.

Jay Fox looked up from one of his big black notebooks as I walked into his grandstand box. "Well, if it isn't the world traveler," he said. "How are you, Shifty? How was the trip?"

"Eventful." I sat down next to him. "Where is everybody?"

"Arnie went to the can," Jay said. "He's feeling rotten, got a flu bug or something, but he didn't want to miss the double. He's alive to an eight-to-one shot he got a good tip on from somebody. Angles is around, too, only he's a basket case these days. He's on a losing streak."

"And how are you doing?"

"Trading dollars, Shifty. It's been a slow meet. Mediocre horses, small fields, low odds. I'm waiting for Del Mar, when the good two-year-olds show up."

"That's six weeks away."

"I'm always waiting for Del Mar, Shifty."

"You got a horse for me today?"

"Not till the feature, if you can wait that long. The third choice in the morning line. He should go off at four or five to one. He'll wire the field, Shifty, if he breaks good. He's the lone speed."

Arnie Wolfenden showed up, shuffling along the aisle toward the box like a man on his last legs. "Shifty, welcome back," he said, easing himself into the seat behind Jay. "I figured you'd be coming home about now. How was Italy?"

"Fascinating," I said. "A lot happened to me."

"Yeah, well, you'll tell us all about it sometime, only not today," he said. "I feel like shit."

"Jay told me. Why don't you go home?"

"What? And miss my eight-to-one shot? What's the matter with you? You've been away too long."

"Did you take something?" Jay asked.

"Two aspirins. It didn't help. Even when I'm feeling good these days I don't feel good. At my age, when you get up in the morning, everything is stiff except the one thing that ought to be."

Angles Beltrami came hurrying down the aisle to join us, his dark Italian face set in a scowl. He shoved past me into the box and sat down. "Jesus Christ, you ever notice?" he said. "Whenever you lose, there's always some guy comes up to you to tell you what a big bet he had on the winner. Everybody does this to me. Then, when you get a winner, nobody wants to hear about it."

"Hello, Angles, how are you?" I said.

He looked at me and blinked. "Hiya, Shifty, who do you like in here?" He waved a hand toward the track, where the horses entered in the second race were filing past us on their way to the starting gate. "I got a tip on the two."

"Who from?" Arnie asked.

"Winkles, the clocker."

"He's a congenital liar," Arnie said.

"How do you know?"

"I can tell. It's easy."

"Yeah? How can you tell?"

"Watch him. It happens every time he opens his mouth."

"Hey, Angles," Jay said. "Shifty's been away, or didn't you notice?"

Angles focused on me, looking mildly puzzled. "Oh, yeah. Where you been, Shifty?"

"Italy."

"No shit. You go racing there?"

"Once, in Rome. I went to the Italian Derby."

"Yeah? That's nice." Angles stood up. "I got to get a bet down on the two. I almost forgot."

No one asked me about Italy again. It was as if I had never been away at all. Arnie's eight-to-one shot won the second race, after which he went home to recover from the flu. Angles lost every race and disappeared penniless in a cloud of losing tickets after the seventh. Jay's speed horse won the feature, paying $7.20 for every two-dollar bet on him and enriching me by over a hundred dollars. It was a nice way to come home.

Over the next few days I told myself I ought to be calling my agent, the irrepressible Happy Hal Mancuso, to get myself some work, but I couldn't make myself do it. I was still winding down from the fantastic roller-coaster ride I had been on in Italy and I needed some time to readjust. I called Jake Dawson to find out how he and Bobby Jo were getting along and was told they were working things out. Bobby Jo was going to stay on the farm and work with the horses again. She was looking forward to it, but eventually, she told me after Jake put her on the phone, she was planning to get her own place somewhere, not too far away. She sounded at peace with herself. That night I sent her a check for five thousand dollars with a note telling her to use the money to help get herself settled. I told her I'd made it betting on Tiberio to win the Derby and that it was small recompense for what Adriano had done to her. I hope she'll be okay.

I sent Francesca a postcard with a picture of horses breaking out of a starting gate. She sent me back a copy of Scarponi's story in *Mezzanotte*, which had a photograph of Dawson hugging Bobby Jo in her wheelchair. One of these days I'll find somebody to translate it for me.

I think about Italy a lot. I remember the faces, the voices, the smells, the great sights, above all, the food and the music. Confronted daily by the lunacies of the goings-on in my own country, the eccentricities of that far more ancient civilization seem gentle, even endearing, to me. Every day I scan the newspapers for stories from Italy, but am rarely rewarded. One day I did come across an item in the L.A. *Times* about the continuing investigation into what the press calls Kickback City. Luca Barone was mentioned as the latest big shot to be arrested; he was awaiting trial. I hope they put him away forever.